LEGACY

ELLERY KANE

BALBOA
PRESS

A DIVISION OF HAY HOUSE

Cover Design: Giovanni Auriemma
Book Development Editing/Consulting: AnnCastro Studio
with Ann Castro, Jae Gravely, Katrina A. Martin.

Balboa Press books may be ordered through booksellers or by contacting:

Balboa Press
A Division of Hay House
1663 Liberty Drive
Bloomington, IN 47403
www.balboapress.com
1 (877) 407-4847

Any people depicted in stock imagery provided by Thinkstock are models, and such images are being used for illustrative purposes only. Certain stock imagery © Thinkstock.

Print information is available on the last page.

ISBN: 978-1-4525-2040-7 (sc)
ISBN: 978-1-4525-2042-1 (hc)
ISBN: 978-1-4525-2041-4 (e)

Library of Congress Control Number: 2014914994

Balboa Press rev. date: 09/24/2015

To my parents—for furnishing me with all the raw materials to write this book: faith in myself; courage to seek adventures; laughter, even in hard times; curiosity about the world around me; and the understanding that only comes with loss; but most of all, love.

"What's past is prologue."
—William Shakespeare, *The Tempest*

PROLOGUE

THE FIRST TIME I KISSED someone, it wasn't at all like I had imagined—and trust me when I say that I had spent hours imagining it. It was a summer night just after my seventeenth birthday. We were sitting side by side in the empty football stadium. I can still feel the bleachers, cold and hard beneath my legs. My elbow was touching the side of his body. I could feel how warm he was. He didn't move, but just let me touch him. The air between us was thick with anticipation. And then, just like that, his lips were on mine. In a few seconds, a wall that had once seemed impenetrable was crossed. I was no longer unkissed.

* * *

The first time I killed someone, it wasn't at all like I had imagined. It was as quick and as effortless as snipping a string. I squeezed the trigger, and the man fell back. It was so dark that I could barely see the outline of his face. I watched him for a long time, waiting for something. *What was I waiting for?* The man didn't move, except for a brief shudder. It seemed for a moment as if I too had stopped breathing. But in the cold I could see my breath visible in small white puffs. I waited for the world to open up and swallow me, but nothing came. In the corner where I hid, I saw a small brown bird hopping. He reached the edge of my vision and took flight. It was only me who had changed.

CHAPTER ONE

THE CROSSING

WHEN I LAST SAW MY mother, we were standing on the Golden Gate Bridge. It was deserted. People were no longer allowed to travel into the city. It was too dangerous. On that morning, the fog was heavy—its wet, white fingers lacing themselves through the burnt red cables. My mother and I walked across the bridge, neither of us speaking. We had to move quickly since there were regular patrols. When we neared the now-vacant tollbooths, my mother handed me a backpack. I finally looked at her. Her expression was stone, but her eyes were heavy with worry. I tried to mirror her strength, but I fought back tears.

"Can't you come with me?" I asked, already knowing the answer. We had planned this for months. I knew there were no other options.

"Lex," she said my name sympathetically as if I were a small child asking for something impossible, "when you find them, give them this." She pressed a small computer flash drive into my hand and took me into her arms. "I'm so proud of you, my girl. No matter what happens, remember that."

I tried to control my breathing, but I felt as if I was drowning. For as long as I could remember, I saw my mother as the tether that grounded me to my world. Without her, I was a feather blown by the wind. I wanted to tell her that, but it would have felt too much like saying good-bye.

I whispered, "I know."

My mother let go first and began walking away. Ahead of me, I saw only fog. I walked toward the tollbooths, then past them. My legs felt like heavy bags of sand. I imagined that, after a few steps, my mother turned and watched me until I disappeared behind layers of whiteness. But I'm not sure because I couldn't look back.

CHAPTER TWO

EMOVERE

MY FIRST VIEW OF SAN Francisco was from my parents' car window as we crossed the Bay Bridge. I was almost eight years old, and we had just moved from Los Angeles. My mother, a forensic psychiatrist, had accepted a research position at Zenigenic, an up-and-coming pharmaceutical company. My father had eagerly pointed at the city, grinning as I gasped. I rolled down the window and let the cold air rush in. Ever since that first drive across the bridge, San Francisco always looked the same to me: surreal, as if each building had been carefully crafted from clay and arranged alongside the ocean by an unseen hand.

As I walked hurriedly into the heart of downtown, my mind was reeling. Nothing my mother told me could have prepared me for the city now. It was desolate in every way.

On either side of me were storefronts—most were looted and graffitied. Stepping over shards of glass, I slipped inside one of the darkened buildings. The air was cold and rancid, rank with decay and desperation. Near the doorway, shelves of groceries were overturned. Bottles were smashed, their empty shells scattered across the floor. An army of ants marched in a zigzag formation, carrying molded crumbs up the wall. I dodged puddles of congealed liquid and a frenzy of mice as I filled my backpack with a few extra cans of food and a box of cereal. Along with the supplies my mother had given me, I had enough to survive for several weeks.

I continued down Market Street, once believed to be the home of the Resistance, then I turned left. I knew exactly where I was headed. My mother and I had selected the perfect hiding place.

I tried to stay focused, but my eyes were drawn to the destruction. In the middle of the sidewalk was an overturned car, its burnt shell crumbling. Nearby, the entrance to the underground BART railway system was boarded shut and marked with large red letters. *DANGER: KEEP OUT BY ORDER OF THE GUARDIAN FORCE.* Posted on almost every building were notices of mandatory evacuation.

Up ahead of me, a stately white building beckoned—the San Francisco Public Library, one of the few remaining libraries in the country. The only consistent noise was my footsteps crunching over glass and debris. I stopped moving and surveyed the area intently, watching, listening. From somewhere unseen, I heard the distant howl of a dog. No other sounds. Even though I had expected this, it still unnerved me.

The last news broadcast from San Francisco was over a year ago. News media were no longer allowed inside the city. The one remaining government-sponsored television station, SFTV, had released propaganda—that's what my mother called it—which reported that San Francisco had been significantly damaged by the rebellion of the Resistance. But, in the days leading up to my walk across the Golden Gate, my mother had received a report from the Resistance that it was the Guardian Force that had bombed portions of the Bay Bridge, making the city that much less accessible.

That night my mother and I sat huddled at the kitchen table, both of us dreading the inevitable.

"It's time, Mom," I said. "If we wait any longer, there will be no way into the city."

I studied my mother's face. To me, she had once been radiant, her eyes always smiling. In the years since my father had left, she looked increasingly tired.

My mother nodded. "I know. But it's just . . ."

She searched for the right words, but there were none. "It's dangerous. I should go with you."

We both knew that was impossible. As one of the faces of the Resistance, my mother would be recognized easily.

She touched my hand. "You know, I can't lose you."

My mother's words still cautioning me, I approached the library with trepidation. Just outside the door was a familiar reminder of my mother's career at Zenigenic: a small vending machine, marked with a large, metallic Z. The machines dotted most street corners in the city and doled out emotion-stimulating and inhibiting drugs, like the kind my mother had been tasked to develop.

One of those was Emovere, which in its earliest form targeted the brain's amygdala. While on the drug, patients felt little to no fear. I remember as a girl watching a recorded demonstration of an Emovere clinical trial. An expressionless man walked to the edge of what he perceived to be a tall building. When instructed by researchers, he stepped from the edge and plummeted into a net 50 feet below. He never screamed.

Operated by biometric identification, the machines could recognize a user and distribute medication with the simple press of a fingerprint. Mental illness was not a requirement, only the desire to alter one's emotional state. It seemed that almost everyone was eager to feel or *not* to feel something—a sentiment captured in Zenigenic's slogan, "How do *you* want to feel today?"

This machine was unique. It drew me in. Taped to the front, side by side, were rows of flyers branded by the Resistance. Looking back at me from each faded paper was an image of my mother. The outer glass was cracked. All the medication stolen long ago, even before Emovere was banned by the government. I contemplated my mother's face—*surely, it was a sign*—hoping to be reassured, but I only felt more alone. The picture had been chosen strategically from her discarded Zenigenic badge. The caption below read *Emovere Kills: Knightley Calls It Biggest Regret.*

Now it haunted her, a relentless ghost, but Emovere was once my mother's crowning achievement. Its development catapulted her into the spotlight as one of the nation's eminent psychiatric researchers. Looking back, I could see now that it was also the tipping point, the turn in the road, the single step that sent all of our lives into a free fall.

The library door was already cracked open, a thin beam of sunlight cast onto a nearby bookcase. Giving the door a gentle push, I tiptoed inside.

CHAPTER THREE

QUIN

THE FIRST TIME I SAW Quin, I was on the edge of sleep, thinking of my mother. She would read to me every night, then run her fingers through my hair until I fell asleep. That world, the world containing my mother, had died so long ago—*was it really only twenty days?*—that sometimes I believed it had happened to someone else, not me. When I thought of my old life, I imagined it far above me, like a child's lost balloon. At first there was the hope of grabbing it, recovering it, bringing it safely back to the clutches of my hand. Then it was out of reach, and I could only watch it and wonder where it would go. Finally, the tiny dot of it disappeared, and I realized it was never mine to begin with.

I sat upright, nearly hitting my head on the desk—a graffitied table hidden in the library's stacks—where I slept. At first, I thought it was a dream. *How long had I been sleeping?* A pinprick of light darted across the library floor. I held my breath.

In the twenty days, now twenty-one, that I had been in the library, a small brown bird fluttering near the doorway had been the only sign of life. I heard muffled footsteps and a *click-click-click* sound, like nails tapping on glass.

Cursing myself for getting too comfortable, I fumbled for the backpack my mother had given to me, rifling hurriedly through its contents—a few remaining cans of food and granola bars, a flashlight, a map of the city, a wad of money that had so far been useless, a change of clothing, and toothpaste—until I found it . . . the *gun*.

When I slept, I usually kept it close to me, but tonight, *of all nights*, I had forgotten.

I positioned myself behind the metal stacks, concealing the gun close to my side. It was heavy and cold. My mother had taught me to use it, but firing a weapon seemed like something that someone else would do, some other version of me. Still, I told myself that I was prepared to. I had to be.

Through the darkness, I saw a boot. A brownish black tail—a dog? Panic started to make its way into my throat, my heart thumping as fast as a hummingbird's. For a moment, I wondered if it was possible to die of fear.

In my mind, I heard my mother's voice, "Fear serves a purpose."

She first spoke those words when I was ten. An earthquake had startled me from sleep. A picture above my dresser crashed to the floor. Yet my mother was calm.

"Are you afraid?"

I couldn't speak, but I nodded.

"Good," she said, holding me close to her. "It's okay to be afraid. Fear is your body's way of telling you something important." Even then, I bristled at the irony in my mother's words.

"Artos, come," said a man's stern voice, followed by a *click–click–click* of what I could only assume were Artos' nails on the library floor. It had been so long since I'd heard a voice other than my own. It was both horrifying and exhilarating. For the rest of the night, I stayed close to the stacks, coaching myself to control my breathing—a trick my mother had taught me. Twice I forced myself to peer into the darkness, expecting something monstrous to meet my gaze. There was nothing.

I didn't see him again until two days later. I had almost begun to believe I had imagined him. I replayed that terrifying night visit again and again in my mind, searching for some clue. My mother had told me to be cautious—to wait, to watch, to be certain. I *had* to be certain.

When I saw him again, it was by chance. It was near dawn, and the rising orange sun cast an eerie light through the library. I was washing my face in the library's bathroom, allowing myself a quick glance in the mirror. I had the kind of face that people were always saying they recognized. My mother told me it was a compliment, that I made others feel comfortable, familiar. But I suspected my face was simply ordinary, so ordinary that it was practically interchangeable.

My long, dark hair was pulled back into a matted ponytail. I moved closer to the mirror and looked into my own eyes. My father always told me that they were like my mother's, kind and bright. As I leaned in, the locket my mother gave me for my eighteenth birthday clinked against the mirror. In it were two faces, both of them smiling—my parents. The gift was unexpected because, by then, my mother's savings had diminished and most of the jewelry stores in the Bay Area had been forced to close.

A faint noise from outside startled me. I froze. Crouching below the window, I peered over the sill and saw him. He was standing near the library's entrance with Artos, a German Shepherd, at his side. I tried to memorize him. He was tall with dark hair that was cut short, but had grown longish at the ends. His clothing was plain, and he wore military-style boots. His shoulders were broad and strong. I couldn't see his face. He was looking out, away from me, at something just beyond my vision. On the inside of his forearm, I saw the outline of a familiar tattoo. I drew in a breath.

Back at the safety of my desk, I tried to make sense of it. The tattoo could only mean he was a member of the Guardian Force and couldn't be trusted. My mother warned me that all Guardian officers and military personnel were under the influence of Emovere since the federal government had awarded Zenigenic a confidential contract. With Emovere, the government had virtually eliminated occurrences of posttraumatic stress. If you can't feel fear, then you won't be haunted by it.

Still, there was something about the way he moved—cautiously, carefully—that made me wonder.

CHAPTER FOUR

FREEDOM

LEAVING THE LIBRARY WAS A risk, but after seeing the tattooed man for the second time, I began to feel a sense of urgency. My mother warned me to guard against my impatience, but it was growing more and more difficult to wait.

"Remember," my mother had chided, "they will come to you."

The Resistance, wherever, *whatever* it was, wasn't to be sought out. After my mother began to speak out publicly about the dangers of Emovere, she was contacted by the Resistance. By then, the government had placed significant restrictions on the public's use of emotion-altering medications, including Emovere. Still, for a price, it was accessible to those who wanted it. And many did.

I peered cautiously out of the library door into the street. It was nearing twilight, and a light rain had begun to fall. Papers blew into the doorway around my feet, most of them posters promoting the Resistance. I clutched my jacket tighter around me. I had no plan. I felt tentative, like a caged animal that had just discovered freedom lay beyond a broken latch. Uncertain, I stepped into the rain, leaving the library behind me.

I headed south. The rain was coming down harder now, stinging my skin. The air felt electric, as if my apprehension was a tangible, steady buzz. I passed familiar streets. At Powell Street, a cable car was overturned, branded in red spray paint with the mark of the Resistance: The Bowl of Hygeia—the Greek symbol of pharmacy—cracked and turned on its side, with a skull tumbling from within it. It was a striking image, both derisive and foreboding.

Most of the stores in this part of the city had been vacant long before the Resistance began. People could no longer afford luxuries. One of the shops was familiar: a toy store where my father had taken me while we waited for my mother to finish a meeting. Back then, it seemed we were always waiting for my mother. After her role in developing Emovere, she became somewhat of a celebrity, appearing on news shows and chatting with her supporters on social media. At home, my mother never boasted about her success, but she didn't have to. It was as apparent and ever-present as her shadow.

As I peered into the toy store's rain-fogged windows, I had a flash of my father, swinging me by the arms in a circle, both of us laughing. I had few memories of him, so I guarded them preciously. He left when I was ten. The last time I saw him, I was lingering in the doorway of my bedroom, looking out into the kitchen where my parents stood, arguing.

"I don't think you know what you're doing—what the consequences could be. Do you even care?" My father's face was red with anger, but he looked defeated. Their arguments had grown more frequent, yet each was the same as the last. My father wanted my mother to resign from her position at Zenigenic.

"Of course, I care." My mother lowered her voice. "You *know* I care."

"I don't know *anything* about you anymore."

My father turned from my mother. When his eyes briefly met mine, I saw that he felt satisfied and then, ashamed. When I returned from school the next day, he was gone. In the years that followed, I came to understand why he left my mother. She could be distant and selfish at times. But I never forgave him for leaving me.

It was almost dark by now, and the remaining light cast shadows around me. They danced eerily at the edges of my vision. I walked faster. I had hoped that by leaving the library, I would discover something to direct me to the Resistance. I saw now that there was nothing here.

What if my mother had been wrong about everything? How could she let me come here alone? For the first time in a long time, I allowed myself to feel angry with her. I turned back toward the library. The rain had subsided, but I was wet and cold. I started to run.

As I ran, I caught broken glimpses of myself in what remained of the store windows. I looked wild, careless. Fear began to tug at me, whispering at first, then speaking urgently. I could hear the soft, methodical thud of what sounded like footsteps behind me. I ran faster, not daring to look. By the time I reached the library, I was certain that at any moment someone, *something*, was just a fingertip's length behind me. As I approached the door, I took one quick look back to ready myself. The street was empty and blanketed in darkness.

CHAPTER FIVE

THE FIRST TIME

WHOOSH! I SLAMMED THE LIBRARY door shut, sending leaves and papers swirling about the room. I pressed my back into the wall, breathing heavily. In the library, it was as dark as a cave. I reached for the light switch, flicking it on and off and on again. Nothing.

It's just a blackout, I told myself, squinting into the blackness. The government reported that California's frequent power outages were caused by the country's crumbling infrastructure. My mother, on the other hand, was convinced that the blackouts were manufactured to keep us in a constant state of uncertainty. I wasn't sure what to believe.

From above my head, a familiar brown bird swooped past me. I squealed with surprise and began laughing. *How was I ever going to be worthy of the Resistance if I couldn't manage a bird?*

"You almost gave me a heart attack," I said aloud, my words echoing in the empty room.

I removed my jacket and left it in a wet heap near the door. I turned on my flashlight, sending a thin yellow beam of light through the room. Though my brief adventure had been unsuccessful, I felt a small sense of accomplishment. I had stepped out into the world and returned intact.

Just as my body began to relax, I felt a sudden, sharp impact to my side. I doubled over. The flashlight slid across the floor, striking the wall with a thud. *Run. Run! RUN!* My brain screamed at me, but, for an instant, I couldn't move. Finally, instinct took over. I scrambled to my feet, trying to reach the gun concealed in the back of my pants. I heard a man's heavy breathing and felt him reaching for me through the darkness. He struck me again, this time in the chest. I felt dizzy. He grabbed at my shirt, and there it was—the black-inked badge on his inner left forearm. A Guardian! He pulled me closer toward him. I landed a solid kick to his knee, then ran toward the back of the library, hiding in a small alcove.

He followed.

I waited.

The man moved clumsily in the dark. As he neared the alcove, I could see he wasn't who I thought he was. He had long blond hair and was heavily muscled. He wore a dark uniform and carried handcuffs and a weapon at his side. Unlike the other tattooed man, he moved without concern as if he couldn't be harmed. Though I couldn't be certain, I suspected he was under the influence of Emovere. His lack of fear was a weakness. He wouldn't anticipate danger.

Time seemed to slow, my senses heightened by my terror. I saw only the man, plodding toward me, his boots causing thunderous echoes in my ears. *Tunnel vision*, I thought to myself, remembering my mother's description of the body's response to fear. I steadied my breathing and considered the gun in my hand. *What choice did I have?* I squeezed the trigger, and the man fell back.

CHAPTER SIX

FOUND

TEN LONG MINUTES LATER, I found the Resistance. Or rather, *they* found me. I hadn't moved from the alcove. I felt heavy inside, my stomach a churning pit of rocks. I had never killed anything larger than a spider—until now. My eyes were drawn to the dead man. He lay face down with his head turned unnaturally to the side. A river of blood snaked its way from underneath him. It was painful to look at him, yet I found it hard to look away.

When my mother told me about her early research with criminals, most of them murderers, I hung on every word, waiting for the *why*. The *why* fascinated me so much more than the *how*. Each case was a riddle I needed to solve, to understand how such things were possible. But I was always disappointed—the *why* never completely satisfying me. Now I understood. *I* was a murderer . . . no different from the men my mother had studied.

In the distance, I heard the rumble of an engine. It steadily grew louder and then stopped. I knew I should be afraid, but I felt numb. The library door creaked as it swung open, and I heard the *click-click-click* that had awakened me nights before—along with the sound of approaching footsteps.

"Where are you?" The man's voice was gruff and demanding, almost a growl.

I said nothing. I tried to be as still and silent as a stone. I could hear Artos sniffing the ground feverishly.

"We don't have much time. In case you didn't notice, you killed a Guardian."

His words surprised me. Wasn't *he* a Guardian?

"Okay," he said. "It's your choice. They'll be here to arrest you any minute now, but I guess you can handle it." Strange, but his sarcasm made me smile.

"Who are you?" my voice croaked.

"I'm here to help you. Right now, that's all you need to know."

I thought of my mother. She had sent me here. She had trusted me. I had to trust myself. I stood slowly, steadying myself against the wall. My legs felt like rubber.

"I'm here," I said, taking a step from behind the alcove. "I'm here."

CHAPTER SEVEN

FIRST IMPRESSIONS

"WE GOTTA GO," HE SAID, looking around nervously.

Now that I could see his face, I saw that he was young, about my age. But there was a seriousness about him that made him seem older, as if life had already written "sadness" on his slate. He had strong features with a faint beard shadowing his jawline.

"Get your stuff," he directed harshly.

As he spoke, he walked purposefully to the dead man. He kneeled beside him and removed a needle and vial from his jacket pocket. Taking the man's arm in his hand, he inserted the needle and withdrew a sample of blood. He moved efficiently, as if he'd done this many times before. He probably had. The thought unnerved me.

Then he searched the dead man's clothing. He removed his cellular telephone, quickly snapping out and pocketing its tiny memory card. He discarded the telephone's shell in the corner. Last, he produced something from the man's pocket. It was the flash drive my mother had given me. I instantly felt foolish for leaving it behind, unprotected.

"Do you know what this is?" he asked.

"No." It was the truth. My mother had not told me. I could only wonder.

I walked toward the door, retrieving my still-wet jacket and backpack. My mother had always been good at keeping secrets. I recalled a conversation we had years earlier. In school, we were studying the human brain. I asked my mother why so many people wanted to alter their emotions. What I really wanted to ask was, "Why are *you* helping them do it?" But I knew she would be hurt.

"Not everyone is like us, Lex," she told me. "Their emotions get the best of them. Feelings are a bit like a wild animal—unpredictable—and they can be dangerous if you can't control them."

I never told my mother that, for months after my father left, I cried every night as I fell asleep, letting my tears dead-end into my pillowcase. I guess I had my secrets too.

"My mother gave it to me. I should keep it." My voice sounded more forceful than I had intended.

"Yes, you should *keep* it." He raised his eyebrows at me, scolding me. Even worse, I deserved it.

He stood by the door, Artos looking up at him anxiously. "Are you ready?" he asked me, begrudgingly handing me the flash drive.

"Can you at least tell me your name?" I tried to sneak a glance at his left forearm, but it was covered by his jacket sleeve.

He rolled his eyes. "Quin McAllister," he said, exasperated. Though his expression was cold, there was a glimpse of warmth underneath.

"And this is Artos." At the sound of his name, Artos' tail pendulummed back and forth.

"Alexandra," I offered without being asked, "but everyone calls me Lex."

It wasn't the whole truth. Most people called me Lexi, a nickname I hated. Hearing it, I couldn't help but picture myself as a small, fluffy dog. My whole fifth grade year, an awful boy named Jeffrey had called me Sexy Lexi—a name made even more humiliating by its obvious contrast to my then-awkward appearance. The truth was that only my parents called me Lex.

"Lex," he repeated. I felt warmth, an instant rush of precious memories. I saw my mother's face.

"So you're Lex." He smirked. "Daughter of the *great* Dr. Knightley. I was expecting someone a bit more . . ." His voice trailed off as he studied me.

My face felt hot. I wasn't used to being examined so intently by the opposite sex. The last time I had been this close to a boy my own age, he had kissed me. My first kiss. My *only* kiss. It seemed a lifetime ago.

My mother referred to me as a "late bloomer," an expression I despised. I imagined myself as a cold, hard seed in the ground, waiting impatiently while life sprung up around me.

"Don't worry," she had said. "It will happen." *It* being my blooming, of course. Though she always reassured me, when I told her about the kiss, I sensed that she was relieved.

I met Quin's stare. The warmth I had felt disappeared. I felt exposed.

"A bit more *what?*" Inwardly, I groaned. I sounded like a child seeking approval.

"Let's go," Quin said, ignoring my question. He opened the door and waited. Artos trotted out obediently.

"Where are we going?" My voice seemed small.

Quin said nothing, but his silence felt like a reprimand. I didn't like him, but I trusted him without knowing why.

CHAPTER EIGHT

WHAT LIES BENEATH

WE RODE IN SILENCE, ARTOS between us. I shivered. My clothing was still wet, and the night air was cold. I petted Artos' head gently, and he licked my hand. At least Artos liked me. The truck—apparently abandoned by someone fleeing the city—smelled of stale beer and cigarettes. Adhered to the dashboard was a small paper calendar: March 2040, over one year ago, when a mandatory evacuation order forced most people from the city.

When my mother and I first received word of the evacuation, we weren't surprised. SFTV had been documenting the increasing unrest in San Francisco for years. Though small Resistance factions had developed across the country, the political climate in California made San Francisco a fitting home for its headquarters. For several years, the Resistance held regular protest rallies in front of several of the major pharmaceutical companies.

When the rallies became volatile, the federal government established the Guardian Force to maintain order in the city. Still, the Resistance marched and bedlam followed—looting and graffiti became commonplace, as did violent clashes between protestors and the Guardian Force. Citizens were urged, and eventually mandated, to leave the city for their own protection.

"How did you know where to find me?" I asked. The question had been gnawing at the back of my brain all night.

"How do you think? We were watching you." He glanced sideways at me, waiting for my reaction.

I paused, carefully considering his use of the word *we*.

"I saw you," I said. "But . . ." I stopped myself. It was still too soon to tell him that I had seen his tattoo.

Quin appeared unfazed. He gestured with his head. "We're here."

Here was nowhere really—the middle of The Embarcadero, a main thoroughfare that ran right next to the ocean. Quin left the truck parked in an alleyway between two buildings. We walked a circuitous route toward the Financial District with Quin silently alerting me to several overhead surveillance cameras. Artos stayed close to Quin's side, his ears perked and alert. At the corner of Market and Embarcadero, Quin turned to me and pointed ahead, smirking again.

"Welcome to the Resistance headquarters."

His words were intended to shock me, and they did. The Resistance had been right underneath me all along. Literally.

CHAPTER NINE

WATCHED

QUIN WAS POINTING TO THE boarded entrance of the underground BART railway station. He easily removed one of the boards, which had been left loosened. The eerie quiet of the city made sense now. As is often the case, life was happening underground. For a moment, I felt the ache of melancholy. I wished my mother could be here with me. Things felt less real to me without her.

"After you," he said, gesturing toward the staircase.

Artos and I began walking down the stairs. Behind us, Quin carefully placed the board back in its position and followed. Just at the foot of the staircase was a large steel door with a keypad. Quin placed his thumb into the device and typed in a code. The door opened.

The sprawling BART station had been given a second life. In the middle of the wall up ahead, the mark of the Resistance was painted in bold red. At the center, there was a control station of sorts with at least twenty monitors capturing various portions of the city from above. Several armed men were stationed nearby. They acknowledged Quin with a nod.

Quin pointed to the monitors. "The government has its eyes all over the city. Our computer engineer, Hiro, was able to tap into their surveillance system. We see *what* they see, *when* they see it."

I wondered how long the Resistance had been watching me. *Had they witnessed my first night in the library? Had they seen me hiding from Quin? Or my wild run through the rain? Had they known I was in danger?*

I followed Quin. He effortlessly scaled the turnstiles that blocked our entrance, then offered his hand.

"I can do it myself," I said, glad that my mother had insisted on our daily workouts—pushups, sit-ups, and a five-mile run in a park near our home.

"Suit yourself," he replied, not glancing back.

He continued walking through a long, sterile corridor and down an unmoving escalator onto the pedestrian platform. I remembered standing here when the trains were still running, hearing the roar and feeling the cold rush of air sliding past me as they approached. Now, there was only stillness and silence.

The trains were shut down more than one year prior to the evacuation. It was one of the government's first attempts to quell the Resistance. SFTV reported that members of the Resistance were targeting stations near the pharmaceutical companies, vandalizing trains and accosting passengers. My mother and I had watched from the West Oakland station as the last train returned from San Francisco.

Quin's voice interrupted my memory. "You'll meet everyone tomorrow," he said. "I'll show you where you can sleep tonight."

Artos was already running excitedly down the tracks. In his wake, birds scattered frantically. Quin hopped down from the platform and started walking into the black tunnel ahead.

"Down there? You've got to be kidding me." I laughed, but inside I was wondering if I had made a fatal error in coming here, putting my faith in Quin, with his Guardian tattoo.

Reading my thoughts, Quin replied, "Trust me."

If I didn't go with him, I would be spending the night on the platform alone. Or *worse*, back in the bleakness of the city. I hesitated, then began walking. Quin produced a small flashlight from his jacket before we headed straight into the darkness.

CHAPTER TEN

PERKS

ABOUT ONE HUNDRED YARDS AHEAD, Quin opened another door with his fingerprint. Inside was a tunnel that widened into a series of rooms. Each door was branded with the mark of the Resistance.

"How is this possible?" I wondered aloud.

Not surprisingly, Quin didn't answer. It seemed that he carefully chose when to speak and when to be silent. I was almost starting to like that about him.

He led me into a small, sparse room with a twin-sized bed and its own bathroom.

"Our visitors stay here," he explained. Though I didn't dare say it, I doubted the Resistance typically entertained visitors.

"I'll give you a moment to settle in," he said. "But first, I'll need your weapon. Visitors aren't authorized to carry guns."

Though I knew it was probably foolhardy, handing the gun to Quin felt like releasing the heaviest of burdens. After he left, I sat down on the bed, letting the day sink into my mind. It seemed impossible so much had happened in one day. But even at eighteen, I already knew life was like that. Sometimes a day can contain a lifetime.

My brain was buzzing with questions, annoying little flies that I tried to swat unsuccessfully. I managed to silence my thoughts long enough to enjoy a hot shower. I changed into the dry clothing in my backpack, slipping my mother's flash drive into my pocket. I would not let it out of my sight again.

On the desk near the bed, I placed the one possession that I treasured most: an anthology of poetry that belonged to my mother. I had read it so many times, it seemed as if the words were my own. My mother's favorite poem—Mary Oliver's "Wild Geese"—was dog-eared. When I thought of my mother folding the corner of that page for me, I felt a pit deep in my stomach. I sat down on the edge of the bed. The mattress was firm, unyielding, but far more comfortable than the library floor.

A short time later, Quin returned with a sandwich and a glass of water. He sat down on the bed next to me with Artos at his feet. He seemed more relaxed. I could feel the warmth from his body. He smelled like summer. He had taken off his jacket, and my eyes instantly went to his inner forearm—the black-inked badge clearly visible now. Quin rubbed his finger across the tattoo. I averted my eyes, but I knew that I had been caught.

"You can ask me about it, if you want," he said.

"Well, that's new," I joked.

Quin laughed, his brown eyes crinkling at the corners. He looked his age again, his seriousness momentarily dissolved. "I guess I can be a bit difficult at times."

"Difficult? Is that how you would describe it?" I met his eyes for a moment, and we both smiled.

I quickly looked away. I didn't want him to think that I was flirting. *Was I flirting?*

"You have some better words, I presume?" Quin teased, gesturing at my book on the table. "Haven't seen someone with one of those in a while."

I nodded. Traditional books were almost obsolete since most information was digital, stored on small computer tablets. "My mother gave it to me."

"So . . ." I was tentative, trying to select the least offensive words. "You're a Guardian?" I finally asked, practically whispering the word *Guardian* as if invoking it held some mysterious power.

Quin took a breath. His brow furrowed. "I *was* a Guardian . . . but not anymore."

"Why?" I asked. That same small question that really was so big. "Why did you become a Guardian?"

"Let's just say that being a Guardian comes with certain perks."

"Like Emovere?" As soon as I spoke the words, I immediately regretted them. Though his face remained expressionless, Quin's eyes were not as skilled at deception. "Sorry," I muttered.

"More like food and shelter," Quin replied. "I was only sixteen and homeless when they recruited me."

I looked at him quizzically. I hadn't expected that. "What about your family?"

"Gone," he said. He disguised it well, but I heard a tangible ache in his voice. I knew better than to press for more.

Quin slipped back into his stony silence, then stood and walked to the doorway. "Try to get some sleep. Tomorrow will be busy."

I nodded, but I couldn't imagine a day any busier than this one.

"Artos, stay," he commanded. As Quin closed the door, Artos whined and then settled near the foot of my bed.

Taking the book of poetry from the desk, my fingers easily found my mother's dog-eared page. Once I skimmed past the first few lines, I thought of Quin as I read.

CHAPTER ELEVEN

MAX AND ELANA

I JOLTED AWAKE. FOR A brief moment, I panicked, my surroundings still unfamiliar. Through the small rectangular window in the door, I could see Quin's face. Looking up at him, Artos sat patiently, but expectantly. I stumbled to the door, hoping I was somewhat presentable.

"Did I wake you?" Quin asked politely, as if it wasn't completely obvious. He wore blue jeans and a gray T-shirt that fit snugly against the curves of his biceps.

I smiled sheepishly and glanced at the clock on the wall. It read 8:30, but it seemed as if I had been sleeping for days—yesterday, a dream I had only now awakened from.

"Get dressed," Quin said. "I want to show you around. There are a lot of people waiting to meet you."

I felt my stomach churn. I was finally going to see the faces of the Resistance.

About thirty minutes later, Quin returned, and we revisited our path from the previous night. As we walked, he showed me the rest of the sleeping quarters and the dining hall. Apparently, many of the Resistance shared a room with a roommate since most of the quarters contained two beds.

"Everyone here has a job," he said. "We have technology experts, ex-military, scientists, nurses, cooks. We're like a community. No one is more important than anyone else."

"What's your job?" I asked.

"Surveillance."

"Why did you choose that?" I wondered aloud. I couldn't imagine Quin selecting a job that required patience.

"It's slightly calmer than my last gig," he answered, grinning at me and turning his hand to reveal his Guardian tattoo.

He pointed to a secure door on my right. "This room may interest you. It's our laboratory."

I peered inside. Large-screen computers lined the walls. In the center stood a workstation, apparently used to analyze blood and chemicals. A colorful diagram of the brain hung on the wall.

Quin also pointed out the armory and the kitchen, both of which had been well stocked in the days leading up to the evacuation. Though I saw no one, I had the sense we were being watched closely by hidden eyes.

"Where is everyone?" I asked.

Quin gestured down the long, dark tunnel in the opposite direction of my room. "The Map Room. It's where we keep the maps of the city and the underground BART tunnels. We usually meet there. They announce upcoming meetings over the intercom." Quin pointed to several small speakers mounted down the wall of the tunnel.

"And we have these for when we're authorized to leave headquarters." He showed off a walkie-talkie clasped to his waistband.

Quin continued down the tunnel, stopping when he came to a large window. "Here's the control room. I have some people I'd like you to meet."

Inside, a stocky young man with spiky blond hair sat perched on the edge of a desk, carefully scrutinizing the screen displays. Next to him, a girl read a magazine on a computer tablet. Quin knocked softly on the thick glass.

"Q, my man!" yelled Spiky, his voice barely audible through the glass. He opened the door and embraced Quin. The girl rose to her feet, also smiling at Quin. He grinned back at her, nudging her teasingly in the side with his elbow. I watched more intently than I cared to admit. Quin seemed different with them, lighter somehow.

"Lex." Quin looked over his shoulder at me. "These are my friends, Max and Elana."

Before either of them spoke, I noticed they both had Guardian tattoos.

Max, aka Spiky, extended his hand. "Maximillian Powers, surveillance extraordinaire at your service." He grinned, shaking my hand vigorously.

Elana and I studied each other cautiously, the way girls do. There was no other way to say it—Elana was stunning. She had peridot-colored eyes and long, red hair that coursed in waves down her shoulders. She wore no make-up, her skin bare except for a smattering of freckles. Her petite frame curved in all the right places, making my athletic build seem ungainly and hulking by comparison. I had known girls like her in school. Boys gravitated toward them, orbiting them like the sun. Next to her, I was practically invisible—a cold, gray star that was merely waiting to fall.

She spoke first. I was prepared to despise her, but her voice was soft and warm. "Elana Hamilton." She offered her hand. "It's so nice to finally meet you. I feel like I know you already." She cast her eyes downward and gave a timid smile.

Max chuckled. "Well, we do know a lot about you."

I looked at Max quizzically.

Quin explained, "Max, Elana, and I were in charge of your surveillance. After your mother told us you'd be coming, we followed you into the city and took turns watching you. We tried to warn your mother that it was unsafe. You got lucky, Lex. *Really* lucky."

Max and Elana glanced nervously at each other, as if they were sharing a distressing memory.

"The morning you crossed the bridge, there was a blackout. We lost the feed from the surveillance cameras, and I'm guessing the Guardians did too. Otherwise . . ." Quin's voice trailed off.

Max put his hand on my shoulder. His voice was thick with sarcasm. "Let's just say, we wouldn't have had the pleasure of meeting you."

I tried to absorb the impact of Max's words. Without that power outage, it would have been over. The Guardians would have taken me. I shuddered as an image of the dead man flashed in my mind.

"So you couldn't see me on those?" I gestured toward the control booth.

As I spoke, several members of the Resistance passed by, one of the men calling out to Elana. "Hey there, Red," he teased, smiling at her. Elana's body tensed instantly. She didn't acknowledge the man. Instead, she looked only at me. I noticed that both Quin and Max eyed the man with annoyance.

"No," Elana answered my question. "That's why it took the Guardians so long to find you. As soon as you left the library, their cameras spotted you."

With each answer, my questions multiplied. They were now a determined army marching through my brain.

"If you knew where I was and knew that I was in danger, why would you leave me there?" Though my question was directed to all of them, I looked only at Quin.

He sighed. "We had orders. We had to know that we could trust you."

"I guess I passed the test then, huh?" My voice sounded angrier than I expected, and it silenced them.

Max was the first to speak. "You sure did. I bet your mom would be proud."

I knew he was trying to make me feel better, so I let him.

"Your mom's gonna want to meet *this* guy," Max said, slapping Quin on the back and laughing.

Quin stiffened. His face instantly hardened like a shell. I looked to Max for an explanation.

"He didn't tell you?" Max asked, his voice incredulous.

When I didn't respond, he turned to Quin, "You didn't tell her?"

"Tell me what?"

Quin looked from Max to me. His eyes were brimming with shame. "We'll talk about it later," he said. Without another word, he turned and walked out of sight. Elana followed after him.

Quin's words echoed in my head. Even though I hardly knew him, I knew enough to know that when he said *later*, he meant *never*.

CHAPTER TWELVE

BY CHOICE

MAX AND I GLANCED AWKWARDLY at each other. "Well, I guess I know how to break up a party," he joked.

"Is he always like this?"

"If by *this*, you mean moody, but strikingly handsome, then yes. Unfortunately, he is." Max grinned, and I instantly realized why Quin considered him a friend.

"Can I ask you something?" I had to know if Max and Elana had also been Guardians, and why there seemed to be so many of those tattoos around here in the headquarters of their enemy.

I pointed to his left forearm.

"This old thing, huh? I'm thinking of turning it into something— something tough, like a dragon." We both laughed.

"So you were a Guardian like Quin?"

"Sort of," he said. "Elana and I are Guardian rejects. We didn't meet their expectations. Apparently, our scouting reports were greatly exaggerated."

I listened intently. My mother had taught me to fear the Guardians, but she had told me very little about them. I only knew they were a highly specialized military police force that secretly used Emovere to suppress fear. SFTV lionized the Guardian Force as a collection of elite heroes. Their standards for selection were reportedly very high—and their methods for identifying recruits, mysterious. There was never any mention of Emovere, of course.

"This may seem kind of personal, but why were you rejected?"

Max paused for a long time. "Apparently, I am . . . *homosexual.*" He pronounced the word like it was foreign to him. "The Guardians have a pretty antiquated view of the world. I guess they thought I'd be too busy checking out Quin to fight the Resistance." He gave a sly smile. "Come to think of it, they were probably right."

I laughed. I had never heard the word *homosexual* said aloud until now, but I had read the term in one of my mother's old psychology textbooks. The word was simply no longer used in conversation. In most places—especially in San Francisco—sexuality was a non-issue.

"And Elana?" I couldn't imagine Elana was anything but perfect in every way. I tried to convince myself I didn't care that she had gone after Quin. *Why should I care?*

"She didn't pass the final intelligence screening. It's very difficult. Most recruits fail that stage. Besides, Elana could *never* have been a Guardian. Even when they gave her Emovere, she was still far too tentative."

Max's words triggered a vague recollection of one of my mother's articles. In it, she had explained how severe past trauma made some individuals partially immune to Emovere's effects, requiring a higher dosage to achieve the desired results. The cause of their immunity was unclear but, anecdotally, my mother had observed that women were more likely to be Emovere resistant. I wondered if Elana, like Quin, had been through something irrevocable.

"How did you end up here?" I asked.

"The Resistance came looking for us. Obviously, because of what we knew, we were an asset to them."

"I can't imagine the Guardians being too pleased with that," I said.

Max looked down, his expression heavy with emotion. "No. There haven't been any defectors since Quin over a year ago."

I considered his words with trepidation. The Guardian qualification standards were overly demanding, making it highly unlikely that no one else had been rejected. But if they hadn't defected to the Resistance, then where had they gone? *What had happened to them?* I couldn't ask the question. I feared the answer was unthinkable. Instead I chose another question, one that had been nagging at me since the night before.

"What about Quin?" I asked. If I didn't get the answer from Max, I would certainly never get it from Quin.

"Quin is kind of amazing." Max smirked. "He breezed through the training. He was a member of the Guardian Force for two years."

"So what happened?"

Max's face grew serious. "Don't ever tell Quin that I told you this. As you can tell, he's very . . . *private*."

"I'm sensing that," I said, half-smiling at him. "It's just between us," I added, eager for his answer.

Max leaned toward me, his voice barely audible. "Quin is the only member of the Guardian Force to have ever left by choice."

CHAPTER THIRTEEN

ALCATRAZ

I SPENT ALMOST AN HOUR with Max, watching the camera feeds. Most parts of the city were under surveillance, but thanks to Guardian dropouts like Max and Elana, the Resistance had learned the location of most of the cameras and was able to avoid them.

Once every thirty minutes, a Guardian helicopter circled past the Golden Gate Bridge, ensuring there were no trespassers. Surprisingly, the cameras had no view of the Bay Bridge or its surroundings, and it had been too dark the previous night for me to see it. I wondered if the information my mother had received about its bombing was accurate. Aside from the helicopter's predictable flight, there was no other movement to speak of.

"Pretty boring, huh?" Max leaned back in his chair, dangerously close to tipping it.

I nodded.

"Why can't we see the Bay Bridge?" I asked.

Max gave a sly smile. "Why do you think?" He answered his own question. "It's a little too close to home for the Guardians. They probably don't want to risk the cameras."

"Close to *home*?" The Guardian Force headquarters had been a mystery to my mother and me.

Max nodded, leaning even further back in his chair.

"Alcatraz," he said matter-of-factly. Then he laughed, shaking his head. "The irony."

Alcatraz! It truly *was* ironic. Almost ten years ago, the government had closed Alcatraz to the public after concern was raised about the possibility of radioactive material in the soil. Since then, SFTV had periodically chronicled the government's efforts to rehabilitate the state park. After a while, we heard nothing more about it. It made perfect sense—the Guardian Force hiding their indiscretions behind ancient prison walls.

"So how did you end up training to be a Guardian?" I asked.

Max sat upright in his chair, jolted by my question. "*They* found me. Not that I had any other offers. They told me that they knew a lot about me and thought I would be a good candidate. I was in a group home at the time."

"A group home?" I looked at Max with concern.

"Yeah, your typical sob story." He smiled. "Boy gets abused. Boy gets neglected. Boy runs away. Boy goes to a group home."

"Max, that's really awful," I said. I was beginning to suspect that Max's bold personality was a cover. "Do your parents know you're here?"

"I doubt they care." Max sighed. "My dad left us when I was a kid. Haven't seen him since. My mom couldn't really handle it. She started taking Eupho a lot. She was totally checked out. It was pretty bad."

Eupho was slang for Euphoractamine, a popular emotion-altering substance. It induced feelings of intense pleasure or euphoria.

Max shook his head as if to shake off a memory. "Then she met my stepdad—and things went from pretty bad to a lot worse. My mom got pregnant with my brother, and I think my stepdad just saw me as an unpleasant reminder of my mother's past. One of his favorite pastimes was using me as a punching bag." Max shadow boxed in my direction. "After I ran away, I told my social worker I wasn't going back home, so I went to the Oak Valley Home for Boys."

I shook my head, giving him a sympathetic look.

"Isn't it funny how those places always have nice-sounding names, like you're going on a permanent camping trip?" Max said, laughing. "That's when the Guardians found me. It seemed like they already knew that nobody would come looking for me."

I was about to ask Max if he knew how the Guardians had learned so much about him, but Quin returned, alone.

"Well, hello, Sunshine," Max teased Quin. "How kind of you to return for our guest."

Quin's mouth turned up slightly at the corners in a half smile. When he looked at me, his face was contrite, though he didn't apologize.

"C'mon, Lex," he said. "They're ready for you."

CHAPTER FOURTEEN

SUPER SOLDIER

I STOOD NEXT TO QUIN at the front of the Map Room. At least three hundred pairs of eyes stared back at me. The last time I had been in front of a crowd this size, I was graduating from high school, giving my valedictory address. I remembered trying desperately to find my mother's face in a sea of faces, beads of sweat pooling underneath my long hair. Stalling, I had cleared my throat into the microphone, sending my nerves cascading in echoes throughout the stadium. Finally, when I implored myself to begin speaking, I saw her.

Now, in this sea of faces, only two were familiar: Max and Elana. I was grateful they had taken seats near the front. I tried to focus on them, but it was impossible. The faces of the Resistance were everywhere: Men and women, young and old, all races. I mentally tallied the number of Guardian tattoos, losing count at seventeen. Though the room was filled with chatter, a steady drum of voices, I often heard my last name. Curious heads turned in my direction, their eyes lingering for longer than was polite. I felt spotlighted, so I looked back at them. I wondered what they'd been told about me.

I glanced at Quin. As usual, he appeared calm, almost bored. He leaned in toward me, so close that I could feel his warm breath on my cheek.

"Apparently, you're quite the celebrity," he said quietly, his face softening into an easy smile. There was something about Quin smiling at me that felt a lot like finding my mother's face in the crowd.

"*Apparently*," I replied. "Too bad you missed your chance for an autograph."

Quin chuckled. I noticed that Max and Elana were watching us intently. Max whispered something to Elana, and she nodded.

Quin nudged my arm and gestured toward a man, standing at the back of the room.

"That's Augustus Porter," he said, his voice reverent. "Before the economy tanked, he was a successful investment banker. He's the elected leader of the Resistance."

Augustus Porter. I repeated the name in my head. It was unfamiliar to me, but then again, up until yesterday, the entire Resistance had been an enigma. My mother's contacts with the Resistance had been infrequent. Text messages to her emergency-only cell were always initiated by them and shrouded in secrecy. I doubted she had ever heard the name, Augustus Porter.

Augustus had the look of an aging athlete. He was tall and wiry, towering above most of the crowd. His skin was the color of candied chocolate, and he had a thick, graying beard. To say the least, he had a presence—the kind of person who changes the room just by entering it. Augustus walked toward Quin and me, the crowd parting as he passed through it.

"Hello, Ms. Knightley." He extended his hand. "Gus Porter. It's a pleasure to finally meet you." His voice was deep and booming like a bass drum. "When we heard about your mother's plan, we were quite concerned. I'm glad you've proven yourself to be tougher than we expected."

I smiled graciously, masking my annoyance. *Was that a compliment?*

"Thank you. It's a relief to be here," I said. That was true, at least.

"I'd like you to meet the Council, the governing body of the Resistance." Augustus gestured toward the group accompanying him. He named them one by one. "Cason Caruso, our strategist; Dr. Shana Bell, psychiatrist; Hiro Chen, computer and technology specialist; and Vera Bullock, pharmaceutical consultant."

Augustus paused, smiling. He put an arm around Quin. "And, of course, you've already met Mr. McAllister. He's our expert on all matters Guardian." Quin's face brightened.

"Nice to meet you all," I said, shaking their hands. Their faces were welcoming, all but Cason Caruso. Giving me a single nod of his bald head, he turned from me, disinterested. He wore a permanent scowl with a firmly set jaw as if bolted into place.

Augustus opened his arms toward the crowd. They quieted as he spoke. "Members of the Resistance, today is a landmark day in our cause. As you may have already heard, we have with us here, Ms. Alexandra Knightley, daughter of the esteemed Dr. Victoria Knightley. Dr. Knightley has been instrumental in promoting the views of the Resistance and has been working closely with us since the city was evacuated. Her daughter is here to assist us."

The crowd began to buzz, a small hive of chattering voices.

Augustus turned to me and addressed me directly. His gaze was intense. "Most likely, you have been given a great deal of misinformation by the media. The things you will hear today may shock you. You may have trouble believing them, but you can trust that the Resistance speaks the truth."

I nodded, but inside my stomach churned with an uneasy doubt. Though I wanted to believe him, my mother had taught me to be skeptical. "We aren't lie detectors, Lex," she always cautioned. Through her work with criminals, my mother had learned quickly how effortlessly people lied and, even worse, how easy it was to be duped.

Behind Augustus, a large projector screen came to life. For a brief moment, I stopped breathing. On the screen was the face of the dead man. The picture appeared to have been obtained from a social media website. In it, the dead man was clearly alive, posing for the camera. I wanted to look at Quin. I wanted to look away—anywhere, but at the dead man's face. Concealing my horror, I kept my eyes focused on the screen as Augustus spoke.

"Last night, in our efforts to rescue Alexandra, a member of the Guardian Force was killed by our surveillance team. His name was Elliot Barnes. He was twenty. We were fortunate to obtain a sample of his blood and his cell phone data."

A new screen appeared. Thankfully, the dead man—Elliot—was not on it. Instead there was a graph marked *Levels and Composition of Emovere.* I tried to focus on it, but I was distracted by Augustus' lies.

I had killed Elliot. *Was he trying to protect me?* And the word *rescue* infuriated me. Quin had admitted he was under orders to allow me to fend for myself as a test of my trustworthiness.

"Consistent with our prior data, Mr. Barnes had large amounts of Emovere in his blood. As you can see, comparing our prior samples, the levels of Emovere have been steadily increasing among members of the Guardian Force. Additionally, we detected the presence of other emotion-enhancing substances, including Agitor."

My assumption about Elliot had been correct, but I hadn't expected him to be under the influence of other substances. Agitor was known as a particularly potent drug for enhancing stimulation and excitement.

Augustus continued. "These results are further proof that our suspicions about the government's motives in establishing the Guardian Force are correct."

Augustus looked directly at me as he spoke. "The Guardians are not a military police force. They are an experimental group serving only one purpose."

Another screen appeared. It was black except for two words in large red, block print: *Super Soldier.*

CHAPTER FIFTEEN

A WARNING

AS THE CROWD DISPERSED, A few members of the Resistance lingered behind to shake my hand. I felt like an impostor. Attention had always come easily to my mother. She reveled in it, soaking up accolades like a sponge. For me, as for my father, it had always been more comfortable to stand just outside the spotlight. Besides, I had done nothing to warrant attention except shooting Elliot. No one but Quin and I (and Augustus?) knew that.

Most of the Resistance was gracious and welcoming, but I knew some viewed my mother's participation in the movement as too little, way too late. An older woman approached me, her brow narrowed in a hard line of contempt. As she neared, I could see that time and sadness had weathered her face. I smiled, trying to preempt the storm that I could see gaining strength inside her. She did not return my gesture.

"Alexandra, is it?" she asked, her voice already irritated.

"Yes, ma'am." I tried to be polite.

"In my opinion, your mother started this whole mess. Wasn't she the one who helped to develop Emovere in the first place?" The woman didn't wait for a response. "Now she wants to jump off that bandwagon onto ours, and we're supposed to say, *Thank you, Dr. Knightley. We're so honored, Dr. Knightley.* I don't think so. We don't need her kind of help."

"I understand why you feel that way," I said, parroting a phrase I heard my mother use often. She told me that expressing understanding disarms anger. I hoped it would work.

"Do you? Do you understand?"

An obvious miscalculation. My words had only strengthened her storm. I sighed, exasperated. I noticed Augustus watching us, listening intently, while pretending not to.

"No," I admitted to her. "I guess I don't understand, but I would like to." My voice was small and contrite.

Just like that, the storm passed and her face calmed.

"I'm sorry," she said. "I don't mean to come off so angry. I'm really not like this all the time." She offered a meager smile. "My name is Sharon Cloverdale. I have—I mean *had*—a son named Michael. He was in the US Army Special Forces. Remember those bombings we had a while back in Chicago?"

I nodded. It was impossible to forget. Radical forces had bombed several major landmarks in the city, resulting in mass casualties. It was one of several precipitating events that sent our economy into a tailspin.

"After Chicago, he was selected to be part of the tactical team that went to the Middle East. He was given Emovere prior to his deployment. The doctors said it was their recommended prophylactic treatment for PTSD. No side effects."

Her face contorted with grief. "After that, I lost my son. He didn't die right away, but he was never the same. He walked around like a zombie, like there was nothing there anymore." She waved her hand in front of her face. "Then he killed himself—or at least, that's what we think. He drove his car into a wall."

"I'm so sorry," I said to her. "It might be hard for you to believe, but I know my mother is too."

She nodded, but I knew my words offered no comfort.

"I'm here for him," she said. "There are a lot of us here for someone. I hope you'll tell your mother that."

"I will," I called after her. She was already walking away.

I took a breath. Sharon's sorrow-fueled anger had stung just as if I had been slapped. I looked around the room. Only Augustus remained, but Quin lingered by the doorway, just within my sight. I was glad he hadn't left me alone with Augustus—something about him seemed false.

Still, I was inclined to believe his accusations against the government. When the economy collapsed, the government worked quickly to shore up the pharmaceutical companies. My mother often referred to these companies as the government's puppets because of the lucrative defense contracts they had been awarded. By that time, my mother had resigned from her position at Zenigenic. Her research had begun to suggest that Emovere could be highly addictive to some and induce aggressive episodes in others. When she approached the company with her concerns, they immediately demanded her resignation. So it wasn't a stretch to imagine the government partnering with the pharmaceutical industry to create an undefeatable and unempathetic soldier: fearless, aggressive, and unrelenting.

"A penny for your thoughts, Ms. Knightley." Augustus stood over me, looking down.

I chose my words carefully. "It's a lot to take in," I admitted, "but I'm not surprised."

"Well then, your mother has certainly taught you well." He paused, surveying the now-empty room. "Quin tells me that you have something for me . . . from your mother."

Again, my stomach flip-flopped. I hesitated but produced the flash drive from my pocket. I had been keeping it close to me. I could still remember the feel of my mother's hands as she pressed it into mine. She *had* wanted the Resistance to have it.

I offered the flash drive to Augustus. As it was swallowed by his large hand, I immediately regretted surrendering it so easily.

"Who else knows about this?" Augustus asked.

"Just Quin," I said. I glanced toward the doorway, but he was gone.

"Let's keep it that way." Augustus' lips smiled as he spoke, but his eyes were dead and cold, faintly reptilian. I couldn't help but feel as if his words were a warning.

CHAPTER SIXTEEN

TOGETHER?

WHEN I LEFT THE ROOM, I was surprised to see Elana waiting for me. She was alone. I felt disappointed. I needed to talk to Quin.

"Are you okay?" she asked. "You look a little pale."

"I'm fine," I lied.

As we walked back toward the control booth, Elana touched my arm. "I just wanted to apologize for earlier, for leaving like that."

"It's okay," I said. "You were just being a good friend to Quin." As I spoke the word, I immediately wondered if *friend* was an accurate descriptor of their relationship.

"Quin has his moments," Elana chuckled.

"So are you two . . . *together*?" Inside, I cursed my own boldness. Though I wasn't entirely sure why, my breathing was momentarily suspended as I awaited her answer.

Elana laughed again, throwing her head back.

"Quin, Max, and I were all recruited at the same time," she explained. "I was only sixteen. I would be lying if I said that I didn't fall for him."

My heart dropped fast, like a hard stone down into my stomach.

"We had . . . a moment, if you want to call it that, but it didn't last long. I guess I needed a lot of reassurance, and Quin isn't exactly the reassuring type."

I looked at Elana . . . her face was radiant. *What could she possibly need to be reassured of?* The girls I had known in school like her moved with a kind of effortless confidence. I could see now that Elana was not like that. Something deep inside her was broken.

"Quin has been through a lot," Elana said. "We all have, but Quin especially."

Elana sensed my curiosity.

"Be patient with him," she said gently, placing her hand on my shoulder. "He'll tell you. I can see that he wants to trust you."

Though I tried to hide it, I knew she could see how much I wanted to believe her.

CHAPTER SEVENTEEN

SIGHTSEEING

AFTER I LEFT ELANA, I returned to the control booth. Quin and Max were exchanging a computer tablet between them, engrossed in a game of Scrabble.

Max glanced up and waved me over. "Here she comes, our local celebrity," he joked, his eyes twinkling at me.

Quin snickered.

I rolled my eyes and shook my head at them.

"We've been waiting for you," Max added. "Augustus wants us to take you on a quick tour of the city—a little sightseeing of the Guardians' handiwork."

I gave him a puzzled look, inwardly recoiling at the mention of Augustus' name.

"What do you mean?" I asked.

"You'll see," Max offered cryptically.

A few minutes later, they were both geared up, guns and walkie-talkies strapped to their waistbands. I still wanted to talk to Quin about the meeting, but I held back. I couldn't help but notice that he seemed less-than-excited about our excursion. He hardly spoke to me until we were outside, walking up Market Street, retracing our circuitous route from the night before. Making sure we avoided the surveillance cameras, Max walked a few steps ahead of us.

"Did you give Augustus the flash drive?" he asked me.

I nodded, still feeling annoyed with myself.

"So," he began, "your mother didn't tell you what was on it?" I was surprised at his interest.

"No," I replied. "My mother is kind of a mystery sometimes. She hasn't told me much about her work lately."

"Oh." Quin sounded disappointed.

His voice hesitant, he asked, "Does she still work with *criminals*?"

I turned to him, considering his face carefully. "Do you know a lot about my mother?" It seemed that he did.

Before Zenigenic, my mother had spent years studying criminals. She had developed a drug—Crim-X—for the government that was supposed to reduce crime by suppressing emotions like anger and excitement. Her work allowed for the release of many inmates previously evaluated as high risk.

A few years after the first group of five hundred inmates was released, one of the men, Inmate 243, committed murder. The other inmates were returned to prison, and the project was abandoned. My mother rarely spoke of that time in her life, even to me, so Quin's question was a curious surprise.

Quin shook his head rapidly. "Uh . . . no . . . not really. Just what I've heard," he stammered. I saw Max glance back at us, directing a raised eyebrow toward Quin.

Max's comment from the morning about Quin and my mother nagged at me. "What have you heard?" I asked.

Quin didn't answer. He pointed up ahead. "Stop one on your tour, Ms. Knightley," he announced.

Up ahead, I saw a familiar scene. It was the overturned, graffitied cable car at the intersection of Market and Powell Street. Max hoisted himself up on the car, showboating for a moment, his arms outstretched.

"Fellow San Franciscans, lend me your ears." Max's voice was intentionally dramatic.

I giggled, but Quin seemed perturbed.

"Max." Quin admonished with a disapproving look.

Almost immediately, Max jumped down, giving me a little bow. "Sorry, *Dad*," he said sarcastically, narrowing his eyes at Quin.

"Wasn't there a rally here a while before the city was evacuated?" I asked, vividly recalling an SFTV news broadcast from one of the protests where shooting had erupted in the crowd.

Quin nodded solemnly, something dark passing across his face.

"That's why Augustus wanted us to take you to this spot," Max explained. "A man was killed here during that rally. The Guardian Force made it look like the Resistance was responsible."

"How?" I asked, unable to conceal my bewilderment.

I noticed that Quin had walked away from us. He was standing on the sidewalk, absent-mindedly kicking at some of the debris with his boot.

Max glanced cautiously in his direction before answering. "By having one of the Guardians dress up as a protestor and fire the shot. That way, the public would fear the Resistance, and the government could justify their plan for evacuating the city."

I raised my eyebrows in surprise, my eyes widening.

"It wasn't the only time," Max added. "There are a few more unfortunate stops on this tour."

I shook my head in disgust at everything I had learned today about the Guardian Force. I desperately wished I could talk to my mother. She would know what to do—she always did. I began to wonder if she had known all along about the true purpose of the Guardians.

Quin was already walking briskly ahead of us. I trotted to catch up to him.

"You never answered my question . . . about my mother," I reminded him.

"You're *persistent*, you know that?" Somehow, he made it sound like a bad thing. Even so, I nodded, smiling at him.

"What about your dad?" he asked, deliberately changing the subject. "I haven't heard *anything* about him."

I furrowed my brow at Quin. "I wouldn't have to be so *persistent*, if you weren't so *evasive*," I teased.

"Fair enough," he said flatly.

Even though he didn't deserve a reply, I answered him anyway. "My dad left us when I was ten. My mom and I haven't heard from him since then. I wish there was more to tell."

Quin was silenced briefly by my revelation.

"I'm sorry," he said. "I just assumed that . . ." He left his thought unfinished.

"My life was *perfect*?" I guessed at his assumption.

"Something like that," he admitted, shrugging.

Max stopped and pointed toward a building that had been gutted by fire. "Stop two," he told me.

"The Guardian Force set fire to this building," Max explained. "The government made sure that SFTV would publicly attribute the arson to the Resistance." He pointed to the red mark of the Resistance, blazing red on all the surrounding buildings.

Turning toward Quin, I carefully considered how to word my next question. "When you were a Guardian, did you ever *participate*?" I asked, gesturing to the building.

Quin's jaw tensed. I saw Max eyeing him closely, the way I had seen my mother watchfully attend to a boiling pot on the stove. There was no answer from Quin, but his silence spoke for him.

On our way back, Quin was distant, removed, even from Max. He walked ahead of us, brooding.

"Guess he didn't like the tour," Max joked with me, loud enough for Quin to hear him.

Quin turned, his expression softening. He caught my eye and winked at me conspiratorially as he grabbed Max, placing him in a pretend headlock.

"The tour was fantastic." Quin's voice was steeped with exaggerated excitement, and I giggled. Rubbing Max's head with his knuckle, he added, "It was the annoying tour guide I didn't like."

CHAPTER EIGHTEEN

RUNNING

I WAS SITTING ON MY bed, holding my book open to the dog-eared page. Only my eyes were reading. My mind was in a million other places. I had been prepared to fear the Guardian Force, but I was unnerved by what I had learned. Whatever their purpose, they were ruthless. Even more surprising, I hadn't expected to distrust the leader of the Resistance, but Augustus had given me an uneasy feeling that I couldn't ignore. He seemed as smooth and slick as oil. Another lesson from my mother: Never disregard that small, but insistent voice inside of you.

And there was something else I kept turning over and over in my mind like a stone. Quin, Max, and Elana had all been recruited as teenagers by the Guardian Force: Max from a group home, Quin from the streets—and Elana, I was still uncertain about, though I knew that she had demonstrated resistance to Emovere. Perhaps it was only an unlucky coincidence, but I couldn't help but think that long before the Guardians came looking for them, each had experienced something painful, something that couldn't be taken back. *Was that why the Guardians had recruited them?*

Mid-thought, I was halted by Quin's voice.

"I'm taking Artos for a run. Do you want to come?" Quin stood in the doorway, wearing shorts and a T-shirt. Artos was prancing, trying to contain his anticipation.

"Outside?"

"Not exactly." Quin smirked at me, running his hand through his dark brown hair, his eyes mischievous. I had to admit, Max was right—Quin was handsome—the unreachable kind of boy who, in my old life, I would have longed for from afar.

"I brought some clothes for you. These are Elana's." He held out a small bag with a shirt, shorts, and sneakers. "I'll meet you at the platform in ten minutes."

I felt eager to be alone with Quin. I was intent upon asking him about the meeting, but somewhere in my butterflied stomach, I knew that wasn't the only reason. When I arrived at the platform, Quin and Artos were standing below on the train tracks. Quin was jogging in place, holding a flashlight, and Artos was jumping eagerly next to him.

"Ready for this?" he asked me, his voice issuing a challenge. "I should warn you that I'm pretty fast."

"I would expect nothing less." I smiled at him.

Running through the tunnels was surprisingly exhilarating. Except for the small circle of light from Quin's flashlight, we were shadowed in darkness. After terrorizing a few unlucky birds, Artos trotted obediently next to us. Quin ran effortlessly. His breathing was steady and calm. I tried to match his pace, but he hadn't exaggerated. He *was* fast. After the first mile, Quin slowed his stride and turned to me.

"What did you think about the meeting?" he asked. I was surprised, but grateful that he had brought it up unprompted. He'd already been clear about his disdain for my *persistence*.

Uncertain how to sum up my thoughts for him, I began with the easiest question.

"Why did Augustus lie about how Elliot died?"

"He didn't lie," Quin replied. He kept running, his pace a steady trot.

After a few minutes of silence, I realized that Quin had no intention of offering more.

"You know, you don't have to make every conversation so difficult," I said, annoyed.

Quin stopped and turned to face me. "He didn't lie. He *wouldn't* lie." His voice was stern. "I told him that I killed Elliot."

"But why?" I asked.

"You ask that a lot, you know." I sensed that Quin wanted to trust me, but couldn't. His restraint protected him, like a turtle's shell hiding its soft underbelly.

"I know. Bad habit," I said. "But I'm trying to figure you out."

Quin took a breath. "I've done things, Lex, bad things. I've hurt people. If you knew what I did, you probably wouldn't like me."

I felt a dull ache, like a hammer strike to my chest, as I heard the shame in Quin's voice. I wanted to touch him, but I held back. "What makes you think I like you?" I asked, trying to lighten his mood.

Quin gave a half-hearted smile.

"I've hurt people too, you know," I said. I thought of Elliot, who was just a young man like Max or Quin, probably with a story equally as painful.

Quin nodded in agreement, but it seemed forced. As I turned from him, ready to resume our run, his voice stopped me.

"You don't hurt people, Lex. That's not what you do. That's what *I* do, and that's why I lied." His voice was hard as nails, matter-of-fact, as if it was a speech he had practiced many times alone.

I offered no response. We ran another four miles in silence, both of us entirely alone with our thoughts. I remembered Elana's words. Quin *had* been through a lot. The question was *what?*

CHAPTER NINETEEN

BULLET TO THE HEAD

QUIN AND I RETURNED TO chaos, the hallways thick with the members of the Resistance. They were scrambling like ants. As we dodged anxious faces, I caught snippets of conversations. "Ten bodies . . . bullet to the head . . . Guardians . . ."

Quin and I exchanged a look.

"We should see Augustus." He said it without thinking, as if Augustus was the answer to every question. Quin wore his distrust for others like a badge, yet it appeared he trusted Augustus without exception. It worried me.

I followed Quin past the Map Room, down another long corridor, and through two more secured doors to a third. Outside, several armed members of the Resistance stood guard.

"Hey, Quin," a guard said in a low voice, gesturing us over. "We tried to find you. Augustus is meeting with the rest of the Council."

He opened the door and ushered us in.

Inside, around a large table, five chairs were filled. A sixth sat empty. Augustus presided at the head, of course. As we entered, I watched him cast a look of disappointment toward Quin. Immediately, Quin's shoulders slumped, his head hung downward like a scolded puppy. Just as he was about to take the sixth seat, which was meant for him, Augustus turned his cold eyes toward us and spoke.

"Mr. McAllister, would you care to enlighten us as to your whereabouts for the past hour?" Augustus' voice was different than before. He was no longer charming.

Quin avoided Augustus' eyes. "I'm sorry, Augustus. There's no excuse."

"You're right. There is no excuse."

His words cut Quin like the strike of a whip, fast and deep. Dr. Bell and Vera Bullock lowered their eyes, embarrassed for Quin. Only Cason continued to stare at him, a look of amusement on his face.

With that, Augustus was finished with Quin and turned his lash to me.

"Ms. Knightley, this meeting is for Council members only. I'm afraid I must ask you to leave."

I looked to Quin for support, but he refused to meet my eyes. I touched his shoulder gently, and he nodded at me, expressionless.

"Go," he said.

CHAPTER TWENTY

AT THEIR HEARTS

LATER THAT EVENING, THE RESISTANCE reconvened in the Map Room. I immediately noticed that Quin was absent. I found a seat next to Max and Elana.

"Where's Quin?" I asked with concern, unable to shake the way he had cowered to Augustus.

Max shook his head. "He's been restricted from the meeting. Punishment."

"*Punishment?*" I asked incredulously.

Elana nodded. "Augustus has always taken a *special* interest in Quin." Her tone suggested disapproval. "Right after Augustus was elected, he found Quin living on the street. He made him the youngest Council member. I think Quin views him as a father."

Augustus cleared his throat and began speaking before she could say anymore. Cason joined him at the front of the room, his face chiseled and emotionless.

"Members of the Resistance, we have a matter of great concern. Today, during our regular patrols, we discovered the bodies of ten Guardian Force recruits washed ashore near Pier 33. Mr. Caruso has confirmed through his sources outside the city that at least five of them had been recently extricated from the Guardian program. We suspect, with further investigation, we will confirm that all of the casualties failed to meet Guardian Force standards and were rejected for further experimentation. Each was killed with a single bullet to the back of the head. As you know, this is the second such discovery in the past month. We believe that, by ordering these executions, the leader of the Guardian Force, General Jamison Ryker, has intended to send us a message. But we will not be deterred in our cause."

I glanced at Max, remembering our conversation from the morning and the question I had left unasked. Now I had the answer and wished that I didn't.

Augustus continued, "I know that those of you who have defected are anxious to learn the identities of the victims. We will obtain and disseminate the information as soon as we are able."

From the back of the room, a man's thundering voice demanded, "What are we going to do about it?"

Another voice joined. "We can't just let them get away with it!"

And another shouted, "We've been passive for too long. What are we waiting for?"

Suddenly, the room was alive with anger. I snuck a look at Augustus. He appeared annoyed, as if he was in the middle of a swarm of mosquitoes that he couldn't swat fast enough.

"Quiet!" Cason's voice commandeered the crowd. Still, his face was stoic.

With the room momentarily silenced, Augustus spoke, raising his voice slightly—enough to appear powerful, but not so much as to seem threatening. I sensed that he was skilled at manipulation. "I understand all of your concerns. When you elected me your leader, you entrusted me to carry out the vision of the Resistance. An attack at this time would be unwise and would lead to the deaths of many of the Guardian Force, whom we know to be innocent victims of a cruel and dangerous experiment. We must be patient. When we are ready, we will strike them at their hearts."

After the meeting, I approached Augustus. In this public forum, I hoped he would wear his charming face.

"How can I help you, Ms. Knightley?" He was pleasant, but the tone of his voice suggested that he had no intention of helping me.

"I was hoping that I could speak to my mother and let her know that I've arrived safely. It's been almost a month since I saw her." I allowed my eyes to fill with tears.

Augustus looked directly at me, examining me. "I have already spoken with her. She is aware of your arrival."

I knew he was lying. I rapid-fired questions at him, but they fell away, leaving him unscathed.

"Why didn't you tell me? I have to talk to her. What did she say to you?"

No response.

"What's on that flash drive? I almost died getting it here. I have a right to know."

Nothing.

I felt a wave of rage swelling up inside me, crashing over my sadness, enveloping it. I quickly wiped away a tear.

"Ms. Knightley, this is a secure compound. We cannot risk our safety by overindulging our emotions. Your mother understands that. You would do well to follow her example. As long as it is safe to do so, you will speak to your mother soon. You have my word."

Afterward, I sat by myself on the floor in a corner of the room. The tile felt cold beneath my legs. I buried my face in my hands, my tears marking tiny tracks down my cheeks. All those nights in the empty library, and I had never felt so alone. I tried to imagine my mother's face, but it was blurred, misshapen, a puzzle I could no longer solve. I forced myself to consider the unthinkable—I might never see her again. The thought was nearly paralyzing, like sinking through cold mud. I wondered how long Quin had felt this way before he made an attempt to stop feeling entirely.

A cold nose touched my hand, and I looked up to see Artos' green eyes looking back at me. He licked my face, and I couldn't help but giggle. He plopped down beside me, giving me a long-tongued grin as I rubbed his belly and underneath his thick, nylon collar.

"He likes you," Quin remarked from the doorway.

I wiped my face on my sleeve, embarrassed. Quin sat down next to me on the floor, our legs almost touching.

"What's wrong?" he asked softly.

"Nothing." I sounded like Quin.

"Now who's being difficult?" His boyish laugh soothed me. For a moment, I felt like everything that had gone wrong might be made right again.

"How did you find Artos?" I asked, still stroking his soft fur.

"*He* found me. It was just after I escaped the Guardians. He started following me. I told him to go away, to go home, but he wouldn't stop. After a while, I didn't want him to go away."

Quin reached over and rubbed Artos' head. Artos leaned in, content. "I guess I'm like that with people too," Quin added, smiling at me.

"What happened today with Augustus?" I asked. "He treated you horribly."

Quin shrugged. "He didn't mean anything by it. He's just trying to help me. He's always been tough with me, but I know that he cares. If it wasn't for him, I don't know what would've happened to me. He told the Resistance they could trust me. Even though I had . . ."

He paused. I suspected he was censoring himself. "Even though I'd been a Guardian."

As Quin spoke, I began to understand Augustus' power over him. Whatever Quin had done, he'd convinced himself it was unforgivable.

Even if Quin didn't believe me, I knew I had to confide in someone. The weight of the last few days was too heavy to bear alone. I started with the flash drive and Augustus' warning and finished with his probable lie about my mother and his cold indifference to my tears. Quin listened intently.

When I finished, he tried to comfort me. "If Augustus gave you his word, then it will happen. I trust him, Lex."

Quin put his hand on my knee, sending a flutter through me as if he had softly blown on the dandelion pieces of my heart. It was the first time he'd touched me with intention. I noticed a small scar across his knuckles.

I wanted to ask him why he trusted Augustus—*why*, my favorite question—but I held back. I knew if I pushed him, the sliver of an opening in the wall of Quin would seal up again. Instead, I summoned all of my courage and placed my hand on his.

CHAPTER TWENTY-ONE

EMPATHY

THE FOLLOWING DAY, A DARK unease settled over Resistance headquarters. I hardly left my room, but each time I did, I felt uncertainty hanging over me like a poisonous cloud. Although Augustus had been masterful in squashing the anger of the crowd, his stifling had driven it underground. Each time I entered the dining hall, I saw people huddled in tight groups, speaking purposefully. Unrest was snaking its way through the Resistance like a thick, unwieldy vine.

As for me, my own private upheaval continued. Mostly, I thought of my mother and the flash drive that I had surrendered to Augustus. Though its contents were a mystery to me, it was obviously of great importance to him. In the months following the evacuation of the city, my mother began spending more time alone in our garage, which my father had long ago converted to her office and laboratory. Sometimes she wouldn't emerge until late in the evening, her eyes red and underscored with dark circles. Once, only once, had I asked my mother what she was working on.

"It's better that you don't know, Lex," she said. "I want to protect you as long as I can. So many people have already been hurt."

At the time, I assumed she was thinking of my father and how her ambition had driven him away, pushing him to the periphery of her life until he had no choice but to disappear. But now, I was no longer certain.

Of course, I also thought of Quin. If I closed my eyes, I could still feel the warmth of his hand under mine. The touch had lasted only a few seconds—one thousand one, one thousand two, one thousand three—before he had taken his hand away and stood to say goodnight. It was probably just a friendly gesture, his touching my knee. I told myself it meant nothing to him. Of course, to me, it meant the complete opposite of nothing, and I knew I was in trouble.

Seeking an escape from my nagging thoughts, I decided to explore the *compound,* as Augustus had referred to it. I meandered past the dining hall and the armory. I knew where I was headed. The laboratory was locked, but I caught the eye of a middle-aged woman with wire-rimmed glasses, sitting in front of a computer screen. Hearing my knock, she rushed eagerly to the door.

"Ms. Knightley, it's an honor to meet you," she said. "I admire your mother's work."

I saw that she wore a badge with a familiar logo. Underneath, it read, *Carrie Donovan.* I pointed to it. "Are you Carrie?"

"Yes, of course. I'm so sorry. Carrie Donovan. This is my old work badge from Zenigenic. I wear it to remind me of the destruction science can cause if left unchecked by common sense." Tongue in cheek, she parroted the slogan, *"How do you want to feel today?"*

I chuckled. "I thought the logo looked familiar. How long did you work there?"

"Just one year. It was after your mother had . . . left." She politely omitted the word *resigned.* "My supervisor asked me to misrepresent some of our findings related to Emovere's side effects. When I refused, I was fired."

"What are you working on?" I asked.

"Let me show you," she said excitedly, gesturing me toward the computer. I could tell Carrie was a pure scientist at heart, eager to share her discoveries.

On the screen was a spreadsheet with copious amounts of data. In one of the columns, I instantly recognized a name, Elliot Barnes—the dead man.

"This is a compilation of the blood analyses for all deceased Guardian Force." She said the word *deceased* matter-of-factly as if she was reading it from a book.

She pointed to several columns of the spreadsheet. "As you can see, over time, we have detected increasingly larger amounts of Emovere. In Elliot and the casualties discovered yesterday, the concentration was twenty times the prescribed dose."

I attempted to disguise my horror, but inside, I was aghast. *Twenty times?*

"But what's really interesting," she continued, "is this." She pointed to two additional columns marked *Agitor* and *Substance X*.

As I studied the data curiously, the laboratory door opened and Vera Bullock bounced inside enthusiastically. She had the look of a first-grade teacher, small and plump, her cheeks like apples. Immediately, she walked over to us, nosily glancing over my shoulder at the spreadsheet.

"What are you up to, Alexandra?" she asked. Her tone implied that we knew each other well.

I considered her with uncertainty. She *seemed* harmless.

"Carrie was explaining some of the Guardian Force data that you've all been compiling." I glanced at Carrie nervously, fearing I had shared too much.

"My goodness," Vera replied, shaking her head. "I certainly hope she hasn't overwhelmed you. This information can be quite confusing, even distressing, for someone so young." She patted my shoulder gingerly as if I might break at any moment.

Carrie interrupted. "Luckily for her, Alexandra has had an exceptional teacher in her mother. I'm sure she can handle it. Now, if you'll excuse us, Vera . . ." Carrie turned the computer screen toward her, away from Vera's prying eyes.

Looking scolded, Vera slinked away from the computer and left the room without a word.

"Sorry about that. Vera can be a bit overbearing at times, but she means well."

Carrie turned her attention back to the columns of data. "As you know, we've also detected trace amounts of other emotion-altering drugs in the Guardian Force blood samples, including Agitor. We believe that, in combination with Emovere, Agitor may increase aggression."

I placed my finger on the screen. "What's Substance X?"

Carrie smiled. "That's the million-dollar question, Ms. Knightley. We don't know. Our working hypothesis is that it acts to impair the supramarginal gyrus."

I looked at her quizzically. "The supra-what?"

"I'm sorry," she said, flustered. "I keep forgetting you're not your mother." Carrie laughed, a nervous twitter.

She pointed to a diagram of the brain on the wall behind us. "The supramarginal gyrus is here," she said, putting her finger at the junction of the parietal, temporal, and frontal lobes of the brain.

"What does it do?" I asked.

Carrie paused for a long time. Unsmiling, she replied, "Empathy."

CHAPTER TWENTY-TWO

AMBUSHED

AS I LEFT THE LAB with the word *empathy* drumming in my brain, I saw a group congregating near the outer door that led back to the platform. At the periphery were Max, Quin, and Elana.

I pulled Elana aside. "What's going on?"

She gestured toward a tall and wiry young man with dark-framed glasses. I glanced at his forearm. No tattoo. He was speaking to the group in a hushed tone.

"Markus is leading a small group to investigate the murders at Pier 33. He thinks there may be more . . . *bodies*. We're going with him," she said.

Markus admonished Elana with his stern brow. "It's supposed to be a *secret*, remember?" Looking to me, he added, "Augustus doesn't know."

Elana shrugged. "It's Lex," she said, as if that explained everything. "Besides, I thought she might want to come with us."

Though the idea of disobeying Augustus was appealing, the thought of encountering the Guardians was not. "Um . . . I don't know, Elana . . . I—"

"I'm not sure that's such a good idea," Quin interrupted.

"Why not?" I asked. Now that Quin had challenged me, I suddenly felt brave.

Quin seemed momentarily dumbfounded.

"He's *worried* about you, *Alexandra*." Max teased.

I looked away from Quin, my cheeks reddening.

"Whatever." Quin replied dismissively, turning back toward the group.

Max winked at me. "Get this girl a weapon," he said, chuckling.

Markus handed me a gun. It was heavier than the one my mother had given me. I slipped the gun into my waistband carefully. The idea of firing a gun again unnerved me. But I wasn't about to let Quin see my uncertainty, and I could feel his eyes watching me.

"I think it's safe to leave now," Markus said, consulting his watch. "Augustus is scheduled to be at a meeting in the lab with Dr. Bell for the next hour."

Within a few minutes, we were outside, heading toward The Embarcadero. The fog had set in again, muting the sun with a cold, gray veil. As we neared the water, I could see rows of palm trees, their tall green stalks breaking through the cloud cover. Quin stayed noticeably close to me.

"I think we should split up to cover more ground," Markus said to the group. He pointed to Max, Quin, Elana, and me. "You four come with me. We'll check out Pier 33, while the rest of you head down toward Pier 39. Meet back at headquarters in twenty minutes."

When we arrived at the Pier 33 building, Quin touched my arm and whispered. "Be careful, okay?"

I nodded, feeling a surge of warmth. He *was* worried about me.

From just behind me, Max muttered, "I told you."

"Shhh," Markus hissed. "I hear something."

From just inside the building, there was a rhythmic creaking, an eerie to and fro. The methodical squeak sliced the silence like a razor. *Ambush.* The thought—a hunch, really—came from nowhere, but it resonated through my body.

"Markus," I called, but he was already walking inside. Max and Elana followed him.

I turned to Quin. "What if the Guardians are expecting us?" I asked. He slid his gun from his belt, motioning for me to do the same.

Inside, it was so dark that, for a moment, I could barely see Quin in front of me. I squinted my eyes tight, waiting for them to adjust to the blackness.

Reaching behind him for my arm, Quin pulled me along. "Stay close," he cautioned. From up ahead, I heard the click of a flashlight and a gasp.

Markus was standing at the back of the building, holding the light to one of the metal rafters. Swaying back and forth, a rope around her neck, was a woman's body. On her Guardian Force uniform, the mark of the Resistance was painted in red, an obvious message. Her head hung down lifelessly so I couldn't see her face, but I imagined it was permanently frozen in terror.

Before I could react, a gunshot pierced the air. Markus fell to the ground, clutching his leg. His flashlight rolled into the center of the room before a big, black boot kicked it out of sight.

Quin and I ducked behind a row of shipping containers just in time to dodge a volley of gunfire that pinged against the metal crates. Our eyes connected in a moment of panic.

"We have to get out of here," I said.

Nearby, Max and Elana were concealed by a forklift. Markus was stumbling toward them, firing haphazardly over his shoulder. With relief, he slumped down next to Elana.

Quin fired several shots into the darkness. I knelt next to him, aiming my gun at nothingness. With each successive squeeze of my trigger—one, two, three—I saw Elliot in my mind as he fell. After firing a few times, I sat back on the ground, frustrated with myself. Behind me, my hand touched something hard and rubbery—a tire.

"Any ideas?" Quin asked me, as he leaned from behind the containers to shoot again. Bullets whizzed by like attack bees, viciously stinging the air.

"*One* . . . but it might not work." I pointed downward, lifting the thick tarp to show Quin my discovery—a car.

Quin nodded. "If it works, it's brilliant. If it doesn't, we'll die." He beckoned Max over to us, mouthing the word *run*.

"I'll take that as a compliment," I said, hoisting myself to a crouch and peering under the tarp.

As Quin fired, Max and the others ran toward us.

From the dark corner opposite our hiding place, a Guardian emerged. She stalked toward us, blank-faced, glass-eyed, launching bullet after bullet. When she drew closer, I could see a trail of blood circling her neck, her flesh splayed. Ignoring her wounds, she advanced her fearless onslaught with no apparent concern for herself. Quin took cover, his gun empty, just as Max fired a shot. Her body struck the ground with a sickening thump.

I looked at Quin with relief.

"That was a little too close for comfort," Max said, exhaling. "I hope you two have a plan. I'm almost out of ammo, and I can't even see who I'm shooting at."

"Are you okay?" Quin asked Markus, considering his wounded leg with concern.

Markus shrugged, but his face was contorted in pain. "It's just a graze, but I've been better."

Another round of bullets struck the forklift—their *rat-tat-tatting* was deafening.

"*This* is the plan," Quin announced, pointing to the car, still concealed beneath its cover.

"A *tarp?*" Max asked with disbelief. "A tarp is the plan?" He lifted his head and returned fire.

"It's a car," I told Max.

Deftly, Quin scooted beneath the tarp and out of sight. I heard the click of the door handle opening. Then Quin's voice. "No keys."

"Check under the mat," Max offered.

A few seconds later, Quin's hand appeared from under the tarp. In it was a single key.

One by one, we climbed inside the dark tomb of the car. Max was last. He continued firing until he was out of ammunition. I wedged myself next to Elana in the passenger seat, listening to her rapid breathing.

"Here goes," Quin said. "Get down and hold on tight."

Lowering my head beneath the dashboard, I held my breath until I heard the engine roar to life. Overshadowing its melodious sound was gunfire. I braced myself as Quin floored the accelerator—tires screeching—torpedoing us blindly from the building, casting the tarp high up into the air.

I didn't look up or open my eyes until the car stopped a block from Resistance headquarters. Even so, I knew we were going fast. Each breakneck turn pressed against my body forcefully as if I was being pushed.

We bailed out quickly and ran the rest of the way, Markus leaning on Max and Quin. The other group who had accompanied us was already waiting just outside the door, their faces quizzical and alarmed.

"What are you going to tell Augustus?" I asked Markus, once we were safely inside.

Glancing sidelong at Quin, Max suggested, "I think you should tell him you got hit by a reckless driver."

Quin volleyed back at him. "You have to admit, if we hadn't almost died, that would've been kind of fun."

I narrowed my eyes at Quin skeptically. *Fun?*

"How'd you learn to drive like that?" I asked.

Quin grinned back at me slyly, but didn't answer.

Max chuckled. "What is that old saying? *Drive it like you stole it.* You know something about that, right, Quin?"

Quin shook his head, laughing. Apparently, in another life—the one I could only guess about—he had been a car thief. I wasn't sure how to feel about that. Like a lot of things about Quin, it was double-edged, both exciting and unnerving.

Turning his eyes to me, Quin's smile softened. "That was a really good idea, Lex. I'm glad you came."

"Looks like she didn't need protecting after all," Max said, punching Quin in the arm playfully.

I waited for Quin to agree. He said nothing, but even better—*so much better*—he slipped his arm around my shoulders and gave me a tight squeeze.

My contentment evaporated like smoke when I saw Augustus and Cason standing by the platform, glowering. They were already lecturing Markus as we approached.

Augustus addressed Quin, "Were you involved in this unauthorized mission as well, Mr. McAllister?"

Quin gave a solemn nod.

Shaking his head disapprovingly, Augustus said, "You continue to *disappoint* me, Quin." Augustus seemed to have masterful command of all of Quin's buttons, pushing them at will.

"And Ms. Knightley, Ms. Hamilton, were you involved as well?"

Cason laughed, appraising Elana and me with a patronizing once-over. "Doubtful," he concluded.

I looked down at my feet. Before either of us could answer, Quin spoke for us. "No, they weren't there."

I started to protest, but Augustus turned back to Markus and Quin, apparently satisfied. "Well then, let's discuss your transgressions in my office . . . *in private.*"

CHAPTER TWENTY-THREE

BLACKOUT

I WAS RETURNING TO MY room the following evening when the Resistance went dark. The blackouts had been more frequent in the last few days, usually lasting two or more hours. During an outage, we were instructed to return to our sleeping quarters since each room was equipped with a battery-powered lantern. As I fumbled with my flashlight, I heard a familiar voice in my ear.

"Meet me at the entrance in five minutes." It was Quin.

Five and a half minutes later, I stood with Quin, outside headquarters for the third time since my arrival. We had exited through a side door, marked EMERGENCY ONLY, the alarm dead, along with the lights. The frigid evening air was a shock to my body, but it felt invigorating. Quin shivered and zipped the leather jacket he had been wearing the night we met.

"I want to show you something," he said, "but we have to be fast."

"Are you sure you want to do this, Quin? Augustus is already furious with you."

He shrugged. "He'll get over it. Besides, as long as we're back before the power comes on, we have nothing to worry about."

We speed-walked for more than a mile into the heart of the city. I followed closely behind Quin. We cautiously dodged the cameras' all-seeing eyes, even though it was likely the blackout had cut the Guardians' surveillance feed. As we neared Telegraph Hill, the path grew increasingly steeper. My legs burned, and the frigid air stung my lungs.

Quin shined his flashlight upward, spotlighting Coit Tower, which shot up into the evening sky like the tail of a comet. Not even this once-majestic landmark had escaped destruction. At the base of the tower, I could see graffiti and crumbling rock. Quin pushed his shoulder into the tower's door several times before it opened with a thud. Inside, the air was stale and bitterly cold.

"This way." Quin pointed up a spiraling staircase. When we reached the observation deck, Quin extinguished his flashlight. The soft glow from the setting sun barely illuminated the city. From up here, I could almost forget the desolation below. But as I looked toward the Bay Bridge, I gasped. The reports that my mother and I had heard were correct. The highway was split into two distinct pieces with only sky in between them. A portion of the bridge had fallen away and was frozen in a sharp descent toward the water.

I looked over my shoulder expecting to see Quin, eager to ask him about the bridge. But he was kneeling on the opposite end of the deck in a spot where the concrete was broken away.

"What are you doing?" I asked.

Quin didn't answer, but began moving aside some of the broken pieces of stone. The sky was almost dark now, concealing him in shadow. I saw him slip something into his jacket, then pick up another smaller object before standing to face me.

"You said that you couldn't figure me out. That's because you don't know anything about me." Quin took a step toward me, his hand extended. "*This* is something about me." He handed me a book of poetry. It was so well-worn that its cover was soft.

"It was my mother's," he said. "Just like your book. This is the only part of her I have left. Before I joined the Guardians, I used to come up here a lot to escape from the world. Right after I went AWOL, I hid the book here. I figured it would be safer."

I knew Quin had hidden something else here—*something* he had concealed in his jacket. But I bit my tongue, holding my question until the time felt right.

Just like my book, Quin's book had a dog-eared page. I flipped to it: Robert Frost's "The Road Not Taken."

"Was this her favorite?" I asked.

Quin smiled. "No, it's mine."

"I never figured you for a poet," I joked.

Quin laughed, but only for a moment. Then his face became serious. "There's *a lot* you don't know about me, Lex. I'm sorry that I haven't . . . that I couldn't . . . that I can't . . . be more . . . open with you." His face looked defeated as he stumbled over his words.

I shrugged, giving him a sympathetic smile. "You're trying, Quin. That counts for something."

He gave a half-hearted nod. I handed back his mother's book, and he pocketed it inside his jacket.

"Have you ever taken Emovere?" he asked.

"Never," I answered. I was surprised by the directness of his question. "What's it like?"

He sighed. "At first, it's exhilarating, freeing. You feel like nothing can stop you, like something heavy was lifted from your shoulders, and you can stand up tall again."

Quin paused, choosing his words carefully, "With everything that had happened to me, it was a welcome relief. But after a while, you just feel numb, even after you stop taking it. The worst part is that it starts to feel good to be numb."

I was surprised by his description. Even though my mother's research had shown that Emovere could be addictive, no published studies had found any lasting effects once the drug was discontinued. I wondered if the pharmaceutical companies were experimenting with the drug's composition. I made a mental note to ask Carrie later.

"That's not supposed to happen," I said.

"I know," Quin conceded. "When I was recruited by the Guardians, they assured me I could stop at any time, that there would be no side effects. But there's a reason no one else has left the Guardian Force. No one wants to stop taking Emovere."

"Do you know why you were recruited by the Guardians?" I had to know if Quin shared my hypothesis that the Guardians selected vulnerable candidates, young people who had suffered trauma.

"I have a pretty good idea," Quin answered cryptically. The tone of his voice was final, like the shutting of a door, and I knew that the subject was closed.

"It's taken me a long time to *want* to *feel* again," he said. "That's part of the reason why I'm so . . ." He searched for the right word.

"Difficult?" I smiled at him, remembering the night that we met.

"I thought you were supposed to come up with a better word," he teased.

Laughing, I turned back toward the city, placing my hands on the concrete railing. By now, the sun had fallen almost completely below the horizon. "How about *complicated*?" I offered.

As I spoke, I could feel Quin approaching from behind. He came close and then closer, standing directly behind me, but not touching me. The warmth of his body radiated in the space between us. I had a flash of my first kiss, my *only* kiss. I closed my eyes and stood very still, hoping that if I didn't move, Quin wouldn't either. One thousand one, one thousand two, one thousand three, and he was gone. The cold air rushed in behind me.

"Lex, we have to go."

"I know," I said, recalling Augustus' verbal lashing after our last venture beyond headquarters. We began to walk toward the staircase.

"Hey," I said, "what else did you put in your jacket?"

Quin chuckled. "You're pretty hard to keep secrets from, you know."

I raised my eyebrows at him with expectation.

"It's something else about me," he offered. "But I'm not ready to show you yet. One step at a time, okay?"

Just before we began our descent, I watched in alarm as across the city in small, random pockets, lights began to flicker.

CHAPTER TWENTY-FOUR

A BOY'S WEAKNESS

FOR THE SECOND TIME THAT week, Quin and I ran side by side, this time with urgency. Unlike before, I had no trouble matching his pace. Adrenaline was coursing through me, my legs fueled by panic. No matter how fast we ran, I knew the damage was already done. Once the power was restored, the silent alarm from the emergency exit door would have sent an alert straight to Augustus. He would be waiting for us.

As we turned the final corner toward headquarters, a voice stopped my heart. Twenty feet behind us stood a man, a Guardian. For a moment, I couldn't feel my body. It seemed like my head had detached itself and was floating away.

"You're under arrest by order of the Guardian Force." The man's voice sounded as flat as a cracker, but his lips were turned in an unnatural smile. Immediately, I wondered what combination of Emovere, Agitor, and Substance X had created his eerie mismatch of emotion.

The man continued walking methodically toward us, his gun raised and ready to fire. I glanced at Quin. His face was the same as the night we had met, tight and hardened. Just as the man was within an arm's length, Quin turned suddenly, grabbed and twisted the man's hand, and struck him in the face. The gun clunked down the sidewalk, and I ran to retrieve it.

When I turned back, Quin had pinned the man to the ground with his knee and was pointing his own weapon at the man's head. Though he struggled, the man had no expression. He wasn't fearless, which might imply that he was brave. Nor proud, which might imply that he was a martyr. Nor apathetic, which might imply that he harbored a death wish. He was simply a blank slate. I tried to remember the face of the man stepping from the ledge during my mother's clinical trial. Had he been *so* expressionless?

Quin looked me, his eyes pained. "Run, Lex," he said, in a quiet voice that was more suggestion than command.

I didn't run, and I didn't turn away. I readied myself for the gunshot that never came.

Instead, Quin hit the man across the face with the end of his weapon, rendering him unconscious. He stood and walked to me. "I can't shoot him," he confessed. He sounded surprised, as if he was observing some other, unexpected version of himself.

"It's okay," I reassured him.

"*Is it*, Ms. Knightley?" From behind us, another voice, this one familiar.

Augustus didn't wait for my response. Without hesitating, he approached the Guardian and shot him, once, twice, three times. After the first shot, the man's body contorted, and I turned away, flinching with each successive explosion. When I finally looked at Augustus, he appeared satisfied, but bored, as if he had completed some mundane activity, like drinking his morning coffee.

"I hope it was worth it, Ms. Knightley." Augustus addressed only me, as if Quin was invisible. I knew his indifference would hurt Quin more than even his harshest words.

Augustus turned and pointed with intention back toward headquarters. We both began walking. He continued speaking, still addressing me alone. "Do you know how long it's been since I've been *forced* to shoot someone? Is this the sort of thing you bring out in others, Ms. Knightley?"

We entered through the emergency door. Two armed members of the Resistance stood inside, while a third exited. I assumed he was tasked with managing the body.

"Since your arrival here, you have compromised the security of this compound on multiple occasions. You have taken advantage of a boy's weakness." He glanced at Quin, waiting to see the stinging bite of his words as they made impact.

Quin looked pale. I was surprised when he spoke. "It's not her fault, Augustus. I asked her to leave with me. It was *my* decision. Besides, no one *forced* you to kill him."

Augustus pretended that Quin was on mute, but I felt a small surge of elation—Quin had finally stood up to Augustus, if only for a moment.

Augustus turned to the armed men. "Please escort Ms. Knightley back to her sleeping quarters."

I began walking down the long corridor, one man on either side of me. When we reached the door, I turned back to look at Quin before they shuffled me away. Augustus was facing him, speaking quietly. I couldn't hear him, but I didn't need to. Whatever he was saying had been carefully honed to a point, cold and sharp as a blade, each word a knife strike to Quin's heart.

CHAPTER TWENTY-FIVE

WORST THING

IN THE THREE DAYS THAT followed, most of the Resistance began to subtly avoid me. I wasn't sure what Augustus had told them, but the day after the blackout, there had been a meeting in the Map Room. I wasn't invited. I was certain Augustus had used me as a distraction, a way to refocus the Resistance and quell their dissidence. I spent most of my time with Elana and Max, who thankfully ignored whatever lies Augustus had manufactured. I was concerned their loyalty might place their positions in jeopardy. But they reassured me that, in time, Augustus would forgive me as would everyone else.

Forgive—that word burned like acid in my throat. Though Augustus' opinion was as useless to me as a single shoe, I had already learned the most important principle of my new home: So goes Augustus, so goes the Resistance.

Quin was avoiding me too, sort of. The day after Coit Tower, Max told me that Augustus had warned Quin about seeing me alone again. Augustus believed that Quin was changing and not for the better. I wondered what Quin believed. When we were in a room together, I often caught him looking at me. His gaze intense, but warm. He instantly pretended to be doing something else, avoiding my eyes. Max and Elana noticed too.

The three of us sat together in the dining hall. Quin several tables away, alone.

"Is it me or is Quin totally checking you out right now?" Max teased.

I blushed. As I slowly turned my head to look, Quin quickly got up from the table and left the room. Max and Elana laughed loudly.

"I'm glad you both find this so funny," I said sarcastically, smiling at them.

"It's just that Quin doesn't act this way . . . *ever*," Elana observed. I wondered if she was remembering her *moment* with sixteen-year-old Quin.

As she spoke, Markus walked up from behind her. His leg was wrapped in a thick bandage, still healing from his encounter with the Guardian Force.

"Hi, Elana," he said, glancing over his shoulder and winking at her. Just as she had that first day I met her, Elana tensed. She was as still and watchful as a small animal in the woods anticipating the first sign of danger.

"Hi, Markus," she said, not looking at him.

After Markus passed by, taking a seat at another table, Max spoke, "He's not going to bite you, Elana. At least, not yet." Chuckling to himself, he nudged her in the side with his elbow, and she playfully nudged him back, her uneasiness gone.

After lunch that afternoon, Elana asked if we could speak alone. We returned to my room.

"Has Quin told you about himself yet?" Elana asked.

"Partly," I said, unsure if that was even true. "A small part."

"Well, that's more than he shares with most. It's one of the things that Quin and I have in common. We hide our true selves, even from the people who care about us. That's actually why I wanted to talk to you."

"Okay," I said. I was deeply curious. In some ways, Elana was more guarded than Quin, relying on her outer beauty as a convenient and glittering diversion.

"I have a theory," she explained. "The Guardians chose me for a reason. The same reason they chose Max and Quin and all the others."

I nodded, and Elana continued.

"When I was a little girl, I was a free spirit. I was always dancing or skipping or hopping, never *walking* anywhere. I loved horses. I rode every day." Elana spoke slowly, as if she was sifting through stacks of old memories. "I was seven when my grandfather started touching me. At first, he told me it was a game. I *loved* games. While my grandmother was picking tomatoes, he told me to find him, and I did. He was in the bedroom. Afterward, he cried and told me I was so beautiful, the most beautiful little girl he'd ever seen. I thought that was the worst thing that could ever happen to me. Like everybody gets a *worst thing*, you know, and that was mine."

Elana paused to look at me as if she was afraid of my reaction. I sensed she had told this story before, maybe more than once, to someone who didn't understand. Her eyes were brimming with tears, but she didn't allow them to fall.

"I was fourteen when it happened again," Elana said. "Everybody says it's not your fault, but when it keeps happening to you, you start to wonder. I was at a party, drunk. There was this boy I liked. He and his friends used their cell phones to video me doing stuff with them, sexual stuff. They posted it online. It was everywhere. After that, I thought there was no way I could live in this world, like I was an alien. Once I thought of jumping from the Golden Gate, just stepping right out into the fog and disappearing, but I couldn't. That's when I did *this*."

She pointed to a scar that traced its way like a tiny river across her right wrist. I hadn't noticed it before. I had always been drawn to her left arm, the one marked with the Guardian badge.

At that moment, I most wished I was my mother. If there was a right thing to say, she would have said it. Instead, I put my arm around Elana.

"Do Max and Quin know?"

"Sort of," she said. "They know about what happened when I was a little girl. It seems so long ago, like it happened to someone else. I couldn't tell anybody here about the other thing, but sometimes I feel like people know just by looking at me." Elana's shame was tangible. It marred her face like a corrosive acid seeping from her pores.

"Do you think the Guardian Force knew about what happened to you?" I was starting to reconsider my mother's theory that the government monitored and mined electronic data to keep a close watch over its citizens. I had always rolled my eyes, dismissing my mother, but Elana's story made me wonder.

Elana nodded. "When the Guardians recruited me, just like Max and Quin, they told me they had been watching me, that they knew things about me, that I was smart and brave. Of course, I wanted to believe them. But I think what they knew was that I wanted to escape more than anything else—not leave, like run away—but escape from everything inside me."

I sighed. "Emovere."

"Exactly."

CHAPTER TWENTY-SIX

THE SECOND TIME

AFTER MY CONVERSATION WITH ELANA, my mind was on autopilot, replaying her story again and again. If Elana and I were correct, then the Guardian Force recruited only trauma survivors. They were especially vulnerable because Emovere suppressed fear and self-doubt in all its forms. If the recruits weren't rejected by the Guardian Force when they failed to meet its impossible standards, by the time they wanted out—*if* they wanted out—it was probably too late. Elana had told me that, like Quin, both she and Max had experienced intense withdrawals from Emovere.

I headed to the laboratory to talk to Carrie, hoping she could support my hunches with something tangible, something scientific. When I knocked, Carrie hesitated, a look of concern on her face. She approached the door with caution as if I was contaminated.

"I'm not supposed to let you in here," she said, her voice meek. "Augustus told us you put the Resistance in danger with your poor judgment."

"Do you believe him?"

"Augustus doesn't lie," she said matter-of-factly.

I was beginning to wonder what sort of strange voodoo Augustus practiced. It seemed that his scheming was completely invisible, cloaked in equal parts by his charm and confidence.

"I don't want to get in trouble," Carrie whispered. "I'm already a bit of an outcast here," she said, pointing to her Zenigenic badge.

I could see I wasn't going to win this argument. "I don't want you to get in trouble, Carrie. I just wanted to talk with you about a few things."

We stood at the door while I told her about my theory about the Guardian Force's recruiting strategy and what Quin had shared about Emovere's lasting side effects. She listened intently, nodding as I spoke.

Before I finished, Carrie interrupted. Her voice suddenly sounded stilted and rehearsed. "I'll have to talk to you later, Lex."

Behind me, a man in a lab coat approached. Flanking him were two Council members, Vera and Dr. Bell. Their eyes darted between me and Carrie, then exchanged a look of concern.

"Later," I agreed.

On my way back to my room, Max stopped me. "Lex!" he called out from the control booth, gesturing me over with his hand. "I was just about to look for you. I thought you should know that Quin is taking Artos for a walk in the tunnels . . . *right now.*"

"Why would I want to know that?" Quin had expressed no interest in talking to me in thirty-six hours.

Max said nothing more, but grinned and handed me a flashlight.

I walked to the platform. Ensuring that I was alone, I jumped down and headed into the tunnel. I walked quickly. The anticipation of seeing Quin was like a steady drum pounding in my chest. After about fifteen minutes, I saw a flashlight up ahead flick on and off, on and off, and on. Quin.

Artos bounded toward me, his wagging tail a giveaway for his pure exuberance.

"Sit," Quin instructed him, and Artos reluctantly lowered himself to the ground. Quin was standing near the side of the tunnel, his flashlight illuminating part of his face. As I got closer, I could see his skin was smooth, freshly shaven. I took a position opposite him, near the other wall. He turned off his flashlight, leaving my single beam of light streaming between us.

"Hey," I said softly.

"Hey, yourself."

I smiled. It was impossible to be mad at him.

Right away, his words surprised me. "I had to see you," he said. "I'm sorry that I've been avoiding you. Augustus thinks that—"

I interrupted him. "I know what Augustus thinks, Quin. What do *you* think?"

Quin took a step toward me. "Remember the other thing that I put in my jacket? I want you to see it." He handed me a small computer tablet. I started to open it.

"No," he said panicked. "Don't look at it now."

"Okay. What is it?"

"It's everything. It's me . . . kind of like *The Book of Quin*." We both laughed. "It's my file from the Guardian Force. I stole it when I ran away." Quin paused. "I'll understand if you don't want to talk to me anymore after you read it."

"Quin," I said his name gently, but firmly. "That's not possible, no matter what it is." With one hand, I cradled the tablet close to my body, holding my flashlight in the other.

Quin took another step toward me and then another, until we were almost touching. He leaned toward me, and I breathed in summer and a hint of shaving cream. From the moment we had sat side by side on my bed on the night we met, some part of me knew that Quin would *happen* to me. He was unavoidable.

"I really want to kiss you right now," he whispered.

Little jolts of electricity pinged through me. "Are you asking my permission?"

"No." He smirked. "Just giving you fair warning."

I nodded, suddenly feeling nervous. "I might be really bad at it," I said. In my mind, I silently added . . . *not like Elana* and *it's only my second kiss.*

"Lex, that's not possible," he said mimicking my earlier words. Quin reached down the length of my arm, letting his fingers lightly graze my wrist. He clicked off my flashlight, leaving us in darkness. A current of anticipation hummed between us like a live wire. One thousand one, one thousand two, one thousand—his lips were soft and warm.

I dropped my flashlight. I don't think Quin even noticed. Reaching just underneath his shirt, I pulled him closer to me. His skin radiated heat. Quin sighed softly in my ear, his kisses becoming more insistent. Then, suddenly, he stopped, taking a step away from me. He turned his flashlight on and, for a moment, the light shined directly on me, a jarring spotlight.

"What's wrong? Why did you stop?" I asked, instantly feeling foolish.

Quin's face was clouded, a sign of a storm brewing within. "I don't know. I guess I just don't want to hurt you."

Thinking of the tablet I held in my arm, I reached for Quin's hand, taking it in mine. Even more than hurting me, I suspected he feared something else—being unlovable.

"We can go slow," I said, reassuring both of us.

We walked back together until we reached the part of the tunnel where the platform's lights started to cast a glow.

Quin spoke, "We should probably go separately from here. There's a Council meeting tonight."

"Right." I agreed, but nonetheless, his eagerness to please Augustus irritated me.

Before I left, Quin gently nudged me with his elbow and grinned. "You know, you *were* pretty bad at that. I think you're gonna need a lot more practice." He winked at me.

CHAPTER TWENTY-SEVEN

THE BOOK OF QUIN

I PRACTICALLY RAN BACK TO my room. I couldn't wait to open the tablet that contained the *whys*, the clues to finally solve the mystery that was Quin. And he was a mystery to me, *most of all to me.* But as soon as I got back, I felt hesitant. *What if Quin was right? What if he had done something unforgivable?*

I closed my eyes. I could still smell Quin on my clothing . . . could still feel his need, so insistent. I remembered what Elana had told me about falling for Quin. Like Elana, I felt myself tumbling down in a delicious and dizzying spin that I didn't want to stop. Whatever it was, I could accept it. I opened *The Book of Quin.*

On the first screen in large block letters, it read:

Property of the United States Federal Government, Guardian Force

Unauthorized possession of this tablet is a federal offense punishable by a $250,000 fine or a minimum of seven years in a federal penitentiary.

"Great," I said aloud to myself—another felony. I scrolled to the next page. At the top, it was marked with the badge of the Guardian Force. It read:

Name: Quin Evan McAllister
Identification Code: Legacy 243
Date of Birth: 6/6/2021

Recruitment Date: 1/12/2038
Age: 16
Height: 6'2"
Weight: 180 lb.
Full Scale IQ: 130 (superior range)

Skills Test Results

	Pre-Protocol	Post-Protocol
Propensity to aggression	80th percentile, high average	95th percentile, superior
Risk-taking behavior	85th percentile, high average	99th percentile, superior
Problem-solving	95th percentile, superior	No change
Empathy	85th percentile, high average	60th percentile, average
Verbal communication	30th percentile, low	No change
Athleticism	98th percentile, superior	99th percentile, superior
Leadership	95th percentile, superior	No change

As I read, I couldn't help but smile. That was Quin alright. I could only assume "post-protocol" implied post-Emovere. Based on Quin's results, it seemed that whatever drugs he had been administered increased his aggression and his propensity to take risks, while decreasing his capacity to understand the feelings of others. I thought of my mother's early research with criminals. Individuals who met the criteria for psychopathy often demonstrated those same qualities. I wondered if Substance X had been part of Quin's protocol, but even more, I wondered if the effects were permanent.

The next few pages were highly technical and difficult to understand, but they appeared to describe the laboratory findings associated with Quin's response to Emovere. The top of each page was marked with Zenigenic's logo. I was relieved there was no mention of Agitor or any other emotion-altering substance.

Next was a response to Quin's requests for release from the Guardian Force.

> **Dear Mr. McAllister,**
>   **This is to confirm that you requested your release from the Guardian Force on 1/5/40, 2/2/40, and 3/1/40. Unfortunately, your requests have been denied based on the terms of your contract. This letter serves as a reminder of your agreement of confidentiality with regard to all matters related to your service in the Guardian Force. Any breach of this agreement is a federal offense and is punishable based on the terms of your contract. Additionally, we would like to remind you of your contractual obligation to consent to the administration of Emovere and any other substances we deem related to the success of your mission. We thank you for your service to your country and wish you continued success as a Guardian.**
>   **Sincerely,**
>   **General Jamison Ryker**

I continued to the next page. There was a picture attached, marked with a time stamp—1/3/40—shortly before Quin's first request for release. It appeared to be taken at a riot on Market Street. As I examined the image more closely, I gasped. Standing on a car and holding a rifle was a wild-eyed Quin. His Guardian tattoo was covered with a red bandana, and he wore the mark of the Resistance on his shirt. He was barely recognizable. The attached document read:

> **On 1/3/40, Legacy 243 was given orders to carry out a confidential mission at a Resistance protest rally. Prior to the mission, Legacy 243 was administered 500 milligrams of Emovere. Legacy 243 completed his mission without error. He is to be commended for his service and advanced in the program.**

As I scrolled the next few pages, I saw several similar notations, dated 1/29/40 and 2/14/40. Attached to those documents was an Internet article documenting a shooting death and a serious gunshot wound, both of which occurred at protest rallies in San Francisco. The article indicated that the shooter's identity was unknown, but he was believed to be a member of the Resistance.

I took a breath. Quin *had* hurt people—for the government in order to make it appear that the Resistance was dangerous. As Max had explained during our morbid sightsee, if the public feared the Resistance, it would confirm the need for the Guardian Force and help to promote the government's hidden agenda. Quin's demeanor that day—mercurial and reluctant—made complete sense now.

On the next page, I saw a picture of Quin, dated 6/1/35, at age thirteen. He wasn't smiling, and his eyes were troubled. Attached was his juvenile criminal history. He had many arrests for trespassing, shoplifting, vandalism, auto theft, and loitering. His last arrest, at age fourteen, was for destruction of property. He had punched his fist through the wall at the Riverbend Home for Boys, causing several hundred dollars in damage and requiring stitches in his hand. I thought of the thin scar on Quin's knuckles, and then the one on Elana's wrist. No matter how hard they had tried to escape it, the past had left its mark.

Beginning at age seven, Quin had been in foster care—at least five homes, most of which he ran away from. In one of the reports, his foster mother noted, "Quin has two personalities. Sometimes he's a little boy, always wanting my attention. At other times, he's moody, like a powder keg, ready to explode at any minute."

Most of his foster parents agreed that Quin pushed them away before they ever had a chance to get to know him. That sounded familiar. When Quin turned sixteen, he escaped from Riverbend a final time, and his case was closed. I suspected he had run away to San Francisco.

Quin's school records were spotty, his grades all over the map. His report cards had a theme: Shows promise, has potential, but doesn't apply himself. Quin changed schools a lot, and he had a lot of absences. In the fifth grade, and again in the seventh, he was suspended for fighting. His eleventh-grade report card was his last.

Quin had been evaluated by a parade of psychologists. By the time he was fourteen, Quin was labeled with a plethora of disorders, including reactive attachment disorder, bipolar disorder, attention deficit disorder, and posttraumatic stress disorder. Most of the reports appeared to concur that Quin, the adolescent, had been irrevocably shaped when he was just a boy.

The next page was older, its type antiquated. It was a Los Angeles County police report dated 5/23/28. Quin was almost seven. It read:

> **On 5/23/28, Officer Rollins responded to the 700 block of Willow Court at 1800 hours, after receiving a 911 call with a report of a domestic disturbance. Upon arrival at the scene, Officer Rollins made contact with suspect George McAllister and his sons, Quin McAllister (age six) and Colton McAllister (age two). The minors were unharmed and were immediately placed in the care and custody of Los Angeles County Child Protective Services.**
>
> **Officer Rollins observed that Mr. McAllister's clothing was covered in blood. Inside the home, officers located the body of the victim, Angela McAllister (wife of the suspect). A knife lying near the body also was secured as evidence. Upon observation, pending the coroner's report, Mrs. McAllister evidenced at least ten stab wounds to the upper torso and neck.**
>
> **Mr. McAllister spontaneously reported to Officer Rollins that he stabbed his wife during an argument, after he returned home to discover her talking on the telephone to another man while his sons played unsupervised in the next room. Mr. McAllister also advised investigators that he is a participant in a government research trial, taking the experimental drug, Crim-X. His medication was seized into evidence. Mr. McAllister was placed under arrest and transported to the Los Angeles County Jail.**

There was more in this section, but I couldn't read it. I didn't have to—I already knew. Quin's father was Inmate 243, making Quin *Legacy* 243. Max had been right. My mother would want to meet Quin. After all, he was part of her legacy too.

I wondered if any other Legacies had been recruited for the Guardian Force. It made sense. If the government wanted to find trauma victims, what better place to start than with the children of inmates who were at high risk for violence? The idea was sinister, twisted, but brilliant.

There was also a picture—a mug shot—of George McAllister. He was handsome. He had Quin's strong jaw, but his eyes were not Quin's. They were small and black, like marbles.

Next, was a Child Protective Services document confirming the termination of parental rights for George McAllister, followed by a certificate of adoption for Colton. Quin's brother had found a permanent family when he was just two. Quin had been left completely alone.

The final pages of the tablet were the hardest to read. They were written by my mother: confidential psychiatric evaluations of George McAllister both prior to and following his experimental release from prison, after he had fatally stabbed his wife. According to my mother, Mr. McAllister likely suffered from psychopathy, which may have made him less sensitive to Crim-X. Mr. McAllister had a long history of violence beginning at a young age. In the years leading up to the murder, he was arrested at least five times for domestic violence. During my mother's interview, Mr. McAllister showed little remorse for the murder of his wife, telling her that Angela had always known how to push his buttons. After his conviction, he was sentenced to the Dellencourt Correctional Facility for high-risk offenders, serving life in prison with the possibility of parole. Now, Quin's father was almost forty.

The last folder on the tablet contained a picture: Quin, celebrating his fifth birthday. The image appeared to have been taken from his mother's social media page. Its caption read: *Happy fifth birthday to the best little boy a mom could ask for.* Under the type, Quin sat on his mother's lap, in front of a cake, a silly paper birthday hat on his head. His smile was mischievous, but innocent. He had his mother's eyes.

I closed *The Book of Quin*, concealing it beneath my mattress, and cried for a long time.

CHAPTER TWENTY-EIGHT

GONE

I DIDN'T SLEEP MUCH THAT night, not that I expected to. When exhaustion finally overtook me, I dreamed of Quin. I was walking down a long, dark tunnel. A little boy was sitting at the end, his back to me. I could hear him crying. I knew it was Quin. I had to get to him, to protect him. As I drew nearer, he grew older before my eyes. Now, he was *my* Quin. I touched his shoulder, and he turned around. His face was his own, but his eyes were black and beady, bird-like. He was covered in blood. I tried to scream, but I couldn't.

I was awake, but the dream lingered in my body, leaving me shaken. I looked at the clock. It was almost morning.

I heard a noise at the door.

"Quin?" I whispered. There was no response, but the sound of a persistent scratching.

"Quin?" I said again, louder this time. The scratching continued followed by a plaintive whimper.

I went to the door, opening it cautiously. It was Artos. Across his nose, there was a deep gash. His paws were bloody, and he was shaking and whining. I took him inside the room, wrapping him in a towel. He was inconsolable.

Leaving Artos inside, I softly padded down the hallway toward Quin and Max's room. I stopped when I heard voices.

"Nothing here," a man said, followed by radio static. His footsteps gradually faded to silence.

Moving quickly, I peered inside the small window at the top of the door. Max lay on his side, sleeping peacefully. Quin's bed was neatly made, empty. Panic came like a wave, nearly knocking me off my feet.

I had known from the moment that I saw Artos alone. Quin was gone.

CHAPTER TWENTY-NINE

THE ESSENTIALITY OF HONESTY

EARLY THAT MORNING, BEFORE DAWN, Augustus called for a meeting of the Resistance. With Artos safely hidden in my bathroom, I walked to the Map Room, my mind in a fog. I was overcome by a sense of impending doom. Quin would never leave Artos, not voluntarily.

Elana beckoned me over. "Have you seen Quin?" she asked, her voice weighted with worry. "Max said he never came back from the Council meeting last night."

When our eyes met, I knew Elana could see my dread. I shook my head. "Artos . . ." I wanted to cry, but I couldn't. "He's hurt."

Augustus interrupted us, his tone solemn. "Please take your seats." He faced the anxious crowd and began speaking. I squinted up at him. *Was there a bruise on his face?*

"Last night, I was forced to make a very difficult decision to expel Quin McAllister from our headquarters. As you all know, Mr. McAllister was a Council member and a trusted friend. I considered him like a son."

My mind had gone blank after Augustus said the word *expel*. I was present, but not there—hearing, but not listening.

"When I was elected to lead the Resistance, we agreed on the importance, the *essentiality* of honesty. Mr. McAllister has lied to us, to *me*." Augustus' head turned toward me. His face was a blur.

"Approximately one week ago, Mr. McAllister was given orders to surveil Ms. Knightley. He reported to me that, during his surveillance, he observed Guardian Force recruit Elliot Barnes posing a grave danger to Ms. Knightley. He indicated that he used necessary force to curtail that threat. However, it has come to my attention that Mr. Barnes was not killed by Mr. McAllister."

I felt dizzy. The room started to spin in a slow motion pirouette. Heat began to rise from my chest as if my heart was a burning coal. I grabbed Elana's arm to steady myself.

"Are you okay?" she whispered.

I tried to answer, but the words wouldn't come. My breath was staccato, short unsatisfying gasps.

Augustus continued, "The truth is that Mr. Barnes was shot and killed by Ms. Knightley. Due to Mr. McAllister's dishonesty and his reckless behavior in the past few days, I had no choice but to demand that he resign his Council position and vacate the Resistance. Mr. McAllister left willingly and with full knowledge of his wrongdoings."

I could see Elana's face looking at mine, but it was distorted as if I was seeing her through a fun house mirror.

"Regrettably, I must warn you all that Mr. McAllister is emotionally unstable, and he poses a danger to . . ."

Though Augustus' mouth continued to move, the room began to fade. I felt a pull, an insistent tug of a warm, soundless nothing. Then, everything went black.

CHAPTER THIRTY

A LITTLE VISIT

I WOKE TO AN UNFAMILIAR voice. It was soft and kind.

"Alexandra? Can you hear me?"

I tried to nod.

"You're in the infirmary. I'm Maria, your nurse. Would you like some water?"

"Yes," I croaked.

Maria had strong hands. I could feel them on my back, urging me to sit up.

"What happened to me?" I asked, taking a drink. The water felt ice cold on my lips. It still hurt to open my eyes.

Max's voice answered, "You hit the floor like a prize fighter, down for the count."

"Max!" Elana chided him. "You had a panic attack, Lex. You fainted."

A panic attack—that was a first. Instantly, I saw my mother's face. There was a time, long before I was born, before she was psychiatrist, that she had panic attacks. She told me the story in bits and pieces, clearly omitting the *why*. She was in medical school at the time, and it began as nervousness. In the middle of her rounds, she would simply freeze. She started staying home some days. And then, for a while, she *couldn't* leave at all. I wondered if this panic had been in me all along, lying dormant, a seed just waiting for the right moment to burst open.

I took a breath and opened my eyes. Everything came rushing back at once: Artos bleeding, Quin expelled, Augustus with a bruise on his face.

"We have to find Quin," I said, sitting up with a sudden surge of energy.

Upon hearing Quin's name, Maria walked away hurriedly. Elana and Max exchanged a look.

"We're under lockdown," Elana whispered in my ear, "because of Quin." I could see that she had been crying.

Max added incredulously, "Augustus called him unstable, said that he may even be using Emovere again. Can you believe that?"

"That's ridiculous," I replied, shaking my head. "You *know* that, right?"

They both nodded at me. Elana pressed a small piece of paper into my hand, closing my fingers around it. "It's from Carrie," she mouthed.

From behind her, Augustus approached. I slipped the paper underneath me.

"You gave us all quite a scare, Ms. Knightley." Augustus made his tone sound fatherly. "Mr. Powers, Ms. Hamilton, may I have a word in private with Alexandra?"

I immediately turned to Elana, my eyes silently pleading with her— *don't leave me alone with him.* My stomach began to flip-flop. For the first time, I realized that I was afraid of Augustus. Now that his face was close to mine, I could see a purplish discoloration on his cheek. It was definitely a bruise.

Elana looked back at me sympathetically. "We'll be right outside, Lex," she said, as they walked away.

Augustus was silent until the door had closed behind them. "Well, Ms. Knightley, you certainly have shaken things up around here." He looked at me with disgust as if I was a bug he was planning to squash with his shoe.

"You can drop the concerned father act now," I said, surprised at my own boldness. "Why is your face bruised?"

Augustus didn't answer, not that I expected him to. He pulled the curtain around my bed shut and sat down on my bedside, inches separating us. I squirmed, feeling like a cornered animal.

"I *am* concerned, Ms. Knightley. *Very concerned.* And I need your help. Something very important to me, *to both of us*, is missing." He held his hand up to my face, his fingers a few inches apart from each other, indicating that whatever was missing was small. Immediately, I knew: my mother's flash drive.

Maria returned then, peeking around the curtain. I exhaled, just realizing that I had been holding my breath.

"Oh, I'm sorry, Augustus. Just checking in on our patient." She looked over at me and gave a tiny wave.

I watched Augustus' change his face like a mime. He smiled warmly and patted my hand. "We're just having a little visit. I won't keep her long."

When she had left, Augustus' hand encircled my wrist and squeezed tight. I grimaced. In his eyes, past the coldness, I saw a glint of pleasure.

"I don't know what you're talking about," I lied, gritting my teeth. "What *really* happened to Quin?" I spit out the question, trying to ignore the pain.

He kept squeezing, tighter and tighter, until I feared that my wrist would break. Then he let go and walked away.

CHAPTER THIRTY-ONE

THE COUNCIL

I SHOOK OUT MY HAND, watching Augustus' fingerprints slowly fade from my wrist. I felt overwhelmed—my thoughts still jumbled. My mother's flash drive was missing, and Augustus thought I knew where it was. I couldn't help but think it had something to do with Quin. I knew he didn't leave willingly. Right now, he was in the city completely alone. The thought hollowed out my insides. I sat upright, flinging the sheet off my body. I reached beneath me and unfolded Carrie's note.

It read: *You were right. Permanent changes in the frontal lobe and supra. Come by later if you can to discuss.*

I left the infirmary without a word to Maria and returned to my room. Artos was sleeping in the bathtub. He whimpered when I rubbed his head. The gash on his nose was covered in a thick scab.

"What would Quin do?" I whispered to Artos. *What would my mother do?*

I knew the answer already, but it frightened me. I had risked everything—my mother and I *both* had risked everything—for me to get here. But *here*, was nothing like we had imagined. Her flash drive was gone, along with whatever she had so desperately wanted the Resistance to have. Augustus was a fraud. I doubted he even believed in the Resistance cause. And Quin, one of the only people that I trusted, was in danger. Still, I knew if I left here, there would be no more safety. I wished I hadn't surrendered my gun so easily to Quin that first night. The Resistance armory was guarded like a fortress.

I began packing up the things that remained: my mother's book of poetry, my clothing, and Quin's tablet from under my mattress. As I packed, I heard soft and steady thuds outside my door, the sound of boots approaching. Stuffing my backpack under the bed, I went to the window and peered out. One of the armed men from the night of Coit Tower stood outside. He positioned himself facing the door, his eyes briefly connecting with mine. His hardened expression didn't waver. I should have known—Augustus would never let me leave. Whatever it was he believed I was hiding from him, he wanted it back. But more than that, he wanted to punish me.

I opened the door without a word or glance to the armed man and began walking.

"Hey," he called out. "Where are you going?" His voice was annoyed.

I didn't look back. I feigned confidence, keeping my steps brisk and even, my shoulders back, and my eyes pointed ahead. When he caught up to me, he was breathing heavily.

"You're not allowed to walk around unescorted—Augustus' orders."

"Fine," I said, emotionless. "Escort me to the Map Room. I want to meet with the Council."

Augustus may have the final word, but he wasn't the only word around here. Perhaps I could outsmart him in a public forum or, at the least, find an ally. Since the first meeting, I had little interaction with the other Council members. I didn't know what to expect, but anything was better than facing Augustus alone.

Ten minutes later, I was seated at a table. The five remaining faces of the Council stared back at me. Cason sat to my right, his muscled arms taking up space on either side of him. He wore his usual severe expression. Dr. Shana Bell was on my left. Her layers of make-up aged her beyond her years; her perfume hung in the air, thick and cloying. Hiro Chen sat next to her. His thin face was all angles, framed with wire glasses. He was doodling on a computer tablet with his finger, looking bored and out of place. Vera sat next to Augustus, looking up at him as eager as a puppy.

"How can we help you, Ms. Knightley?" Augustus began, his voice dripping with false concern.

"I would like to leave," I said. As soon as I spoke the words, I knew they were momentous. There was no going back. "Am I being held prisoner here?" I glanced toward the door. Outside, two men stood watch.

Dr. Bell shook her head sympathetically. "Of course not, Alexandra. Don't be silly. We don't operate that way. Augustus told us you had grown *close* to Mr. McAllister. This must be a hard time for you. However . . ." She paused and turned toward her colleagues.

Cason finished her sentence, his voice intense and pounding like a hammer. "We cannot just allow you to walk out." He looked at me condescendingly. "You would be captured easily and would likely be persuaded to give away our position. Or killed." He listed the options methodically, as if they were all the same to him.

"Is that the *only* reason I'm being detained?" I asked.

Augustus turned to me, shooting flares at me with his eyes. I doubted that the Council knew about the existence of the flash drive, much less that it was missing.

No one answered. Augustus' silence was notable.

"You can't force me to stay here," I added. My voice sounded more desperate than I wanted it to.

Looking at Augustus for approval, Vera spoke, "We'd like you to think of this as your new home, at least for a while. We want you to be comfortable here."

Dr. Bell nodded.

I felt defeated, but I tried not to show it.

"What about you, Hiro? Do you have an opinion?" I asked.

Hiro looked surprised, as if speaking was not in his job description. The other Council members appeared visibly uncomfortable.

"Excuse me, Ms. Knightley, but I will direct questions to the Council." Augustus' booming voice leveled the room like a tiny bomb. For a moment, no one spoke.

Without looking up from his computer tablet, Hiro said flatly, "Rule 7.1 should apply here. Members of the Resistance are free to vacate headquarters at any time, but will not be allowed to return."

There was an uncertain silence. I looked at Augustus. He seemed on the verge of eruption.

Cason countered, "That rule applies only to *members* of the Resistance. Ms. Knightley is a *guest*, not a member."

"Exactly," Augustus added quickly and firmly, trying to put a period at the end of the argument.

"Well . . . her mother has spoken out on our behalf," Dr. Bell offered. "That must be worth *something*."

I saw Vera nodding her head.

"You understand that you would not be allowed to return?" Dr. Bell asked. "Even if your life was in danger?"

"I do," I replied without hesitation, sensing the attitude of the room shifting slightly.

Apparently, Augustus felt it too. He stood, towering over us like an angry giant. "This is absolutely ridiculous. If we allow Ms. Knightley to leave, we will be compromising everything that we've worked for. I will not allow it!" He pounded the table with his fist as he spoke.

Hiro jumped in his seat as his tablet bounced from his hands. Vera cowered. Augustus was accustomed to getting his way. I sensed that his tightly wound grip on his perfectly crafted image was loosening.

"Augustus," Dr. Bell's voice was tentative as if she was speaking to a wild animal. "You seem upset."

That was an understatement. Augustus returned to his seat, not speaking. It seemed to require all of his energy to sit quietly.

Dr. Bell glanced at him cautiously before speaking. "We should vote."

CHAPTER THIRTY-TWO

A MUFFIN

THE VOTE WAS 2-3. I lost. Just before Vera cast the deciding vote, Augustus leaned over to her and whispered in her ear. Though she maintained a thin, nervous smile, the rest of her face contorted in fear. Immediately after it was settled, I watched Augustus' charm return, as easily as if he had shed one skin for another.

"Looks like we'll have the pleasure of your company a bit longer, Ms. Knightley," he said, before he slithered away.

As I was being escorted back to my room, I saw Elana peering at me from behind a wall. Worry had paled her face. Our eyes connected, and I mustered a tiny smile.

Later, she and Max came to my room. I heard them asking the guard if they could visit with me. I peered out the window in time to see Elana sweep her auburn hair from her shoulder and smile at the guard. He was transfixed.

"I just wanted to take her a muffin." Elana shrugged, her voice unassuming. "She hasn't eaten all day." She held up a bag for him to inspect.

"Five minutes," the guard answered, his voice hard and flat.

As soon as the door closed behind her, Elana embraced me.

"Lex, what happened? Where did you go?"

"I want to leave," I said. The finality of the words cut like a knife.

"I have to find Quin." I lowered my voice. "Augustus is lying about what happened to him." I hoped they would believe me.

Max and Elana looked at each other, both of their faces a mixture of emotions.

Max started to speak. "Lex, we—"

"Please don't say that Augustus doesn't lie," I interrupted.

Max leaned in close to me. He whispered, "We believe you. Elana told me about Artos. Quin would never leave him behind willingly."

"Time's up," the guard's cold voice sliced through the room.

I rolled my eyes. "That was a fast five minutes."

The guard responded with a dismissive grunt.

Before they left, Elana opened the bag and handed me a muffin. "I thought you might be hungry," she said, her eyes conveying more than her words.

I took a bite of the muffin, peeling back the paper as I ate. Written on the wrapper were four words: *We're coming with you.*

CHAPTER THIRTY-THREE

STEP ONE

I LAY ON MY BED, my eyes fixed on the white ceiling. There were exactly 112 tiles. I had counted them again and again. Time seemed to crawl, each second announcing itself with a loud tock from the clock on the wall. With each tick, I thought of Quin. I had a plan. Now I just had to wait.

At 5 p.m., I asked the guard to escort me to the laboratory. Carrie sat inside, her head down, her focus intense. She jumped when the guard banged on the door.

"You asked to see me," I said casually, hoping that Carrie would catch on.

She blinked a few times before answering. "I did," she said. Her voice tilted up at the end, almost a question. "Of course, I did." She repeated, speaking more confidently this time.

The guard positioned himself on one of the laboratory stools near us. He already seemed bored, tapping his fingers on the counter and examining an empty beaker.

"This way." Carrie gestured me over to the computer.

She opened a file entitled *Brain Images*. On the screen were pictures of at least 50 brains, each labeled with a name.

"We've been able to dissect and compare the brains of long-time Guardian Force officers and new recruits," Carrie explained.

She pulled up a dual screen with two brains opposite each other. One was labeled *Elliot Barnes*—I couldn't seem to escape him. The other belonged to a Brady Johnston.

Carrie pointed to Elliot's brain, a tight graying mass of coils. I felt a deep pang of regret. It was because of me that Elliot had been laid on a table, cut open, and studied like a lab rat.

"Elliot was a member of the Guardian Force for over three years. As I mentioned last time, his blood contained near-toxic levels of Emovere. His brain showed marked changes that appear to have been permanent, including a shrinking of the frontal lobe and supramarginal gyrus."

She pointed to the other brain, belonging to Brady Johnston. "Compare that to *this* brain. Brady was a new recruit. His brain has all the characteristics of a healthy eighteen-year-old. We've seen similar patterns in our other subjects, and we're fairly confident that we can attribute these changes to high levels of Emovere and Substance X."

I felt nauseous. "Do you know when the effects become permanent?" I asked, thinking of Quin. I wasn't sure if he had received Substance X, but he had taken Emovere for at least two years.

Carrie shook her head. "We're not certain. It appears that some brains are less vulnerable to the long-term effects. One might call them resilient."

"My mother always said that some patients had a resistance to Emovere."

Carrie beamed with pride. "Yes, I read your mother's article— brilliant work."

I saw Carrie cast a surreptitious glance toward the guard. He was spinning side to side on the laboratory stool, his mind elsewhere.

"There's one more thing," Carrie said quietly. She reached over and turned on a large projector, casting the dual images of the brains onto a screen. The projector's motor hummed loudly, its drone completely covering our voices.

Carrie leaned in closer to me and continued. "The night you arrived here, Augustus asked me to perform an analysis on the bullet taken from Elliot's body. I was able to determine that it came from a weapon outside of our armory. I think he knew all along that Quin was lying—that you had shot Elliot. I thought you should know."

She flipped off the projector as the guard approached. "Time to go," he said.

As we walked toward the door, I knew it was now or never. Casually, I bumped the laboratory table with my hip, sending two large beakers filled with liquid tumbling to the floor. They broke on impact, glass scattering at our feet.

Carrie's mouth hung open for a moment.

"I'm so sorry," I said to her. "I'm still feeling a bit woozy from this morning."

"Say no more," she said, giving my arm a sympathetic pat. "Sit here." She pointed to one of the nearby stools. Carrie disappeared for a moment behind another door, retrieving a broom and dustpan.

"Can I get a little help with this?" She asked the guard, as she gathered the glass with the broom.

I waited for the right moment. When both of their heads were concealed below the table, I quickly pocketed a small bottle of ether. It was a common laboratory chemical I had seen my mother use many times. She had always warned me to handle it cautiously. It was highly flammable and had the properties of a sedative.

As Carrie walked me to the door, I apologized again, turning back to examine the now-spotless floor.

With a maternal smile, Carrie's voice reassured me, "Like it never happened."

CHAPTER THIRTY-FOUR

A BAD GOOD-BYE

A FEW MINUTES AFTER 7 p.m., just as it had the last five evenings, Resistance headquarters went dark. I heard the guard shuffling nervously outside my room, as if expecting the black out.

"I'm okay," I told him, trying to make my voice sound steady. Inside, my nerves were pinging and pinballing, rapid-fire, through me.

A short time later, I heard him settle back in his chair, just outside the door. Cat-like, I padded across the floor, holding my breath. I knew I had to move quickly and confidently. If I hesitated, it would be over—and worse, Quin would be that much farther from me, almost unreachable.

In my mind, I began a slow count down. On *one*, I opened the door with my foot, reaching my hand around to the guard's face. He cried out in surprise, grasping for my hand, but only for a moment. The ether was already taking its effect. I held the cloth against his mouth for at least thirty seconds to be sure, though it seemed as if a brief eternity passed. Finally, I released him. He slumped limp and unmoving.

Calling softly to Artos, I left the room, backpack in hand. I heard Artos' nails clicking behind me as he followed. It was pitch black, but I couldn't risk using my flashlight. I went by feel, rounding the corner to Elana's room where I slipped a cryptic note under the door.

From there, I headed down the tunnel with Artos. We were both running now. With each step, I thought only of Quin.

For him, leaving here was probably just one of many bad good-byes. I imagined that he had grown accustomed to disappointment, recognizing it like an old friend. In fact, he probably expected it, outsmarted it by pushing everyone away first. But for some reason, Quin had let me in, and I realized now, from the inside, that his walls weren't really as they appeared. Their substance was paper-thin parchment that could be blown down by a mere breath.

Quin was somewhere, *could have been anywhere*, in this abandoned city, but I knew exactly where to find him.

CHAPTER THIRTY-FIVE

COIT TOWER, REVISITED

I BOUNDED UP THE SPIRALING stairs two at a time, Artos following closely behind me. When I reached the entrance to the observation deck, I took a breath, my heart suspended in a brief limbo before slowly opening the door. *Please*, I asked silently to no one in particular.

Quin sat directly opposite with his gun pointed at the door. His eyes looked frightened, but hopeful. On his face, near his temple, I could see a cut and a yellowing bruise. He lowered his weapon. Before either of us could speak, Artos bounded through the door toward Quin, licking his face uncontrollably.

"I missed you too, Artos," Quin said, chuckling and fending off Artos' tongue.

Quin stood, turning his eyes to mine. Relief washed over me in waves. I thought I might cry, but I didn't. I looked only at Quin. His pull was like a magnet. Before my mind had even decided to walk toward him, my feet began moving. I felt his arms around me. He lowered his face, burying it in my shoulder. His warm breath tickled my neck. In a word, Quin felt like home.

"Lex." He pronounced my name deliberately as if saying it for the first time. He pulled away slightly, but kept his eyes on mine. "You found me."

"*And* Artos," I added proudly, omitting the fact that Artos had done most of the finding. "Did you think that I wouldn't?"

Quin didn't respond. He dropped to one knee, and Artos eagerly ran over to him. From under Artos' collar, Quin removed a small object. He held it up for me. It was my mother's flash drive. I gasped in surprise.

"You have a lot of explaining to do, Mr. McAllister." I narrowed my eyes at him in pretend anger.

Quin grinned. "I know," he said. "I guess I should start by saying that you were right."

"That's always a good place to start," I teased.

Quin laughed, and I noticed the way his eyes crinkled at the corners, making his face seem boyish, mischievous. When he laughed, I could see five-year-old Quin looking back at me.

"Augustus lied to me about a lot of things. He's been lying to everyone. After I left you that night, I went to see him. I wanted to talk to him about you."

"About *me?*" I said, taken aback.

"I wanted to tell him that I was done . . . avoiding you." Inside, my heart fluttered as if about to take flight. I was thinking of our kiss. Quin's lips turned up at the corners in a shy smile, hinting that his thoughts were the same.

"When I got to his office, I heard him talking to someone on a cell phone, the emergency one that no one is supposed to use without his permission. He was talking about *this*." Quin held up the flash drive. "He was going to sell it."

"*Sell* it?" I had suspected that Augustus was manipulative—a con artist, an opportunist—but I was shocked by his willingness to betray everyone who trusted him. I knew his disloyalty must have been a bitter shock to Quin.

"To who?" I wondered aloud.

Quin's face darkened. "This is going to sound crazy, but I think he was talking to General Ryker."

Quin paused, allowing the alarm to settle from my face.

"Do you know what's on it?" I asked.

"No," Quin replied, "but it must be something really important if the Guardians want it so badly." I hid my surprise. I had been sure that Quin knew the contents of the flash drive.

Quin continued, "I confronted Augustus. At first, he tried to deny it—to turn it around on me. He said I wasn't myself because of you. He even told me he thought I was using Emovere or something. When I threatened to discuss it with the Council, he hit me." Quin touched the bruise on his temple. It was dark purple in the center, bordered by an ugly yellow. Shaking his head, he added, "I never thought he would deliberately hurt me. I guess that must sound stupid to you."

"Quin, you're not stupid." I reached up and brushed the side of his face gently with my hand. He turned toward my touch. "You looked up to him. He abused your trust."

Quin sighed and shrugged his shoulders. "Yeah, the story of my life," he muttered. I imagined that he was thinking of his father.

"So how did you get the flash drive?"

"Well . . . I hit him back." Quin and I shared a satisfied smiled. It gave me more than a small bit of pleasure to imagine Quin's fist connecting with its target.

"Augustus fell and dropped the flash drive. I hit him again, but he kept coming at me. He wasn't going to let me leave that room, Lex." Quin's voice was somber but distant, as if he was reliving a nightmare, scene by scene. For a moment, I tried to imagine the white, hot terror of realizing that someone you trusted was trying to kill you.

"Then Artos got him by the leg and wouldn't let go." Artos pranced at Quin's feet as if celebrating his victory. "So Augustus reached for the lamp on his desk. He knocked it over and cut us with some of the broken glass." Quin looked down to examine the cut on Artos' nose. His wound now completely forgotten, Artos wagged his tail, carefree.

"After that, I ran into the tunnels. I could hear Augustus behind me. I slipped this into Artos' collar—there's a hole, where the fabric is worn from him chewing on it—and I told him to find you. I didn't think I would get away."

We sat in silence, Quin's words sinking into my mind like heavy stones. I shook off a shiver, imagining Quin, bleeding and afraid, sending Artos away from him. I knew then that Quin was brave, the kind of bravery that is only born in a dark place.

Quin spoke first. "I didn't know if you would . . . I mean, I hoped that you would . . ." Quin's voice trailed off, but his eyes finished the sentence for him. He looked down, shuffling his feet nervously.

I looked back at him, disbelieving. After everything that had happened, Quin thought I wouldn't try to find him, that what I knew about him would somehow change the way I felt.

"I care about you, Quin. That hasn't changed—no matter what it says in that stupid file."

He stepped back from me. "Why?" he demanded. "Why do you care about me?"

I smiled. "Isn't that supposed to be my question?"

"I'm beginning to like it," Quin countered. "So?"

I couldn't answer. I might have said I felt safe with him, but that wasn't entirely true. When Quin touched me, it was like heat buzzing in my brain, a cold razor's edge pressed to my skin. It was the kind of feeling I feared, but wanted all at the same time. And how could I explain that to someone, most of all to Quin?

"Why do *you* like *me*?" I asked. I knew it wasn't fair, but surprisingly, Quin didn't protest my question. He turned away from me, leaning out against the observation deck, and answered.

"When I'm with you, everything feels different. Not like the past didn't happen, which is something I wanted for a long time. But like it *happened*, and it's okay that it did."

It was a perfect answer.

"Quin, it *is* okay. That file is not what you said it was. It's not *everything*, and it's certainly not the *Book of Quin*. It's just a few chapters in the story."

"*Important* chapters," he said, unconvinced.

"Fine . . . important ones," I conceded.

I walked over to the railing and stood next to him, both of us looking out into the blackness of the city. "But there are a lot of chapters missing. That file is not Artos or your mother's book of poetry or Max and Elana or . . ." I wanted to say me, but I stopped myself.

Quin didn't reply. His silence felt like disagreement. Frustrated, I sighed and began to walk away, but Quin stopped me, placing a firm hand on my forearm.

"Aren't you forgetting something?" he asked softly.

Before I could answer, his lips were on mine.

CHAPTER THIRTY-SIX

PRACTICE

KISSING QUIN WAS LIKE STANDING on the edge of a soaring precipice, watching pebbles roll and plummet to their death below, only blue sky between me and the ground. Falling felt inevitable, a welcome but fatal exhilaration.

I was most aware of his hands. One was tangled in my hair, holding my head tightly. The other travelled urgently around my waist and up my spine. Quin's hands seemed to have their own life, and it was one of pressing need, eliminating any separation between our bodies. For the first time in my life, I wondered if it was possible to die of bliss. I could understand why Max's mother had become addicted to Euphoractamine. If I could have bottled *this*, whatever *this* feeling was, I would have ached for it in its absence.

Quin brushed his lips against my cheek and buried his face in my hair.

"Practice," he teased.

I laughed, and I could feel his smile against my neck. Quin released me, his face suddenly shy. My body felt instantly cold in the space between us.

"So what now, Ms. Knightley?" Quin's voice was light and playful.

"Well, you're not the only one with a story to tell," I replied. "Your leaving caused quite a stir."

"I would imagine," he said, grinning.

I told Quin about everything that had happened since I had awakened to find him gone—Augustus' early morning meeting and lies to the Resistance, my encounter with the Council, and my escape. I conveniently omitted my panic attack. In part, because I knew Quin would shoulder the blame, and I didn't want him to have anything else to hold over himself. The other part was me. I didn't want to admit I had lost control, that my fear had temporarily taken my body as a helpless hostage.

"There's one more thing," I added. "Max and Elana are coming too. They're meeting us at the Golden Gate Bridge at sunrise."

Quin didn't seem surprised, his thoughts focused elsewhere. "And where exactly are we going?" He looked at me, uncertainly.

"There's only one place left to go." I felt a tug of longing, before I even said it. "Home."

Quin didn't respond, but I watched his face change. He was slowly rebuilding his walls.

"My mother will know what to do," I said, lending my voice more confidence than I felt.

Quin sat down, leaning up against the wall. He patted Artos' head absentmindedly. "Okay," he said, but I knew that it wasn't.

I sat down next to him. "What's wrong?" I asked, touching his shoulder.

He shrugged off my hand and looked straight ahead, avoiding my eyes. His face was as impenetrable as steel.

"What happened to my mom was my fault." He said it evenly as if it was a fact he had learned in school—one not open for debate. "Your mom knows that. How can I even *look* at her?"

"Quin, your *father* murdered your mother. You were only six. How can that *possibly* be your fault?"

"I knew what my dad was like," Quin began. "I had seen him hit her before, throw her around like a rag doll. That day, she told me to watch Colton and play on the floor close to her. I didn't listen. I *never* listened. And now, the things I've done . . . I'm just like him." Quin's voice cracked. He lowered his head, resting it between his knees. I put my hand on his back, rubbing it gently.

"Don't try to make me feel better, Lex," his voice the pained growl of a wounded animal.

I took my hand away and said nothing for a long time. Artos settled in the space between us, laying his head on my lap. I watched Quin's shoulders move up and down. Though he made no sound and I couldn't see his face, I knew he was crying. Words from his Guardian file ran through my head: *The minors were unharmed.* What happened to Quin didn't leave a visible scar. It burned from the inside.

I spoke softly, fingering the locket around my neck, "Sometimes, I think it was my fault that my dad left." I had never said it aloud before, but I couldn't remember a time I hadn't thought it. "He just disappeared, like my mom and I never existed. It's hard to believe he ever *really* loved me."

After I finished, Quin took a breath and looked up. His face was wet, his eyes red. "How could he *not*?" he asked.

CHAPTER THIRTY-SEVEN

A TEST

THE SUN WAS NEWLY BORN, just beginning its slow ascent over the horizon. It was a clear day, the Golden Gate's burnt-red cables cutting through the pinkish blue of morning. Gulls screamed at us from overhead, and I shivered, though the air was warm. Their cries sounded like a warning. Quin stood outside the tollbooth, out of view of a nearby camera, pacing nervously, while Artos chased mice in and out of the booths.

"Where are they?" he asked, a discernible edge in his voice. "We don't have long before there's another helicopter patrol."

As Quin spoke, I heard the rumble of an engine and saw two oversized military vehicles approaching the bridge from San Francisco. I opened my mouth to speak, but before I could utter a sound, Quin pulled me inside the tollbooth and down to the ground. Artos bounded inside after us, his teeth clamped on the tail of a portly rat. Quin tapped Artos' head, and he dropped his catch. I watched as it scuttled across the floor and out of the door.

"Quiet," Quin instructed calmly. I was comforted by his arms around me. They were familiar to me now. I had spent the night like this memorizing the crook of his elbow, the three freckles on his forearm, the inked edges of his Guardian tattoo. I could feel his breathing, slow and controlled.

From the floor of the booth, we could see nothing. But after a minute or so, the engine noise roared past us and stopped abruptly.

Doors slammed, and I heard the sound of boots marching. Then a shrill voice cut the air like the blade of an axe.

"Guardian Recruits, take your assigned positions."

There was more marching, followed by the *click-clacking* of metal against metal. Minutes passed as I watched the second hand on Quin's wristwatch make several rounds.

Quin whispered, "It's a test."

I had to look. I couldn't help it. I loosened myself from Quin's grasp and raised my head slightly. He didn't protest, but pulled me back to him when I gasped.

I had seen at least ten recruits arranged in a line atop the bridge's outer railing. They wore harnesses around their ankles attached to bungee cords. Their hands were bound with thick rope behind their backs. On the bridge, overseeing them was a small but ferocious man, balding with a thick beard.

"Guardian Recruit Legacy 152, jump!"

"Guardian Recruit Greenhorn 341, jump!"

"Guardian Recruit Greenhorn 533, jump!"

One by one, I imagined the recruits jumping without a sound from the bridge, yo-yoing above the ocean some two hundred feet below.

"Guardian Recruit, Greenhorn 558, jump!"

Ten seconds later, the voice spoke again, "Greenhorn 558, do you have a problem following instructions?"

"No, sir," a man's voice replied with a surprising, subtle crackling of fear. I had assumed the Guardian recruits were given Emovere prior to this *test*, which would explain their post-jump silence.

"Good. Then you have exactly five seconds to jump. Count it down for me, Greenhorn."

Quin mouthed a name against my ear. "Ryker."

"Five." The jumper's voice feigned confidence. Perhaps he was thinking he could muster the courage after all.

"Four." There was a hint of doubt. I wondered if he was looking down into the frigid water below.

"Thr-ee." His voice shook slightly, breaking in the middle of the word.

"Two." Now he was whispering. He wasn't going to make the jump, and he knew it.

"One." There was complete silence. Maybe I had been wrong.

For the next five minutes, I heard constant movement outside. There were muted, purposeful voices. Among them was neither General Ryker nor the jumper.

"What happens now?" I whispered to Quin.

"There's a boat waiting for them. Someone unties and unclips them, and a doctor takes their vital signs. It's supposed to tell them how well the Emovere is working."

Quin had obviously done this before, probably many times. I shuddered, imagining him stepping off the bridge into nothing.

After several slamming doors, the engines roared to life again, but remained idling.

"General Ryker, I'm sorry, sir. Please, sir." It was the jumper's voice, Greenhorn 558.

Once again, I lifted my head, peering out at them. General Ryker was conferencing with another man, purposefully ignoring his recruit. Though the jumper was too far away for me to see his expression, his shoulders were slumped and his head lowered. In silence, General Ryker walked over to Greenhorn 558. He calmly swung his feet over the ledge so that he was standing alongside him.

"Greenhorn 558, this is your third failure to complete the jump test. You are dismissed from the Guardian Force." There was a harsh finality in his voice.

I tapped Quin, urging him to look, but he shook his head. I knew whatever was coming was bad.

General Ryker turned away for a moment. I hoped he would unclip the jumper, untie his hands, and help him climb back over the railing. But he didn't. Instead, with all of his strength, he pushed Greenhorn 558 from the bridge. I imagined that he bounced up and down, up and down, up and down, until he was hanging like a spider from a thread.

General Ryker effortlessly scaled the railing and returned to his vehicle, moving with a quiet satisfaction. Once inside the passenger seat, he reached his arm out the window, giving the roof several deliberate taps, signaling their departure.

I sat back down in the booth, exhaling. *How long had I been holding my breath?* Quin didn't speak. He didn't have to. I knew that, like me, he was imagining Greenhorn 558, swinging below us, his hands useless, his eyes likely fixed on the water in a state of despair, knowing better than to hope for a rescue that would never come.

CHAPTER THIRTY-EIGHT

I KNOW HIM

AFTER THE MILITARY VEHICLES SPED away, Quin and I emerged cautiously from the booth. I was worried about Max and Elana. It was already 7:30, the sun well over the horizon, and there was no sign of them. Quin approached the bridge's railing, where Greenhorn 558's cord was clipped.

"We have to help him," he said. "They won't return for at least a week. He'll be dead by then." The frankness of Quin's words told me that Greenhorn 558 wasn't the first recruit to be pushed from the bridge and left behind.

As Quin began to hoist him, pulling him up hand over hand, I saw Elana's face. She was running toward the tollbooths, her cheeks flushed. Max followed closely behind her, along with someone else—Carrie.

"Never thought I'd be so glad to see you two," Max shouted as he approached.

"Can I get a little help here?" Quin asked, struggling to raise the recruit to safety.

Max looked at me quizzically.

"A recruit failed the jump test," I said, gesturing toward the bridge's railing.

Max's eyes opened wide with understanding. With urgency, he ran to Quin's side and began helping him.

Elana and I embraced. "I see you got my note," I said to her.

"Brilliant," she said, showing me the piece of paper where I had written *Meet me at sunrise at the place where you almost stepped into the fog.*

I turned to Carrie. "What are *you* doing here?"

Before Carrie could answer, Elana replied. "She saw us leaving and said she wanted to come."

Carrie nodded. "I've already wasted too much time working for one corrupt organization. I couldn't stand to think I was being used by another." She smiled. "And I must admit I was hoping that I might get a chance to finally meet your mother."

I hugged Carrie. "You will," I said.

Our reunion was short-lived. Over Carrie's shoulder, I watched Quin stand up suddenly, his face ghost-white.

"*You?*" he said, looking down, while Max held tight to the recruit's cord. His voice was filled with venom. "Forget it, Max. Let him go."

Quin swung a leg over the railing and began walking across the bridge away from us. I could see that his fists were clenched tight.

I ran after him, while Elana and Carrie helped Max heave the recruit back onto the bridge. When I glanced back, there was a fourth person standing with them. It was Greenhorn 558.

"Quin!" Quin continued walking without looking back. Artos ran after him.

"Quin!" I yelled again, louder this time. Still walking, he didn't even slow his pace.

"Quin, please don't make me chase you." He stopped suddenly, stonewalled. Without facing me, he spoke.

"*I know him.*" Each word pounded with hatred.

"I see you haven't changed much, McAllister," I heard the recruit's voice behind me, approaching. Max, Elana, and Carrie were walking speedily to keep up with him.

I turned to face Greenhorn 558. He was young, probably eighteen or nineteen. His skin was smooth and tanned, offset by his sandy blond hair. It was shaggy as if he had cut it himself. His eyes were blue like the crayon cornflower. Unlike Quin's, his muscles were thin and wiry. His wrists were rubbed red and raw from the ropes—his black Guardian tattoo a marked contrast. The edges of an arrogant smile played on his lips.

He directed his words toward me, his gaze playful, cocky. Somehow he seemed to know I was one of Quin's soft spots, and he aimed a poison arrow straight for me.

"This guy was always a real hot head," he said to me, gesturing with a nod to Quin. "But—help me out here, Quin—how is it that you always manage to have girls chasing after you? A real ladies man, aren't you?"

Even though it was foolish—I had known Quin for less than a month—the thought of another girl running after him caused me physical pain, like a sucker punch to the stomach.

I watched Quin's face change, revealing an expression I hadn't seen before but recognized instantly. It was rage. It flared like a grenade launched from somewhere deep inside him.

Quin turned to the recruit and punched him squarely in the face. Stunned, the recruit took a few wobbly steps back. Blood trickled from his nose.

"Quin!" Elana admonished him.

Quin immediately looked at me. His eyes were fiery, but ashamed.

"Well, then," the recruit said, holding his hand protectively to his face. "Now that McAllister and I are reacquainted, I guess I should introduce myself." He extended his hand to me, but I didn't accept it.

"We did just save your life," I said harshly. I felt wounded and defensive. "I think a *thank you* is in order."

He shrugged, probably embarrassed at my rebuff. "My apologies," he said. "My name is Edison *Van Sant*." He emphasized his last name, pausing afterward to allow time for a reaction. When there was none, he added, "My friends call me Eddie."

"*Humph*," Quin made a noise of contempt.

"This isn't at all awkward," Max joked. No one laughed. "How exactly do you two *know* each other?"

Quin didn't answer. Typical.

Edison took a step back, safeguarding himself from another meeting with Quin's fist. "McAllister had a thing for my girlfriend. Too bad he wasn't exactly her type, him being *homeless* and all."

I couldn't look away from Quin. I anticipated an explosion, but he kept his fury tightly wound inside him, a ball of pure heat.

Quin looked directly at me and no one else. He spoke slowly, still gritting his teeth. I could see how hard it was for him to contain his boiling indignation. "We were both sixteen. I had just run away here from L.A. and lived in a park across from Edison's house. That's how we met."

Max and Elana looked at each other, their eyes holding a silent conversation. I wanted to touch Quin, but I stayed put, holding my own hands in front of me instead.

Carrie broke the uncomfortable silence. "Shouldn't we probably head over the bridge now? I mean, don't they patrol or something?" She glanced nervously at me. I hoped she wasn't already regretting her decision.

"Carrie's right," I said, and we all began walking in silence.

When we reached the halfway point, I turned and looked toward San Francisco one last time, its skyline still a deceptive façade of grandeur. The last time I traversed this bridge, I had said good-bye to my mother. Now retracing that walk, I realized my good-bye was also to the girl I was then. I had changed without knowing it or inviting it.

Max sidled up alongside me, playfully punching my arm.

"So when did *this* happen?" he asked, his finger a metronome marking time between Quin and me. He grinned his usual, easy-going smirk and, in spite of myself, I smiled back.

CHAPTER THIRTY-NINE

HOME

WITHIN FORTY MINUTES, WE WERE in Marin, a city that abutted the Golden Gate. No different from when I left, the streets were nearly deserted. Unemployment was high, and most people returned straight home from work, venturing out only for necessities. It was safer to stay inside—at least that's what the government wanted us to believe. Though I felt relieved to no longer have to worry about the watchful eyes of the Guardian Force, the wary anticipation of seeing my mother began to work its way into my stomach. I hoped she wouldn't be disappointed in me.

"Where's your house, Lex?" Elana asked.

"It's in Tiburon," I said. It was nearby, a small and quiet seaside town. "We're going to need a car," I added, surveying the sparse parking lots around us.

"One of your specialties—right, McAllister?" Edison couldn't resist a chance to jab at Quin, if only with his words.

I turned to Quin, and he nodded at me. "Wait here," he said, jogging down a side street toward a residential neighborhood.

After Quin was out of earshot, Elana turned to me, speaking loud enough for the group to hear her. "Are we letting *him* come with us?" She gestured toward Edison. "Doesn't he have a home to go back to?" Everyone's eyes rested on him.

Edison shrugged. "I've been disowned," he said flatly. "So I guess the short answer is no."

"If we're going to let you come with us, then you could at least try to be polite," Elana said.

Edison gave her a condescending smile. "Whatever you say, Red."

Elana's face tightened. She rolled her eyes.

"How long since you were recruited by the Guardians?" I asked Edison. I liked him less each time he spoke, but my curiosity wouldn't be denied.

"A few months," he answered. "I failed the jump test three times. Bridges and I don't exactly have the best history."

Before I could ask my favorite question, Quin returned, driving a newer model jeep. The driver's side window was broken.

"The keys were locked inside," he explained.

"Would you like us to start a running tally of your felonies?" Edison asked. Elana and Carrie both turned to him, shooting darts with their eyes.

As we drove, I directed Quin, while Max explained their early morning escape.

"I had to take out a few guards with these babies," Max joked, displaying his fists. His knuckles were bruised and swollen. "I guess my stepdad taught me something after all."

"Did anyone follow you?" Quin asked.

"I don't think so," Max replied. "Carrie disconnected the emergency alarm, and we went out that way, but I'm sure they're looking for us by now."

"Turn here," I told Quin. "It's the last house, the one on the cul-de-sac."

Quin glanced at me. He looked nervous.

"We're here," I announced.

On the porch, I reached into one of my mother's potted plants, long dead, and removed our spare key. I took a deep breath as I turned it in the lock.

"Mom," I called to her cautiously. I had imagined my homecoming many times, but I never expected to feel apprehensive, like a stranger in my own house. Over a month had passed since I had seen her, and I wasn't sure what to expect. I glanced into the kitchen and the living room. Both were empty and dark. I noticed piles of dishes in the sink and a stack of laundry on the dining room table. Then I felt Elana's hand on my shoulder.

My mother stood in the foyer, an odd combination of shock, grief, and gratitude on her face. In the days since I had left her, my mother had aged years. Lines had carved themselves around her eyes, which were darkened like bruises underneath. Her hair and clothing were disheveled as if she had been sleeping for days. Tears pooled in her eyes and fell in a steady stream down her face. She choked back a sob.

"Lex, we'll wait in here." Elana ushered the group into the living room while Artos settled on the mat inside the doorway.

With trepidation, I walked toward my mother. I felt frightened, overwhelmed by her. I had never seen her this way. Even after my father left, my mother never cried in front of me—well, only once. I had returned home early from school and found her in the bedroom at the computer looking at photos from her wedding album. At the time, she had insisted that her eyes were red from a long night in the laboratory, but I knew better. Still, this unhinged version of my mother was entirely alien.

"I thought you were . . ." For a moment, the sentence remained unfinished. "Dead." The word dropped like a boulder from her mouth. My mother took a few steps toward me and touched my face. "He told me you were dead."

My mother's arms blanketed me, holding me so tight that I could barely breathe. After a few seconds, I let myself cry . . . hard. My tears didn't surprise me, but their strength was unexpected. They seemed to flow from a guttural and hidden place, a place where I had secreted *all* my sorrows. My mother didn't let me go for a long time.

When she released me, I asked her, "Who told you I was dead?"

"He wouldn't tell me his name, only that he was the leader of the Resistance and that anonymity was essential for his protection and mine. He said you had been captured and executed by the Guardians."

"Augustus Porter," I told my mother. "That's his name, and he's not who he says he is. I think he's a psychopath like the ones you studied."

My mother's eyes opened wide at the term, but she didn't speak.

"He was going to sell *this* to the Guardians." I handed her the flash drive. She put it in her pocket and shook her head.

"I should have been more careful," she admitted. "I should have told you everything. If the Guardian Force had this, there would be nothing left. Their ability to perfect the super soldier would be limitless."

I was shocked to hear my mother use the term *super soldier*. As I had suspected, she had known much more than she had revealed to me.

"What's on that flash drive?" I asked her.

"We'll talk about it later," she said. Sensing my frustration, she quickly added, "I promise."

We walked together into the living room where we were met with five anxious faces.

"Mom, these are my friends. Without them, I *would* be dead." I introduced them one by one, saving Edison for last. I wasn't sure I could call him a friend.

Carrie spoke first, her face tense with excitement. "Dr. Knightley, it is such a pleasure to finally meet you. I've been following your work since graduate school. I wanted to tell you that you should be so proud of your daughter. She has certainly inherited your love for learning."

My mother put her arm around me as my face reddened. When I glanced at her, I saw that her mask of composure had quickly restored itself. There was no trace of that alien creature with tears in her eyes.

"Let's all go into the kitchen," my mother said. "You must be starving."

Max nodded. "Famished," he said, grinning at me.

For the next few hours, we sat at the kitchen table and told my mother the story of the last thirty-something days. She and Elana cooked pasta—our typical meal since the government started rationing perishable food—while Max and I did most of the talking. My mother listened intently, asking countless questions. Even after we explained to her that many of the Resistance were former Guardian recruits, her eyes frequently darted to the four tattooed arms resting on her table. Carrie took over at the scientific parts, telling my mother about the increasing strength of Emovere and its lasting effects on the brain, along with the use of Agitor and Substance X. We also discussed our theory that the Guardians were recruiting from trauma survivors. Max, Elana, and Quin all fit the profile.

"What about you, Edison?" my mother asked. "Have you been through *something*?"

Her directness took Edison by surprise—his response seemed uncharacteristically polite.

"Yes, ma'am. I have." He didn't elaborate and, surprisingly, my mother didn't push him.

I noticed Quin was quieter than usual. When I tried to catch his eyes, he looked away, but I felt him watching me as I spoke. After we ate, my mother turned her attention to Quin.

"Quin, what was your last name again?" He was seated next to me at the table, and I felt his body tense.

"McAllister." His voice sounded like a young boy's.

"Hmm . . ." My mother was thinking. "That name . . . it sounds awfully familiar. Where are you from?"

Max and I made eye contact across the table, and he raised his eyebrows.

"Mom, it's been a long day," I interjected before Quin could answer or, more likely, *not* answer. "Try not to interrogate everyone."

"It's okay, Lex. I have to tell her sometime," Quin said reluctantly.

"Tell me what?" My mother was curious, as always.

Quin's voice shook nervously as he began speaking. Aside from Max, Elana, and myself, I doubted he had ever explained this part of himself to anyone.

"You know . . . knew . . . my father."

Under the table, I found Quin's hand and interlaced my fingers with his. His palm was sweaty, and he squeezed hard as he spoke.

"He was in prison, when you met him. You were doing an experiment with Crim-X."

My mother looked at Quin, the blood draining from her face. She had seen the ghost of her past in the handsome, brown-eyed boy next to me.

"George McAllister, Inmate 243," she whispered, almost inaudibly.

Quin nodded. "He killed my mother." Quin's hand left mine and went to his face. He covered his eyes.

The room was silent, tomb-like. Even Edison looked subdued. My mother stood and went over to Quin. She knelt next to him and put her arm around him.

"Quin and Colton," she said softly. "I have thought of you so often since I ended that dreadful research trial. I'm so sorry. You can't imagine how sorry I am."

I was surprised. I had always believed the government had forced the closure of the Crim-X experiment, thinking my mother was too proud to ever accept failure.

"When you're ready, Quin, I have some things I would like you to see." My mother rubbed his shoulder and took a breath.

"Now who wants dessert?" she asked, diverting everyone's eyes from Quin but mine. "I've been saving some chocolate ice cream for a special occasion."

CHAPTER FORTY

SOMETHING PRECIOUS

AFTER DESSERT, AS MY MOTHER sat and talked to everyone, I snuck away into my bedroom. It was just as I had left it, but it felt foreign somehow. I sat on the bed, flipping through my journal. Though most people kept their diary on a computer tablet, my mother had encouraged me to handwrite my journal. She always told me there was something satisfying, releasing, about putting pen to paper—and she was right.

My last entry was the day before I left for San Francisco.

April 5, 2041

> *It's 2 a.m. I've been putting off writing for the entire day. Even now, I don't want to write this. If I write it, it will be real. Tomorrow is the day—the day that my life changes. Mom keeps saying she's not worried, but I know she's good at hiding her feelings. Me, on the other hand, I'm a wreck. I have so many thoughts racing through my head that I can hardly write fast enough. What if I can't find the Resistance or they don't find me? What if something happens to Mom while I'm gone? Or worse, what if something happens to me? I don't know if she could bear it. I'm trying my best to see this all as a grand adventure, but the truth is that I'm afraid. For some reason, I've been thinking a lot*

*about Dad lately . . . wondering what he'd say about all of
this, if he'd be proud of me . . .*

There was a soft knock at the door, interrupting my reading. Quin's
face peeked around the doorframe.

"Can I come in?" he asked.

"Sure," I replied, but I felt my cheeks warm with embarrassment.
My room suddenly seemed to belong to a little girl, my stuffed bear
watching us, glass-eyed, from my bed. Quin walked over to my desk,
running his hand absentmindedly across the dark wood. My academic
awards, ribbons, and trophies were stacked side by side. Quin leaned
over to inspect them.

"Pretty impressive, Ms. Knightley," he said, grinning at me.

"I guess." I didn't want him to think I was bragging.

Quin sat down next to me. I was instantly aware of his body in
relation to mine. There were exactly five inches of space between his
thigh and my hand.

"So today was *interesting*," I offered, hoping he would take the bait.

As usual, Quin wasn't biting. He only nodded.

"I'm really proud of you," I said, nudging his shoulder with mine.
"It took a lot of courage to tell my mom."

Quin nodded again. His silence frustrated me, and I sighed.

Even so, I continued—hopeful I would wear him down with the
persistence he so undervalued. "You and Edison obviously have quite a
history. Will you tell me what happened?"

Quin looked down. "If I have to," he said, only half joking. I raised
my eyebrows at him, encouraging him to continue.

"For starters, what he said about me wasn't entirely true. He was a
total jerk, a spoiled rich kid. He lived in this fancy house across from
the park where I slept. He and his friends would go there lots of nights
to get drunk. A couple of times, his girlfriend tried to talk to me or give
me food. Eddie couldn't stand it. He was so jealous. You can probably
guess that this wasn't the first time I hit him." Quin lowered his eyes
and continued. "Anyway, he told the Guardian recruiting officers where
to find me. They had been looking for me for a while."

I could understand why Quin despised Edison. He *did* seem spoiled and was kind of a jerk.

"So you're not a *ladies' man?*" I tried to make my voice sound feather light as if I didn't care at all about the answer.

"Lex," Quin said, chiding me as if I *was* a little girl. "What are you *really* asking?"

I took a breath. I couldn't find the right words. I shrugged, feeling babyish.

"You know who I was then," Quin continued. "I was like a shell of a person, always looking for something or someone to make all of this okay." He gestured toward himself. "I was *really* impulsive . . . even more than I am now. So yes, I've *been with* girls in my past, if that's what you're asking."

The plurality of the word *girls* stung more than I had expected.

"But . . ." Quin's turned to look at me.

"Don't say it didn't mean anything, Quin." I sounded like I was pouting. Maybe I was.

"I wasn't going to say that."

"Oh."

Quin lay back on my bed, perpendicular to my pillows, his feet still on the floor. I could see a thin line of his skin and the point of his hip bone, where his T-shirt met his jeans. My hand wanted to place itself there, but I didn't allow it.

"I was going to say that those girls didn't know anything about me. I was a pretend Quin. You know me, the *real* me, better than anyone has. If we ever . . . if you ever wanted to . . . *do that* . . . it would be different."

I didn't know what to say to Quin. My body felt things I couldn't easily express. I wondered when Quin's communication skills had started to exceed mine.

I lay back beside him, not speaking. He turned toward me, waiting for me to meet his eyes, but I didn't. I was afraid to. I didn't know how or when it happened, but I had given Quin something of mine, something precious. I worried he would break it without meaning to.

Quin pressed his mouth to my ear, his breathing drowning all other sounds until he spoke. His voice was barely a whisper.

"I've never said this to *anyone*." He paused, his breath marking the seconds. "Lex." I had never heard my name sound so heavy with longing. "I'm falling in love with you."

CHAPTER FORTY-ONE

DEMONS

QUIN TOOK MY HEAD IN his hands, turning it toward him, moving his mouth a few inches from my ear to my lips. He tasted like chocolate ice cream. I turned my body toward his and let my hand wander to the spot it had wanted to find—the soft, warm skin just above his waistband, the sharp point of his hip. When I touched him, Quin kissed me harder. I felt powerful, desired.

Still, I was afraid to respond to Quin's *I love you*, uncertain if my hesitation had to do with who Quin was or who I was—or maybe who we were together. I was starting to understand that my father's absence had affected me more than I realized. It was hard for me to trust Quin with all of me and even harder to trust myself.

Quin slipped his arm around my waist and pulled me in close to him, hiding his face in my hair. "You smell so good," he said.

"I do?" I laughed.

Quin nodded, his face still next to mine. I could feel his stubble rubbing against my cheek. "You smell like you," he whispered.

"Lex?" My mother's voice was a splash of cold water. I sat up instantly. "Where are you?" she asked.

Quin stood abruptly and sat in the chair by my desk.

I smoothed my hair. "In here, Mom," I replied.

She opened the door cautiously.

"There you are." She smiled warmly, but there was an edge in her voice. I wondered if it was possible for her to know, just by looking at me, that my mouth had been pressed to Quin's a few seconds ago.

"I'll let you two talk." Quin walked toward the door and out of it, without looking back. The room felt empty without him.

My mother closed the door and sat down next to me. "What a day, huh?" She laughed, making her eyes seem slightly less weary.

"It feels so good to be home," I said.

She nodded and pulled me in close to her.

"Mom, I know this wasn't easy for you. I'm sorry that—"

"Lex, there's nothing to apologize for. I'm just so grateful to have my girl back with me. You should probably get some sleep. You must be exhausted. I've put your friends in the guest room and on the couch."

I yawned. My mother was right, my eyelids did feel heavy. Since I had left, I hadn't once slept through the night. My mother walked to the door, as if to leave, but she paused. She appeared to be considering her words carefully, which she often did.

"Quin." She said his name thoughtfully as if he was a research topic she was studying. "He seems to like you."

I couldn't help my broad grin. I had always failed miserably at keeping secrets from my mother. Even though I had wanted to keep it for myself, at least for a while, I had told her about my first kiss as soon as I had arrived home from the football stadium. The words simply tumbled out of my mouth even as I tried to contain them. Now, I didn't even try to lie to her.

"I like him too, Mom. *A lot.*"

A shadow of worry passed over my mother's face. "I just want you to be careful, Lex. Quin is not like you. He's been through a lot. Things like that don't just go away. They haunt a person."

I bristled inside. I had been through something too. My mother seemed to think that losing my father was like misplacing a sock.

"I *am* being careful, Mom." My voice sounded harsher than I intended. "Quin would never hurt me." Even as I spoke the words, I didn't completely believe them.

She nodded. "I can see why you like him, but I want you to remember something. The past—Quin's past—is not dead. It's very much alive inside him, and I don't want his demons to become yours."

It sounded as if she was speaking from experience, but she didn't elaborate. I resisted the urge to respond. I wanted to tell her that, to me, loving someone required fighting his demons as if they *were* my own. My mother said nothing else. She kissed my forehead and left me alone, my own demons howling inside my head.

CHAPTER FORTY-TWO

A BOY WITH A PAST

I WAS DREAMING AGAIN—THIS TIME of my father. I was walking next to him in a field of tall grass. I had met him in my dreams before, but this was a dream like no other. For the first time, in a dream I knew. I knew that he had left us and yet was still walking there beside me.

I said, "I miss you."

"I know," he replied.

"No, you don't."

He walked away from me until all I could see was the grass waving to me in the wind.

A sound awakened me. Startled, I said a silent *thank you* that I was in my bed at home. I saw a thin bar of light under my door. Someone was awake.

Edison sat at the kitchen table, a glass of water in front of him. His eyes were alert, but red-rimmed as if he hadn't been to sleep at all.

"Hey," he said softly. "I can't sleep. Hope I didn't wake you."

"It's okay." I tried to imagine what it would be like to be Edison, alone in a strange house with people who didn't really like him all that much. I would try to be nice.

"So why don't you like bridges?" I asked.

"You don't waste time with pleasantries, do you?" His voice was harsh, but he grinned.

"I guess not," I admitted.

"I like that," he said. His directness made me feel instantly shy, and I avoided his eyes.

Sensing my discomfort, Edison returned to my question. "I'll tell you what happened, but don't tell McAllister, okay? He already thinks he's better than me."

I hesitated. Promising to withhold something from Quin seemed like a betrayal, but I was so curious that I nodded my agreement.

Edison began, "In high school, I used to drink a lot. I'm sure Quin told you. My father got me out of a lot of close calls with the police. He had *connections*, as they say." I remembered Edison emphasizing his last name when he introduced himself. His father was obviously someone important. "So he told me if I messed up one more time, I was dead to him—cut off."

"What about your mother? Did she feel the same way?"

Edison shook his head. "She left when I was eight, and I haven't seen her since. I don't really blame her though. My dad wasn't exactly a model husband."

I looked at Edison with understanding. As much as it pained me to admit, we had a lot more in common than I would have thought.

"But I messed up anyway. I was driving, totally wasted, and I went right off a bridge."

"Wow. Were you injured?"

Edison gave an ironic chuckle. "That's the twisted part. I was fine. But my friend Connor drowned. I was sitting on the bank of the river when they pulled his body out. His lips were blue."

"When was that?"

"Last year. I got probation. I *killed* my friend, and I got *probation*. My dad hasn't spoken to me since."

I wasn't sure what to say. Edison's self-loathing explained a lot, and I began to realize he didn't repulse me anymore. He was just like Quin and Max, a boy with a past.

CHAPTER FORTY-THREE

ONYX

I AWOKE EARLY THE NEXT morning to the smell of strong coffee. I opened my closet with eager anticipation, excited that I no longer had to choose from one of two outfits. I decided on my favorite T-shirt. The cotton was worn soft and nearly paper thin. It was my father's from Columbia University, where he had studied journalism. He and my mother met there.

I had always assumed I would attend Columbia as well, but after the economy failed, many universities were forced to close. Now I wasn't sure if I would ever go to college. My mother had told me to throw out that T-shirt countless times, but I couldn't part with it. After putting it on, I brushed my hair into a loose ponytail and wandered into the kitchen.

Elana and my mother were sitting side by side at the table, talking quietly. Elana's eyes were glassy, and she held a balled-up tissue as if she had been crying. Artos sat on the floor near her feet, sleeping.

"Good morning, sweetie." My mother's voice was cheerful. "Elana was just telling me a bit about herself."

Elana smiled at me. "Your mom is a good listener, Lex. Just like you."

As I took a seat next to them, Quin and Max walked in from the living room, where they had slept. Max's hair stuck up awkwardly on one side, and his face looked groggy. Quin met my eyes and smiled furtively.

"It's too early for crying," Max joked with Elana, mussing her hair with his hand.

Elana laughed. "Is it too early for a brush?" she asked, mussing Max's hair right back. Somehow Max had a way of making everyone feel lighter.

Quin gently pulled my ponytail as he walked behind me. "Good morning, Alexandra." He enunciated each syllable of my name in a soft, teasing voice, making me wish we were alone.

Carrie and Edison joined us a few minutes later. Carrie lugged an oversized bag marked with the Zenigenic logo. I assumed it held her computer and some of the research data she had taken with her from the lab.

When we were all assembled, my mother addressed the group. "I think we should discuss our next steps," she said. "There are some things I want to show all of you, but first . . ." My mother's voice became faint as she walked out of the room.

She returned with her laptop computer. I hadn't seen it in at least a year. She usually kept it inside her lab and didn't allow me to use it. Neither of us had accessed the Internet since the city had been evacuated, so I was surprised when she opened a search engine website.

"Mom, I thought the Internet was off-limits."

"It is," she said. "But today, we're making an exception."

Into the search bar, she typed a name: *Augustus Porter*. Immediately, over five hundred results were displayed, most of which seemed to be related to Augustus' former life as an investment banker.

My mother opened the first link to an article entitled *Investment Banker Arrested on Reports of Insider Trading*.

She read aloud: "On September 9, 2030, Augustus Porter, a well-known investment banker, was arrested on charges that he illegally traded shares through accounts belonging to his ex-girlfriend to net nearly a one-million-dollar profit. He has been charged with ten counts of fraud and faces up to twenty years in prison. Mr. Porter had no comment."

She scrolled through the search results to find a later article: *Investment Banker Receives Probation, Wall Street Stunned.*

"Wall Street executives expressed their disbelief today after Augustus Porter was acquitted on several charges of fraud. He was convicted of three counts

of making false statements and received two years' probation. After court proceedings concluded, Mr. Porter addressed the media, praising the judge for his just and rational decision. He indicated that he plans to leave the financial industry to pursue a career in politics. Mr. Porter has long maintained his innocence in any financial wrongdoings."

Buried on the fourth page of results was a newspaper article from 2020: *South Bronx Man Arrested for Defrauding the Elderly.*

"Gus Porter, a twenty-year-old resident of the South Bronx, was arrested Friday afternoon after reports that he defrauded at least twenty elderly women. According to some of the victims, they were telephoned by Mr. Porter over a month ago and promised assistance investing their retirement savings. After Mr. Porter collected an initial payment from the women, he did not contact them again, and their money was never invested. Police indicated that Mr. Porter defrauded the victims of upwards of $15,000."

Not surprisingly, a few months later, Augustus was acquitted of the charges. He certainly had a way of wriggling out of tight spots.

Quin shook his head. "I can't believe I fell for him."

"We *all* did," Elana agreed.

My mother turned from the computer, her expression sympathetic. "Don't beat yourselves up. I've evaluated hundreds of criminals like Augustus. He is a con artist. Lies come to him as easily as the truth. He gets by in this world by taking advantage of the goodness in people."

Before my mother closed the computer, she clicked on Augustus' social media profile. "I've got to see what this snake in the grass looks like," she murmured.

It was apparent that Augustus had not accessed the site in several years. Still, he had over ten thousand friends. At the top left corner, baring all his teeth in a captivating smile, was Augustus.

Edison gasped. "Hey!" he exclaimed. "I've seen him before. He was at Guardian headquarters last week. I saw him talking with General Ryker and some of the lieutenants."

My mother sighed. "This is a mess. All those people thinking Augustus is going to help them, when really he's just biding his time, playing both sides."

"What can we do?" I asked. I turned to Quin. "Do you think the Council is on to him?" I already knew the answer. I had witnessed Augustus' power over his colleagues.

Quin shook his head. "I don't think so. They all look up to him, just like I did. He told us he made millions on Wall Street and retired early to start a charity for inner city kids."

Carrie cleared her throat, turning the group's attention to her. "I may have something that can help with Augustus," she said. "Before I left, I emailed Dr. Bell and shared some of my suspicions about him. I know she'll look into it."

Quin gave Carrie a concerned look. "Are you sure that was a good idea? Can we trust her?"

Carrie shrugged. "*I* trust her. She gave up her career at Zenigenic to work for the Resistance after her daughter became addicted to Emovere. I know she believes in this cause—it's personal for her."

I thought of my uncomfortable conversation with Sharon Cloverdale in the Map Room. "If that's true, then I'm sure we can trust her," I reassured Quin.

"I have a feeling that time will take care of Augustus," my mother offered. "You all made a brave step in leaving. People will start to ask questions. Liars like Augustus don't like questions."

She was right. Questioning Augustus seemed to be the surest way to expose him. He had nearly dropped his mask when I had challenged him in front of the Council, but he seemed to have an uncanny ability to land on his feet.

Carrie changed the subject, directing another question to my mother. "Dr. Knightley, can you tell us what you know about the Guardian Force?"

"Absolutely. Let's go to the garage."

I was shocked to see that my mother's laboratory was coated in a thin sheet of dust. She was usually meticulous about maintaining its condition and rarely allowed me inside. I had a feeling that when my mother believed I was dead, she gave up on maintaining a lot of things.

"Please forgive the mess," she said. "I haven't been down here in a while."

She pulled a large box from one of her shelves. It was labeled *Dishes,* in large black letters. Inside there were hundreds of thick file folders. *No dishes.* With my mother's clever disguise, the files had hidden in plain sight for years. I hadn't noticed before, but on that same shelf, there were a lot of *Dishes.*

"These are the Crim-X files," she said. "Each inmate enrolled in the program had one."

I turned my eyes to Quin. His eyebrows were raised slightly, curious. I suspected that his father's file was what my mother had wanted to show him.

"I haven't shared this with anyone," she disclosed. "Not even Lex." She patted my arm sympathetically. "I should have been honest with you from the beginning."

"It's okay," I assured her, even though her secrets always stung bitterly, an unintended betrayal.

She took a breath and began. "The government has been working on developing a super soldier for a long time. Crim-X was their first attempt. I didn't know it at the time, but the research trial was *never* about reducing crime. It was all about finding the *exceptions,* the George McAllisters. The government believed by identifying these men, they could isolate the characteristics of an ideal soldier—one who was not affected by fear, was willing to take extreme risks, and couldn't be swayed by his caring for others. After George was arrested, I asked the government scientists to abandon the program, but they refused. When I started to suspect I was being used, I threatened to go to the media. I took all of these with me when I resigned." She gestured toward the box of files.

We were all speechless, transfixed by my mother's story. Only Carrie didn't seem surprised. Working at Zenigenic, she had likely grown accustomed to the government's subterfuge.

My mother continued, "When I went to work for Zenigenic and helped to create Emovere, I thought I was doing a service to others, helping people control their emotions. I didn't realize the government was already surreptitiously paying the pharmaceutical companies to help with their quest for a super soldier. Once they perfect the dosages, I suspect the Guardian Force and other programs like it will be deployed everywhere that we have an ongoing military presence, including all of the cities that are under martial law. The government is already well on its way with Emovere and Agitor."

"And Substance X," I added.

Carrie shook her head in agreement and turned to the others. "Do you know what medications you were administered?" she asked them.

"I'm pretty sure we only received Emovere," Quin said, gesturing toward himself, Max and Elana. "But there were always rumors that they were lacing it with something . . . to make it more potent."

Edison nodded. "Definitely Emovere—didn't really seem to work so well on me though." He chuckled. "Once you pass the jump test, I think they start Agitor. You have to be pretty advanced before you get Onyx."

"Onyx?" Carrie and my mother asked simultaneously, jarred by Edison's revelation.

"I don't know too much about it," he admitted. "But I heard a rumor that one recruit stabbed his squadron leader while taking it. Apparently, afterward, he told some of his buddies that he liked it—it made him feel good to hurt something. I was told they give it to all the lieutenants in charge of recruit dismissals . . . or should I say *executions*."

I shuddered, thinking of the ten bodies the Resistance had discovered. It was no wonder the lieutenants needed Substance X. They had been tasked to shoot their own.

"Why do they call it Onyx?" Elana wondered.

"That I can answer," Edison said, grinning wickedly. "Ryker said it will turn your heart as black as a stone."

CHAPTER FORTY-FOUR

POINTLESS

LATER THAT MORNING, MAX KNOCKED on my bedroom door. I was lost in thought, trying to imagine how my mother held all those secrets inside of her. Even though it was silly, it angered me, her withholding. It made me wish I was better at walling her out.

"Hey," Max said. "We're taking Artos for a walk. Wanna come?"

"Definitely."

Outside, the air was warm, hinting at spring. Two squirrels darted up a nearby tree, and Artos could barely contain his excitement. Quin gave a quick tug on his leash, and Artos fell into line, composing himself. When we were a block from my house, without a word, Quin slipped his hand into mine.

"How come there's no one holding my hand?" Max teased us. "Who do I talk to about the shortage of available men around here?"

"What about Edison?" Elana offered, and we all laughed.

Feeling guilty, I added, "You know, he's really not *that* bad."

Elana turned her head sharply to look at me, her eyes narrowed. *"Really?"*

Quin said nothing, but out of the corner of my eye, I saw his jaw tense. Inwardly, I cursed myself for opening my mouth.

I couldn't help but notice a few anxious faces peering at us from the neighbors' windows. As we passed, the curtains fell back into place, concealing the occupants inside. Fortunately, our neighborhood was mostly middle-class families, making us less vulnerable to the crimes that had besieged wealthier subdivisions. Still, it wasn't commonplace to see groups of people walking outside, and it must have unnerved them.

"What do you think your mother is planning?" Quin's voice was serious.

"Planning? What do you mean?"

Elana answered for him. "We can't just do nothing, Lex. This whole super soldier thing is scary, and besides, they *used* us. They made us think we were special, elite, when really they just wanted to exploit us."

"I know," I agreed. "But the Resistance is just as corrupt. Why would we risk our lives for any of it? It all seems so pointless."

Quin released my hand. When he turned his eyes to me, I was surprised to find anger there.

"Do you know what's *pointless*, Lex?" he asked, his voice raised. He had never yelled at me before. "My mom died so the government could get what they wanted. My brother was adopted by a family he never met. I have nobody. That's *pointless*."

Quin turned down a side street, yanking Artos with him. We all knew better than to follow him. I instantly felt ashamed.

Elana tried to comfort me. "I understand what you're saying, Lex. Quin . . . well, you know Quin."

As she spoke, my eyes were drawn to a black sedan parked at the end of the block. Max noticed it too. He diverted course, turning sharply back toward my house. With no discussion, Elana and I followed, exchanging a look of concern. The sedan's windows were tinted dark, giving away nothing, but I had a feeling there were eyes inside looking back at us.

Because of my mother's involvement with the Resistance, we had already been the target of ongoing scrutiny by the government. Twice in the last two years, black-suited men had arrived at our door unannounced, asking to speak with my mother. It was the kind of request that allowed for only one answer. Both times, I listened to her quickly dismiss the men, telling them that she was a scientist, not an activist. She put on her best absentminded professor act, claiming she couldn't remember how she had heard of the Resistance and didn't have an inkling as to why they were using her image in propaganda. Thankfully, my mother was a convincing actress.

As we walked back down my street, I allowed myself one casual glance over my shoulder. The sedan was gone.

When we arrived back at the house, Quin was already sitting on the porch, throwing an old tennis ball into the yard for Artos to catch. As we approached, my stomach flip-flopped. Quin stood, Artos' eyes following the ball closely. To Artos that ball was the entire world. I wished I could be so singularly focused. Instead, my insides were a tangle of thoughts and emotions.

"Did you see that car?" Max asked Quin immediately.

Quin shook his head, frowning with unease. "No."

"It's happened before," I explained to them. "The government likes to keep a close eye on my mother. We'll have to be especially careful when we leave the house." I gestured toward my left forearm that, unlike theirs, was unmarked.

They nodded their agreement, and we began walking inside.

"Lex, can I talk to you for a minute?" Quin's voice sounded dejected. I knew he was already punishing himself for raising his voice at me.

We walked in silence to the backyard. I sat down on my old swing set and began pushing myself with my feet, quickly gaining momentum. Quin sat in the empty swing next to me not moving.

"I'm sorry I got angry." He looked down at the ground, making circles in the grass with his feet.

"You were right, Quin. What I said was selfish—I wasn't thinking." I was swinging higher and higher, trying not to cry.

Quin walked behind me and abruptly stopped my swinging, returning my feet to solid ground.

"I yelled at you," he said.

I stood up and turned to him. "People yell at each other sometimes. It's okay."

Quin didn't respond, but he shook his head in disagreement. His face looked pained.

I reached over to him and gently hooked my fingers into his belt loops. In spite of himself, his lips turned up in a slight smile. I pulled his body closer to me, and I heard him catch his breath, surprised.

"I forgive you," I whispered. "Do you forgive me?"

Quin didn't answer, but he kissed me hard, wrapping his hand around my ponytail. I didn't even care if anyone was watching.

"I guess that's a yes . . ." I said before he kissed me again.

CHAPTER FORTY-FIVE

THE FLASH DRIVE

WHEN WE WALKED BACK INSIDE, my mother and Carrie were engrossed in conversation, sitting across from each other at the kitchen table, which was stacked solid with thick file folders.

"Mom, your *friends* are back in town," I told her, interrupting their conversation. "We saw a black car on our walk."

My mother frowned, her face unsettled. "Did they see you?"

I nodded. "I think so. We turned around, but . . ." I shrugged.

"Well, we'll need to be prepared for a visit. Let's just hope they didn't see *those*," her eyes wandered toward Quin's tattooed arm, resting against the back of the dining room chair.

"What were you working on?" I asked, hoping to change the subject. Nothing unnerved me more than the thought of another visit from those black-suited men.

Carrie motioned me over. "Your mother and I were just talking about your theory."

My mother gave me a proud glance. "I think you're right, Lex. The government has been recruiting trauma survivors for the Guardian Force." She paused, then added, "It's a calculated risk."

"Why a risk?" Elana beat me to the question.

My mother's face was excited. She relished teaching opportunities. "Well, on one hand, trauma survivors are ideal candidates for emotion-altering medications. For starters, they are at increased risk for anxiety, making them more likely to abuse or become addicted to Emovere. The government doesn't have to do much convincing, if you know what I mean."

I looked at Quin. He was nodding his head in agreement.

My mother continued. "It's not surprising that they're drawing from the second generation of the Crim-X program as a starting point." We had told my mother about the other Legacies jumping from the bridge.

"But here's where the risk comes in . . ." Her voice trailed off suspensefully. "Trauma survivors are also more likely to be Emovere resistant, like Elana and Edison. The drug doesn't affect their brains in the same way. It's probably a big part of the reason that so many recruits fail."

Elana smiled. She seemed to find comfort in my mother's explanation. "So it's like what makes us weak, also makes us strong."

"Exactly," my mother said. "It's a lot like resilience."

Carrie and I exchanged a look. *Resilience*—that was her word.

My mother reached into her pocket and produced the flash drive, displaying it in her hand for us. "Resilience is what *this* is all about."

Finally, I thought to myself, eyeing the flash drive eagerly.

She inserted the drive into her computer and opened a file entitled *Exceptions*. It contained hundreds of other files, each labeled with a name. She looked at me as she spoke.

"Remember the article I showed you a few years ago?"

I nodded, and my mother continued, addressing the group.

"I wrote an article about the partial immunity to Emovere observed in certain populations. I suspected that their immunity was related to trauma, but I wasn't sure how. What I did know was that if the government had been looking for exceptions, then I should be looking for them too. I went back through our clinical trials and identified all the failures, the subjects who hadn't responded to Emovere in the way that we'd hoped. I noticed a pattern."

My mother opened a graph titled *Elapsed Time from Trauma*. On the x-axis it read *Emovere Resistance*; on the y-axis, *Time since Trauma (in years)*. She pointed to the line that ran across the graph, zig-zagging a bit here and there, but decreasing steadily. "You can see that the less time that has elapsed since a trauma occurred, the more resistant the subjects were to Emovere. I think, in some cases, the recency of the traumatic event is too powerful for the drug to overcome. From what I've learned in the last two days, both Elana and Edison fit this profile."

Elana shifted uncomfortably in her seat, avoiding everyone's eyes. I saw Quin and Max look at each other quizzically, but neither spoke.

My mother's face brightened with excitement. "Using the brain scan and neurotransmitter-release data that I obtained from the exceptions, I created a new drug, a vaccine of sorts. I've been calling it Resilire, the root word for resilience. In theory, it should work to permanently prevent the impact of emotion-altering substances, particularly Emovere."

"In *theory*?" I asked.

My mother nodded. "I've never been able to test it, but I developed a small sample here. I don't have the equipment to produce it in large quantities. That's why I wanted the Resistance to have it. If the drug was mass-produced and administered to Guardian recruits . . ."

Carrie's mouth hung open.

I finished my mother's sentence—"No more super soldiers."

CHAPTER FORTY-SIX

THE IDEAL SUBJECT

"CAN WE TEST IT?" CARRIE asked. The anticipation in her voice was too intense to muffle.

My mother nodded, cautiously. "We can try," she said. "Ideally, we would need a subject who was not Emovere resistant already." She glanced at Elana and Edison. "Someone who *has* been vulnerable to the effects of the drug in the past." She paused. I knew what, or more accurately, *who* she was hinting at.

"Looks like your number's been called, McAllister." Edison didn't try to disguise the pleasure in his voice.

"Mom," I said, irritated. "Quin's not doing it."

"What about me?" Max offered. "I'm pretty sure Emovere worked on me too."

Quin's silence was notable. His eyes were cast downward.

"Quin is the ideal subject," my mother explained. "He was a member of the Guardian Force, so we know he was subject to and responsive to high levels of Emovere." She turned to Quin. "But we certainly don't want to force you, Quin. It's up to you."

I shook my head with disapproval. My mother continued to ignore me.

"What will it be like?" Quin asked, looking cautiously at my mother.

"Quin, you don't have to do it," I said, my voice pleading with him. I imagined that the things he had done while taking Emovere were playing on a slow motion reel in his mind.

My mother patted Quin on the shoulder reassuringly. "We'll administer Resilire first, followed by a small dose of Emovere. I'll monitor your heart rate with an electrocardiograph. Then we'll expose you to a stimulus, something frightening—you can choose. If it works, you'll feel afraid. Your body will show the physiological signs of fear. That's the point—to render the drug useless."

"And if it doesn't?" I asked.

"*If* it doesn't . . . well, then I'm sure Quin will recognize the feeling or lack thereof. It's a small dose so the effects will only last an hour or so." My mother's face was expressionless. "What do you think, Quin?"

In that moment, I hated her.

"I'll do it," he said, boldly.

"Perfect!" my mother exclaimed. "Now we'll need to pick your stimulus."

"I can't watch this," I said. I wasn't sure if I was angrier with my mother for putting Quin in harm's way or Quin, for accepting the risk so readily.

"It'll be okay, Lex." Quin looked at me intently, his eyes adding *please don't be mad at me.*

My mother ushered us out of the room, where we waited anxiously as she and Quin discussed his *stimulus.* I had never seen Quin afraid of anything, and I didn't want to. I knew it would be something terrible from his past.

My mother emerged from the room and whispered briefly to Carrie. Carrie nodded and walked back toward the house. When we entered the lab again, Quin was already sitting in a chair next to the heart rate monitor, wires from the electrodes snaked from under his shirt, connecting to the machine. I couldn't look at him, so I focused on his heartbeat. It was a steady beep. On the table next to him were two small vials and a needle.

After cleaning a spot on Quin's arm with rubbing alcohol, my mother administered the first dose of Resilire, the drug she had created. Quin stared straight ahead as if he was unaffected. But knowing Quin, I suspected his indifference was a mask.

"Now, the Emovere," my mother announced.

Before I could protest, the needle was in Quin's arm.

"Do you feel anything, Quin?" Elana asked almost immediately.

"We need to allow a few minutes for the drugs to take effect," my mother explained.

After five minutes elapsed. I noticed the steady beep of Quin's heart slowed a bit. I considered asking my mother about it, but stopped myself. I didn't want to know.

Carrie returned from the house with a plastic bag in her hand. She passed it to my mother gingerly.

"Okay, Quin, we're going to expose you to the stimulus you selected."

From out of the bag, my mother pulled the largest of our kitchen knives. Its blade was long and razor-sharp. Elana and I both gasped. I should have guessed.

Moving cautiously, my mother placed the knife near Quin's arm. His heart rate continued to beat steadily, no change. She moved the knife closer to his skin, letting the blade lightly graze his wrist. Still nothing. She pressed the flat edge of the blade against his forearm. I watched his skin depress. The beeping increased ever so slightly. My mother set the knife down next to Quin, reaching for her pen to record something in her notebook.

"How can we be sure this is the right stimulus?" I asked, frustrated. I just wanted it to be over. My question hung, unanswered.

Without warning, Edison grabbed the knife from the table. Moving with the speed and precision of an animal clamping down on its prey, he pressed the knife within inches of Quin's neck. I couldn't move or speak, only watch, transfixed.

Quin's eyes were wide, his face drained of color. His breathing stopped for a moment, then quickened, coming in small bursts. Finally, I heard the beep of his heart, drumming insistently.

Edison calmly returned the knife to its resting place. "Somebody had to do it," he said, shrugging.

I watched Quin closely, waiting for his reaction. He was surprisingly self-contained.

No one spoke for a moment. We all watched as Quin's heart rate slowed and returned to normal.

"Dr. Knightley, does that mean it works?" Max asked.

My mother, still shocked, only nodded.

Finally, Quin spoke. I couldn't tell if it was anger or fear, but there was a noticeable quiver in his voice that he covered with sarcasm. "We should've left you dangling a lot longer, Van Sant."

CHAPTER FORTY-SEVEN

BLACK SUITS

WE WERE SITTING AT THE kitchen table, finishing up dinner, when our *expected* unexpected guests arrived. My mother jumped when the doorbell rang.

I peered through the shades to see the black car parked in our driveway. My heart sank straight to my stomach, its contents churning with unease. It may as well have been a hearse.

Quin, Edison, Max, and Elana hurried upstairs and out of sight. Carrie remained in the kitchen, watchful. My mother gave me a reassuring smile.

"Just play along," she whispered before opening the door.

"Good evening, Dr. Knightley." The first man spoke, his voice formal, thinly cloaked in politeness.

"Good evening, gentlemen. May I ask what brings you here?" My mother didn't waver.

The second man replied, "I think you *know*, Dr. Knightley. This is not our first visit. As usual, we would like to ask you a few questions. May we come in?"

I stood behind my mother, hoping to disappear. Though I knew it was impossible, the black-suited men appeared to have the same face—angular, cold, and unyielding.

"Certainly," my mother replied assertively. "I think you'll find that my answers haven't changed."

"Perhaps," said the first black-suited man, looking smugly at his partner, "but we may have some *new* questions."

Instantly, I felt light-headed, his words a sucker punch to the stomach. *What if they had seen the Guardian tattoos? What if they had seen Quin?*

"Please, fire away," my mother countered, as she welcomed the men inside, gesturing them to the living room.

I was certain my mother was completely unprepared to field any questions about my friends, but she remained poised, self-assured. She always told me that confidence was mostly illusion.

The second black-suited man took the first shot. "We received an unusual report this afternoon. Someone spotted your daughter walking with a group of young people." I knew that he was staring at me, but I didn't raise my eyes. They remained fixed on the floor.

"Yes," my mother replied calmly. "This is my daughter, Alexandra."

"Come over, honey," she directed me. I took a breath and walked toward them, taking a seat on the edge of the sofa.

"I believe she was walking with my friend, Carrie Donovan." My mother gestured toward the kitchen, and Carrie gave a timid wave.

The first black-suited man shook his head, unconvinced. "Our report specifically indicated there was a man in the group—a man who fit the description of someone we've been looking for."

On cue, his partner displayed his cellular telephone, an image on the screen. I gulped, covering my shock with an awkward cough. It was Quin. He was wearing his Guardian Force uniform.

The second man turned the screen toward me. "Do you know this man?" he asked.

"No," I lied, the deception slipping easily off my tongue. My mother was correct—lying wasn't as difficult as I anticipated. Though I was grateful, the thought dismayed me.

"This is Quin McAllister. He has been AWOL from the Guardian Force for over a year. He stole government property before running away. As you can imagine, we would very much like to find him."

"Are you sure he's not *here?*" After launching his barbed question toward my mother, the first black-suited man stood and began walking toward the staircase, surveying the room closely.

My mother and I exchanged a glance. Her face was unmoved, but her eyes were panicked. As the man moved ever closer to the staircase, I felt paralyzed, my body stuck to the sofa.

"It was me." I heard Edison speak from the top of the staircase. He was wearing one of my father's old sweatshirts, his Guardian tattoo safely concealed beneath it. "*I* was walking with Alexandra."

"And who exactly are you?" The first man demanded.

"Alexandra's boyfriend," he replied, smirking. "Right, sweetie?" He winked at me, as he descended the stairs. He sauntered casually toward me, kissing me on the cheek.

Taken aback by Edison's boldness, I couldn't help but smile. "Right," I agreed, nodding my head at the men.

"I meant *your name*," the man repeated, sneering at Edison.

"Oh, *that*." Edison laughed. He was good at this. "Brock *Van Sant*." Just as he had on the bridge, Edison paused, waiting. This time, there was a reaction.

"*Van Sant?*" The first black-suited man glanced uncomfortably at his partner. "As in illustrious criminal defense attorney, *Van Sant?*"

"Is there any other?" Edison asked, his face completely serious.

"Umm, I guess not. We didn't realize . . ." Like twins, the faces of the black-suited men became simultaneously submissive.

"It's okay, gentlemen." Edison smiled graciously at them. "So about that picture . . ." He was glancing at the cellular phone in the second man's hand. "May I have a look?"

As Edison studied the picture carefully, I met my mother's eyes. We were both in awe. Edison made my mother's theatrics seem amateurish.

"I know this man," Edison pronounced. For a moment, all feeling left my body. Then he added, "I *used to* know him. I believe he was homeless, living across the street from my family. A real *nuisance*. We were certainly glad when the Guardian Force scooped him up. I'm sorry to hear that he's brought you so much trouble, but I can't say that I'm surprised."

The black-suited men nodded agreeably at Edison, obviously transfixed by his act.

Edison put the final touches on his masterful performance. "We'll certainly contact you if we see him. Do you have a business card?"

The first black-suited man handed Edison a small, white card, which he pocketed with false intent.

"We appreciate your assistance, Mr. Van Sant. It was a pleasure to meet you." Synchronized, the black-suited men made their way toward the door.

My mother and I remained speechless.

"The pleasure was all mine," Edison said, waving at them from the doorway.

After the door closed, Edison and I watched them from the window. When the car's taillights faded from view, Edison collapsed in uncontrollable laughter, tears streaming down his red face.

My mother shook her head in amazement. "That was some performance, Edison," she admitted. "Or should I say, *Brock*."

I giggled, but immediately, I thought of Quin. Feeling guilty, I turned toward the staircase, hoping he was still hidden. But he was standing at the top, looking back at me.

"Academy Award worthy, I'd say," Quin joked, but there was no mistaking his eyes. They were darkened by humiliation.

CHAPTER FORTY-EIGHT

A RUNAWAY TRAIN

THAT NIGHT, I HEARD MY bedroom door creak open, and Quin stood there, sheepishly. He was barefoot, wearing shorts and a T-shirt. His hair was slightly disheveled as if he had already been sleeping.

"What are you doing here?" I whispered.

He held his finger to his lips to shush me and closed the door behind him.

"I just wanted to see you," he said. "Is that okay?"

"Quin . . ." I admonished him, shaking my head, though I was smiling. "You are *trouble*, Mr. McAllister."

He pulled back the covers and climbed into my bed beside me. I felt myself holding my breath. Even though he wasn't touching me *yet*, my skin felt electric. Not trusting myself, I turned away from Quin to face the door. He reached his arm around my waist, just under the edge of my shirt and slid me closer to him. He was so warm.

"I'll just stay for a few minutes," he promised in my ear.

I nodded without speaking. All I could think about was his hand touching my bare skin.

"Are you okay?" I asked, trying to distract myself. "I still can't believe Edison." I wasn't sure which would bother Quin more—Edison's dramatics with the knife or the kiss.

"I'm fine. But I like that you were worried about me." He tickled my side, and I giggled.

"Besides, you only have eyes for me," Quin teased, revealing that it was the kiss on his mind. I hoped he knew that was true.

He snickered to himself. "Has anyone ever called you Lexi?" When he said it, it didn't sound annoying at all. I nodded again.

"What about *Sexy Lexi?*" he said. I knew he was smiling broadly, even though I couldn't see his face.

"Once, this boy did, but in a mean way," I admitted.

"Well, he was on to something," Quin whispered. "You are *so* . . ." He didn't finish the sentence, but pulled me even closer, until there was just my body and his, no separation between us. I did a quick self-assessment: *Athletic? Yes. Cute? Maybe. Sexy? Never.* But his *"so" was* convincing—I halfway believed him.

I measured the time with our breaths, lying very still, trying to resist the force field of Quin. It was an unwinnable battle. Slowly, I turned to face him, placing my hand against his chest. When he kissed me, his eyes were opened into mine.

"Goodnight, Lex."

And just like that, he got up and left me.

My mind was exhausted—I could barely think—but my body was wide awake. It had taken on a life of its own, a life that revolved around Quin. He could stop and start me at any time. The boy I had kissed first had been nothing like him, colorless and watery by comparison. Quin was vivid, indelible, but his intensity frightened me a little. My mother always cautioned me, "Love has to be practical to sustain itself." *Practical* was the last word I would have used to describe my feelings for Quin.

I couldn't lie in bed any longer. I tiptoed to the kitchen and was only slightly surprised to see Edison. He was looking at some of Carrie's research folders.

"What are you doing?" I asked.

"Trying to put myself to sleep." He chuckled. "Figured this would do the trick."

I couldn't help but smile. Edison had a knack for biting humor.

"Can't sleep either?" he asked.

"Nope." I tried to push away the thought of Quin's hand on my waist. "Today was quite a day." I raised my eyebrows at Edison, silently scolding him. He nodded knowingly, casting his eyes downward.

"I hope you don't mind the company," I added, softening my voice. I didn't want to make him feel too guilty. After all, he had dismissed the black-suited men single-handedly, and it was thanks to him that we knew Resilire worked.

"I've had worse," Edison teased.

"So," I began, taking a seat next to him. "You said your mom left when you were eight—do you have any memories of her?" I had always wondered if my miniscule file of recollections of my father was normal.

"Not many," he admitted. "I remember Christmases the most. It was her favorite holiday. She always went all out—probably part of the reason I'm so spoiled." I was surprised to hear him be self-deprecating.

"What about you?" he asked. "I don't see your dad around."

"Same as your mom," I said softly. "He left when I was ten. I don't remember much either. Sometimes I try to recall his voice, but I can't."

Edison nodded with understanding. We sat in silence for a minute or so until he spoke again.

"You and McAllister, huh?" He smirked at me. It was more of a statement than a question.

"Will you tell me about the first time you met Quin?"

Edison rolled his eyes, but he indulged me anyway. "It was pretty memorable," he began, grinning. "It was my sixteenth birthday. As usual, I was drunk. Connor and I went over to the park. We were going to take pictures of ourselves swimming in the fountain—don't ask me where that idea came from." He shook his head. "Anyway, when we got there, we see that there's already this guy in the fountain. Not to spoil the surprise," he smiled widely, baring all his teeth, "but it was Quin. I think he was *bathing*. He was only wearing shorts."

Edison started laughing again, deep belly laughs. He couldn't stop, even after I shushed him. "So . . . ha, ha, ha . . . we . . . ha, ha, ha . . . stole his . . . ha, ha, ha . . . clothes."

His laughter was contagious. Soon I was laughing too. Picturing *my* serious-minded Quin bathing in a fountain was rather comical. For a moment, the heaviness of the last month of my life lifted.

"What's going on, Lex?" Quin demanded from behind us. There was a sharp bite in his voice. I wondered how long he had been standing there.

"Nothing," I said. My voice sounded guilty. "We were just—"

Quin interrupted me. "It doesn't *look* like nothing."

I began again, "We were just—"

"Flirting. It *looked* like you were flirting." Quin's voice grew louder and more assured. And for a moment, I doubted myself. *Had I been flirting?*

"Chill out, McAllister," Edison said with annoyance.

Quin's jaw clenched, and he took a step toward us. "Shut up, Eddie," he growled. "I'm not talking to you."

Edison turned to me, eager to feed Quin's fire. "There you go," he said, gesturing toward Quin. "That's the real him. Not as pretty as you thought, huh?"

I felt something heading for me, pressing down on me like a runaway train, but I couldn't stop it, couldn't slow it down. I knew instantly that it had been headed my way long before I ever saw it coming.

Quin's eyes were dark with rage, just like that day on the bridge. But this time, they were fixed on me. He banged the table with his fist, sending Edison's glass of water and several of Carrie's files tumbling to the ground. "I. Don't. Want. You. Talking. To. Him. Anymore."

Each word was a command in a voice so intense that it shocked me, like the hot sting of a slap to the face. The words didn't seem to come from *my* Quin, but rather some primitive *other*—a vestigial Quin that had been biding its time inside him waiting to be born.

Almost instantly, I could see my fear register on Quin's face. He seemed as stunned as I was, as if he too had been unprepared for the birth of this *other* self.

"What's going on in here?" My mother ran into the room, followed closely by Max, Carrie, and Elana.

Neither Quin nor I spoke.

Edison's voice eagerly filled the uncomfortable silence. "I'd say jealousy, among other things." His tone was mocking. I despised him again.

"I'm sorry," Quin muttered to my mother so fast it was barely audible. "C'mon, Artos."

Quin quickly clasped Artos' leash around his neck. He walked hurriedly to the door without looking up. For a second, or maybe even less than a second, he paused in front of the open doorway. I thought—I hoped—he would turn around, but he didn't.

"Lex, what—" my mother began, her tone a mixture of concern and disapproval.

"Leave me alone." I walked to my room without another word.

CHAPTER FORTY-NINE

BREAKING

I LAY IN BED, NOT sleeping until sunrise. Though I hadn't even closed my eyes, I had convinced myself that the night was a bad dream—until I saw Quin lying on the front porch, Artos curled next to him.

My mother sat at the kitchen table, drumming her fingers nervously. It didn't seem as if she had slept much either. When I came into the room, she looked up but didn't speak to me. After taking two big sips of her coffee, she walked toward the door. I followed her like a puppy.

"Alexandra, stay inside." She was using her authoritative voice. "I need to talk to Quin alone."

I sat at the table, trying not to feel anything. I couldn't hear what they were saying to each other, only the sounds of their voices.

When my mother returned, her face was stoic. "Quin would like to talk to you," she said.

I felt a heavy fog of dread around me as if I was walking to my own execution. Whatever Quin had to say, everything had already changed. I knew there was no going back to the way we had been before.

"Hi," I said, my voice small.

Artos perked up first, his tail flip-flopping against the porch. "Hi, Artos." I gave his head a pat.

Quin still hadn't looked at me, but I could see he had been crying, and his hand was bruised.

"Are you going to look at me?" I asked him.

"I don't know if I can," Quin said. His voice was thin, breakable.

I sat down next to him. "What did you do to your hand?" I already suspected he had punched something. I reached to touch him, but he snapped his hand away.

"You *know*," he confirmed.

"What happened last night?" My question remained in the space between us, unaddressed for a long time.

Then, "I know he was just pretending, but he kissed you on the cheek . . . and then, I saw you laughing with him. I thought maybe you *liked* him, after I told you . . . you know, how I felt about you. I—I couldn't control myself."

"We were just talking, Quin."

"I *know*," he agreed. "I know that now." Quin sighed. "Lex, what if I had hit you?"

"But you didn't. You *wouldn't*. You're not like your father." I wasn't sure if I was trying to convince Quin or myself.

"Do you know that for sure?" Quin asked.

I realized that I couldn't say yes, so I didn't answer at all.

"Because that guy in there last night sounded a lot like my dad. That was *his* thing—he was so jealous. My mom couldn't even smile at another guy without him flying into a complete rage. The day that he killed her, she was on the phone talking to a mechanic about our car. *A mechanic.*"

"What are you trying to tell me?" I already knew the answer.

"I ran away from the Guardian Force because I was becoming him. I was hurting people for no reason, people I didn't even know. To think that I could hurt someone that I . . . that I *love* . . . I won't let it happen." His voice softened at the word *love*, and it made my heart ache.

"Did my mom tell you to do this? To end it with me?" I hoped she had. It was better to feel angry with my mother than to feel *this* way.

Quin shook his head. "She just told me that if I'm going to stay here, I have to learn to control my anger, and she's right. She didn't say anything about you."

"So that's it?" My voice was flat, but I felt something inside me breaking.

Quin didn't answer. He just stared straight ahead.

I reached to touch his face. He let me for a second, then he took my hand and put it back on my lap.

"Lex, please don't make this any harder than it already is."

I stood up. "You know, Quin, it doesn't even really seem that hard for you." I knew it wasn't true, but I wanted to hurt him—needed to *see* it on his face— and I did. But it didn't satisfy me as I'd hoped. Instead, it only added to my anguish.

It took everything in me to walk back inside the house and away from Quin. Each step yanked fiercely at my heart as if it was tied to him with an invisible thread.

CHAPTER FIFTY

FOR THE BEST

WHEN I WALKED BACK INSIDE, Max and Elana were awake.

"Lex, what happened? Are you okay?" Elana asked.

I ignored her, walking past them and back to my room. I pulled back my covers, crawled into bed, and pulled them over my head. I could still smell Quin on my pillowcase. I let the tears come, not even bothering to wipe them away.

I heard my door open and close. I knew it was my mother.

"Go away, Mom," I snarled, without even showing my face.

She sat down on the bed and rubbed my shoulder through the blanket. "Lex, I know you probably don't want to hear this right now, but it's for the best. Quin has a lot of growing up to do, and I think you know that."

"Whatever, Mom. Please stop talking." I couldn't stand knowing that she was right.

My mother didn't listen to me. She kept right on talking. "What he went through as a boy . . . what he saw . . . well, it's going to be hard for him to love someone the right way. Right now, his *need* is so intense that he's going to break anybody who cares about him—and I don't want that to be you."

As she spoke, I could see the lights through the sheets flickering off and on and off again. My room went dark, matching my mood.

"I'm not your patient, Mom. You don't have to use all this psychobabble with me. I understand Quin, probably better than anybody and certainly better than you." I knew that my words would wound her, but I didn't care. I only wanted someone to join me in feeling miserable.

I continued, my anger gaining momentum. "Besides, what do you know about loving someone anyway? You drove away the only person who loved us. You just gave up."

My mother was uncharacteristically silent. I peered at her cautiously from under the covers. Her eyes were welling with tears. More than anything, I wanted to take my words back, rewind and reverse them, tuck them back safely inside my mouth, where I would let them die. But I knew I couldn't.

"You're right, Lex. I didn't handle things properly with your father." I was stunned. She hadn't mentioned him in years.

"I think about that a lot, more than you know. But my mistakes aren't relevant here. You *do* know Quin, so you know that I'm right. I want you to find love—the kind of love that you're looking for. But I'm your mother, and I also have to protect you." She patted me gently on the shoulder and kissed my head.

After she left, I lay there, numb. I had no tears left. Opening the locket around my neck, I studied my father's face. I wondered if what my mother hoped for me was even possible. Did anybody actually find the love they looked for? And if they did, did it last? It seemed to me that someone always ended up giving up or running away or just watching the slow fading of love, like a picture left too long in the sun.

I closed the locket and pulled the covers back over my head.

CHAPTER FIFTY-ONE

DISTURBING

I SPENT THE DAY IN a fog, avoiding everyone. I didn't see Quin again until the next morning. He was sitting at the table with Carrie and my mother, the three of them hunched over Carrie's computer. I could see right away something was wrong.

Quin met my stare first and didn't look away. I wished he had. My eyes were puffy and red from crying. I saw my appearance slowly register on his face. He looked pained, as if someone was pinching his arm under the table.

"Lex," he said, his voice flat.

My mother and Carrie looked up simultaneously. Carrie's concern for me was instantly obvious, while my mother pretended that I looked just fine.

"What's going on?" I asked. I was surprised to hear the sound of my own voice. It was a hoarse croak.

"Augustus," Carrie said, gesturing me over to them.

I sat down next to my mother as far from Quin as possible. I could feel him still watching me, taking my inventory and sizing up the damage.

"Augustus?" I asked. I had hoped I would never have to speak his name again.

My mother nodded and turned Carrie's computer screen toward me. There was an email from Dr. Bell.

> *Dear Carrie,*
> *I have been so worried about you. I hope that wherever you are, you are safe. Since you left, a lot has happened, most*

of it because of you. After I saw your message, I looked at the data you referenced about the bullet that killed Elliot Barnes. Of course, you were right. Augustus knew all along about Quin. It seems as if he lied to turn us against Quin, but I'm still not sure why. Perhaps you know. I can only hope that Quin is safe as well.

After I realized that Augustus couldn't be trusted, Hiro helped me hack into his email account. What we found was . . . well, there are really no words for what we found. You'll have to see it for yourself. I've attached a link to this message, but please be prepared—it is disturbing. We believe that Augustus was planning to use it to blackmail the Guardian Force.

Right away, I convened the Council. We voted for Augustus' removal from his position and planned to demand he leave headquarters immediately. But when we went to find him, he was gone. We haven't seen him since.

I've assumed the leadership role here, but I must admit we are a bit lost. Vera couldn't handle the stress and has resigned from the Council. People are beginning to lose faith that our cause is viable. I'm not sure if this message will reach you, but if it does, please let me know that you are okay.

Take care,
Shana

I sat in stunned silence for a moment before speaking. "I can't believe Augustus ran away."

My mother sighed. "I'm not surprised," she said matter-of-factly. "Snakes like him have a way of sensing danger and slithering right under the nearest rock before it's too late."

"Have you looked at the link yet?" I wondered.

They all shook their heads.

Minutes later, we were all convened around the table, tunnel vision on Carrie's computer screen.

"Here goes," she said, clicking the link, her voice tentative.

It was an amateur video—the camera shaking and jostling, disconnected voices in the background.

"What are we looking at?" my mother asked.

Quin answered her. "It's the Guardian headquarters. It looks like a real-life training exercise. After I became a member of the Guardian Force, I had them monthly to prepare for missions and deployment. They videotaped the exercises for our performance reviews. Usually, if we weren't being tested, we were assigned a role, like acting as a civilian."

"I assume you were administered Emovere beforehand." My mother's voice was more of a statement than a question.

Quin nodded.

The camera stabilized and a hand appeared, holding a white index card. It read:

Training Exercise, January 10, 2041.
Candidates Assessed: Legacy 132; Greenhorn 111;
Legacy 365; Greenhorn 225.
Medications Administered: Emovere (batch #120);
Agitor (batch #32); Onyx (batch #4)

In the background, we heard a man's voice giving the command to begin the exercise. It sounded like General Ryker.

"Ryker," Quin said, confirming my suspicions.

The Guardians advanced stoically and methodically on a group of pretend civilians. One of them spoke. I saw a badge on his jacket that read *Greenhorn 111*. His voice sounded removed, as if he was an unskilled actor.

"You are all under arrest by order of the Guardian Force. Stand up and face the wall."

None of the pretend civilians moved.

Quin commented, "As civilians, we were usually instructed to resist or to refuse to follow instructions, anything to make the exercise more challenging."

Another Guardian, Legacy 365, approached the civilians. He seemed agitated. His jaw was clenched as if he was grinding his teeth.

"We gave you an order." His voice was demanding. I saw him reflexively kick one of the pretend civilians in the stomach. The man doubled over clutching his mid-section, groaning.

The background voices suddenly quieted as if everyone had turned their attention to the training exercise.

Greenhorn 225, a female Guardian, approached her partner and said something too quiet for the camera to record. Legacy 365's fists balled tightly in response. He stiffly walked back toward the rest of the group. Behind him, one of the pretend civilians scurried to help his injured comrade.

At the sound of the movement, Legacy 365 turned back, removing his weapon. The camera fell, likely dropped in panic by its holder, but it continued to record. There was yelling and running, a chaos so fierce that I had to look away. When I turned my eyes back to the screen, I saw Legacy 365 shoot two of the pretend civilians and his partner, Greenhorn 225, before he was restrained by his fellow Guardian Force troops. A single drop of blood spattered onto the camera lens. Seconds later, it went to static, and my mother quickly pressed stop.

Elana ran from the room, crying. Carrie followed closely behind her.

I couldn't help but look at Quin. He was the only one still staring at the computer screen. I watched his face for a moment, but it gave away nothing. He stood up without speaking and walked from the room.

CHAPTER FIFTY-TWO

OKAY

I WENT TO LOOK FOR Elana. I found her sitting on the porch, petting Artos' head methodically, her hand shaking. Quin was sitting next to her, his armed draped protectively around her shoulders. The sight stonewalled me. It felt as if my heart was being twisted and wrung out like a wet towel.

As I joined them, Quin removed his arm, placing it casually by his side. Still, I couldn't *unsee* it. I sat down next to Elana, but she didn't acknowledge my presence. Her face seemed vacated as if she had left her body sitting there, abandoned.

"Elana?" I asked.

She didn't respond, but continued her rhythmic petting, her hand's movement almost involuntary.

I grabbed her arm. "Elana?"

She looked at me and opened her mouth to speak, but no words came.

"Elana, it's okay. It's over. You're okay."

She nodded, but her face seemed blank. My mother came outside, her brow furrowed with concern.

"I think she's in shock," Quin said.

My mother shook her head, her face contorted with guilt. Putting her arm around Elana, she said, "I shouldn't have let her watch that . . . with what she's been through. No one should have watched that."

I turned back toward the house and saw Max standing in the doorway, observing us with unease.

"Is she okay?" he mouthed to me.

I shrugged. *Okay* was relative.

"I think we all need a break," my mother announced, helping Elana back inside.

I followed them, sitting down next to Max in the living room. He flipped on the television. A rerun of a once popular reality show was playing. I was grateful for the distraction, even though I had seen the episode at least ten times. Since the government had assumed control of the media, television programming had changed drastically. Reruns recycled regularly, broken only by twice-a-day broadcasts from SFTV. Each city had its own local broadcast team approved by the government. At the bottom of the screen, a news ticker kept the public apprised of any breaking developments. I nudged Max and pointed.

Government announces short list for military promotion . . . Jamison Ryker thought to be top candidate . . . Ryker currently serves as leader of the Guardian Force in the San Francisco Bay Area . . .

Max raised his eyebrows. "Promoting Ryker? That seems like a not-so-great idea . . . unless you *want* a sadistic psychopath controlling drugged-out people with guns." He snickered at his own vivid description.

Quin and my mother walked in as Max finished speaking. I pointed them to the screen.

My mother nodded. "I saw a few similar reports last week. Apparently Ryker is getting a lot of attention."

"Wow," Quin said, his voice monotone. "With a promotion on the line, he's probably more driven than ever before to get this right. One thing about Ryker—he's hungry for power, and he's persistent. He'll mow down anything or anybody that gets in his way."

Max laughed again. "I guess he's one of those guys who doesn't need Onyx to turn his heart black."

My mother and I both managed a half-smile. Quin's expression was flat, his lips a thin, unchanging dash across his face.

"I'm going to check on Elana," he said, walking toward the guest bedroom. Though I knew I was overreacting, the words stung.

After everyone else had left the room, Max and I remained. He turned off the television and shifted to face me.

"How are you, Lex?" he asked. The hollow tone in his voice told me that he already knew the answer.

I shrugged. I was afraid if I tried to speak, I might cry.

"Quin's a wreck too," he said, shaking his head.

"He *is*?" I asked skeptically. "He looks fine. Besides, he seems pretty preoccupied with Elana. Don't try to make me feel better."

Max chuckled to himself. "He pretty much said the same thing about you . . . minus the Elana part, of course."

"That's ridiculous," I said. "Anyone can see that I'm . . . upset," I said, gesturing toward my face. My eyes felt like sand paper.

"Anyone but Quin, apparently," Max replied, shrugging.

"What did he say to you?" I asked. It was hard to explain—I wanted Quin to be distraught, but the thought of him in pain knotted my stomach.

"Not much. You know Quin, a man of few words. But last night, I woke up in the middle of the night, and he was just sitting there reading that stupid file of his. I asked him what he was doing, and he said, 'Nothing.' But I got the feeling that he was . . ." Max paused, searching for the right words. "I got the feeling he was cataloguing his mistakes. One of his favorite hobbies."

I nodded with understanding. Max knew Quin almost as well as I did.

He added. "I'm sure what happened between the two of you last night is at the top of the list."

I gave Max a doubtful look.

"You know, you're the only one he's ever shown that file to." I detected a hint of jealousy in Max's voice.

"You've never seen it? But you know everything in it."

"Not *everything*," Max replied. "Just what Quin told me." His face was unusually somber.

"What about Elana? Hasn't she seen it?" *Please say no*, I thought, all the while chastising myself for thinking it.

"Nope. Just you."

"I didn't realize," I said, feeling guilty. I knew that Max considered Quin like an older brother. Quin's deliberate withholding must have wounded him, the same way that my mother's secrecy hurt me.

Max confirmed my suspicions. "It's just that I told him everything about me. *Everything.*"

I gave Max a puzzled look. He had always seemed so open about himself. I never imagined that he was hiding something too.

"Remember how I told you that my stepdad didn't like me?"

I nodded.

"It wasn't because he didn't want a stepson." Max's eyes filled with tears, but he quickly composed himself. "He didn't want a *gay* son. His views were no different from the Guardians, but he thought he could 'toughen me up.'" Max made quotation marks in the air with his fingers. "Quin is the only one that knows that—well, now except for you."

Max stood up, shaking his body, casting off the heavy emotion. I stood with him and put my arm around him. "You've been a great friend to Quin . . . and me."

He smiled. "It's a tough job, but somebody has to do it."

Then with seriousness, he added, "I just want you to know that Quin loves you. And he's going to make this right. When he does, will you give him another chance?"

I had already asked myself the same question many times. *Yes or no?* My mind chose one—my heart the other. Neither answer seemed entirely right.

"I don't know, Max," I finally said aloud, letting my eyes speak for my heart.

CHAPTER FIFTY-THREE

FROM THE INSIDE

LATER THAT EVENING, WE MET in the laboratory. The mood was subdued, everyone still affected by the contents of the video. Elana was sitting between Max and Quin—thankfully, closer to Max—listening to Max tell a story. Her face mimicked interest, but I could tell it was forced. Even Max's jovial demeanor was muted.

My mother addressed us all. "First, I want to apologize. I should have watched that video before showing it to all of you. It was far more disturbing than I ever imagined. That was my concern from the beginning, when I resigned from Zenigenic. The drugs we've created are unpredictable. Emotions are like wild beasts. Thinking we can manipulate them, stop and start them with a pill . . . you see what can happen."

Edison was being unusually quiet. I wondered if he had known about the training incident.

"Did you know about this?" I murmured softly to Edison.

Edison nodded. "Sort of," he mouthed. "I heard a rumor. As recruits, we're not allowed to mingle with the full-fledged Guardians, but stories have a way of trickling down."

Quin turned toward our hushed voices, then quickly looked away, whispering something to Elana. Seeing that glow she had—even if it was dampened by this morning's events—in such close proximity to Quin darkened me like an exile to my own sunless room.

Ignoring us, my mother continued speaking. Her tone was intentionally persuasive. "Seeing that video, I think we have no choice but to act. Today, SFTV reported that Ryker is on the short list of candidates for promotion, meaning that he'll be that much more eager to make the Guardian Force a success. If this program goes forward, there will be more of what we saw today. But it will be happening in our cities to people we know. No matter how difficult it is to watch, I think this video has to be seen."

"How?" I asked.

My mother pointed to her computer. "I've been waiting for something like this to happen," she admitted. "If the public knew about the true purpose of the Guardian Force, there would be outrage—maybe enough to pressure the government into abandoning the program."

Edison shook his head. "You don't know Ryker. A little dip in public opinion is not going to stop him. I doubt it would even slow him down."

For once, Quin appeared to agree with Edison, nodding his head. "Dr. Knightley, Ryker is already acting independent of the government, executing his own recruits. If we're going to stop the Guardian Force, it's only going to happen from the inside."

"Well," my mother began, "I thought you might say that." Her face was lit with excitement, the way she always looked before an important presentation.

"Now that we know Resilire works," my mother glanced gratefully at Quin, "and the Resistance has gotten rid of Augustus, there's nothing to stop us from mass-producing it in their lab. Then we just have to figure out a way to administer it to the Guardian Force."

"Oh, *just that*?" Edison smirked.

Quin shot him a look of disdain.

"It does sound kind of far-fetched, Mom." I spoke slowly, trying to soften the impact of my words.

"Not really," Quin said, averting his eyes from mine. "Unless the protocol has changed since I left, every Monday, the Guardian Force—new recruits included—meets for a debriefing. Before the meeting, the entire Force is injected. If we could replace those drugs with this one . . . well, I don't see why it couldn't work."

My mother gave Quin an appreciative nod. She added, "We'll have to think carefully about who should return to San Francisco. As Dr. Bell told us, the Resistance is in a fragile state. I don't think it would be wise for *you* to go," she said, directing her gaze to Quin. "Or myself, for that matter. Lex told me that I'm a bit of a lightning rod for some members of the Resistance." I had told my mother about my difficult conversation with Sharon Cloverdale.

"I'll go," Carrie offered. "It would be an honor."

Smiling broadly at her, my mother replied, "I knew that you would, Carrie. You know the lab, and you're a talented researcher, but we can't let you go alone. Max, would you be willing to accompany her?"

Max looked surprised, but he nodded his agreement. My stomach churned. Everything seemed to be happening so quickly. *Was I the only one with doubt turning my stomach?* I looked around the room. All eyes were attuned to my mother.

"Mom, are you sure this is the only way?" I didn't want to challenge her in front of everyone, but I knew that her ambition sometimes muddled her judgment. "It seems really risky."

Not addressing me directly, my mother asked the group, "Should we vote?"

No one answered, but I knew it was a lost cause. My mother was dynamic. She had a way of drawing people to her.

"It's fine, Mom. We don't need to vote." I folded inward, feeling publicly scolded. I noticed Quin watching me, his expression tender. My spirits brightened a little.

Before we left the lab that night, it was decided. Carrie and Max would return to headquarters the following evening. There, they would proceed with manufacturing Resilire, attempting additional trials to test the drug's efficacy with some of the former Guardian recruits and helping Dr. Bell regroup the Resistance. Carrie would let us know that they had arrived safely, but updates would be limited, due to my mother's suspicions about the government's monitoring of telephone communication. Once a sufficient quantity of the drug was manufactured and the trials had proven successful, we would proceed with the rest of our plan.

On our way back to the house, my mother called to me. She was lingering at the door of the lab, locking it.

"I know what you're thinking," she said, a twinge of guilt in her voice.

"I'm just worried about my friends, nothing more," I replied, trying to reassure her.

"Well, you're right to be worried. It *is* risky. Just like it was risky for you to go alone to San Francisco. But I want you to understand that I'm not the same person I was at Zenigenic. I know a lot of this is my fault, and I take that responsibility seriously." My mother frowned, her face weighed down with regret.

"I know, Mom. I trust you." It was painful to admit, but even as I spoke the words, I wasn't sure I believed them.

CHAPTER FIFTY-FOUR

THE WAITING BEGINS

CARRIE'S TEXT MESSAGE ARRIVED THE following night at midnight. We were all awake. My mother was pacing, checking her telephone obsessively. Elana and I chatted nervously on the couch, trying to distract ourselves. Only Quin and Edison appeared calm, at least on the surface. When my mother's phone dinged to signal a message, we all jumped. It was short, just two words. My mother read it aloud:

Arrived safely.

"Thank goodness," Elana said, relieved. "Now the waiting begins," she added, apprehension quickly returning to her face.

She turned to me, speaking quietly, "Are you okay, Lex? I've been wanting to ask you since the other night."

I saw Quin watching us, pretending not to. "I'm totally fine," I said, loud enough for him to hear. I watched my words make their impact. He sat unmoving for a moment, then left the room. My mother and Edison followed him, wandering into the kitchen for a snack.

I turned back to Elana, giving her a sad smile. "Okay, so I'm not totally fine."

"I've never seen Quin act like that before," she confessed. "I mean, I've seen him get angry, but he was . . . he seemed . . . like—"

"A different person," I offered.

She nodded.

"Elana," I paused, wondering if I should continue. "Why did you and Quin break up?" I spit the words out quickly, driven both by my insatiable curiosity and my newly born insecurity.

Elana sighed. "Are you sure you want to talk about this?"

"Go ahead. It's okay," I said. Inside, I already regretted asking. Not talking about Quin was hard, but talking about him was worse.

"Well, I don't think you could call it a breakup. That would require an *actual* relationship. Quin didn't really do relationships back then. He was kind of a loner. And I was a mess too. Half the time, I avoided boys, kind of like I do now. The other half, I thought their attention was the only thing that mattered, like that was all I was good at. Anyway, we just kissed a few times. I wanted it to be more, but Quin made it pretty clear that wasn't going to happen. It's funny, but I didn't really know anything about him until after we stopped seeing each other."

"Typical Quin," I said, half-smiling. "Thanks for telling me."

"Of course," Elana said. Then she looked down, ashamed. "I know this sounds silly, but I'm envious of you . . ." My stomach tightened at her words.

Sensing my concern, she quickly added, "Not for being with *Quin*, but just for being with *someone*. I don't know if I'll ever be able to just be with a boy and act like myself, not pathetic, like a deer caught in the headlights."

I put my arm around her. "You will. Just give yourself time."

She nodded halfheartedly, her face skeptical.

Elbowing her playfully in the side, the way Max always did, I added, "Besides, love will make anyone a deer in the headlights."

CHAPTER FIFTY-FIVE

CHANGE

FOR THE NEXT FEW WEEKS, Quin didn't avoid me as I had expected—*worse*—he treated me just like everyone else. He spoke to me at breakfast, pleasantries exchanged over toast. Then he usually asked me to go for a run with him and Artos, but we were almost always accompanied by Elana or Edison. Nights were the worst. After dinner, Quin would sit next to me on the sofa, warm and smelling of soap, making fun of the silly reruns. I tried to stop myself, but my eyes always wandered to his hands, willing them closer. He *never, ever* touched me. In one way, I was glad. If Quin had touched me the way he touched everyone else, I would have known it was over. *That* would have been unbearable.

Quin inhabited a universe that I could only observe with wonder. I convinced myself that whatever we had, for Quin, it was only *a* story— one of many that would end and begin again with ease. Despite what Max had told me, I began to doubt that Quin even thought of us at all. On the other hand, I thought of almost nothing else. For me, what I felt for Quin was *the* story, the only one I cared to read.

I noticed Quin had been spending a lot of time in the laboratory with my mother. He was always carrying a new book from her library, and there was a definite theme. So far, he had read *Anger Management for Beginners*, *Rage and Relationships*, *Calming Your Inner Storm*, and *Children of Domestic Violence*, not that I was keeping track. The previous morning, I had seen him with a copy of one of my mother's books,

Getting to Why: Understanding the Criminal Mind. For obvious reasons, it was my favorite.

My mind cluttered with Quin, I wandered outside. My mother was sitting on the porch, drinking a glass of iced tea and enjoying the first warm day of summer. She patted the spot next to her, and I sat down, sighing.

"What's wrong?" she asked. "You've been moping around all day."

I shrugged languidly. "What do you think?"

"Oh, Lex." My mother shook her head and smiled knowingly at me. "*Still?*"

Obviously, my mother expected me to shed Quin as easily as a winter coat. I narrowed my eyes at her with annoyance. "Yes, Mom. *Still.*"

Sensing my upset, she quickly backtracked. "That's not what I meant. It's just been so long since I've been in love. I guess I just forgot how *devastating* it can be."

Devastating. I silently considered the word usually reserved for natural disasters—earthquakes, hurricanes, floods, fires. *Yep, it seemed accurate.* I nodded at my mother.

"Do you think it's possible for people to change?"

She glanced sidelong at me. "People or *Quin?*"

"Both."

She paused, thinking carefully before answering. "Yes and no. I think there are some parts of ourselves that are resistant to change. No matter how hard we try, we just can't make headway—like chipping away at the Grand Canyon. But I've seen people change themselves in revelatory ways. I think the question to ask is 'Does the person *want* to change?'"

With hesitation, I turned toward my mother. In the past few weeks, she had spent more time with Quin than I had. "Well . . . do you think Quin wants to change?"

My mother put her arm around me. I braced myself for a lecture. "Yes," she said. I waited for the *but*—it never came. "I think Quin is just starting to understand that even though he can't change the past, it doesn't have to define him."

I felt relieved by my mother's answer, but a long buried question was nagging at me. "Did Dad want you to change? Is that why he left?"

My mother took a deep breath. She didn't seem surprised, only saddened, as if my question was a dreaded guest she had been expecting for a long time.

"That was part of it," she said. "Your father didn't like my working for Zenigenic. He thought I had lost my moral compass, and he was right. I was so focused on my career. I didn't think about how my choices would affect others—like him and you and Quin and your friends. At the time, I thought he was being so unfair asking me to give up Zenigenic. Now I see I was being just as unfair to him and to you."

"Do you think Dad ever wonders about us?" My voice was heavy with melancholy.

My mother frowned, her eyes distressed, but her response was ambiguous. "I'm sure your father thinks of us as often as we think of him."

Eager to mine my mother for more information about my father, I readied another question, but I was interrupted. Quin and Artos came running up the driveway, both of them breathing heavily. Artos found a spot in the shade, flopping on his belly into the cool grass. Quin collapsed on the stairs, next to me. I silently measured the space between us. Twelve inches. Still, I could feel the heat radiating from his body. He seemed oblivious.

My mother chuckled to herself. "We were just talking about you, Quin."

My body tensed. I gave my mother a look of horror.

"All good I hope," Quin said, his eyes twinkling.

"I'll let Lex fill you in," she offered slyly, already gathering her things and walking toward the door.

Quin sat up, alert. He turned toward me, his eyes curious and warm. It was impossible not to think about kissing him.

"I was just asking my mom if she thought that *people* could change," I said, hoping he wouldn't press me for more.

Quin gave a small nod. "And what do you think? Can *people*?" His voice sounded casual, but his expression wasn't. We both knew we were talking about him.

"I hope so."

CHAPTER FIFTY-SIX

OLD BONES

"LEX, WHERE ARE YOU, HONEY?" I heard my mother calling me from the kitchen.

"Here, Mom," I answered, walking toward the sound of her voice. The house was empty. Everyone else was in our backyard, soaking up the second warm day of summer. For the last few days, the fog had obscured the sun, but now it was high and bright in the sky, just a few wispy clouds trailing around it. I could see Quin and Edison through the window, throwing a football to each other. I smiled to myself. Amazingly, they were actually having a good time together.

"I need to talk to you." My mother's voice sounded unusually serious. "Let's go to the lab."

Sensing that my mother was tense, I instantly felt nervous.

When we walked inside, I noticed two large boxes sitting on the counter. Both of them familiarly labeled in black marker: *Dishes.* One had been opened. The other sat staring at me, not revealing itself. I knew then that we were about to unearth more old bones from my mother's past.

"Sit down, Lex," she instructed.

I sat on a stool at the counter, fidgeting nervously.

"Before I say anymore, I want you to know that I love you." My mother sounded as if she might cry. "I know I haven't always handled things the right way. I haven't always been the best mom, but—"

"You've been a great mom. Just tell me . . . whatever it is."

"You're going to be angry with me," she warned.

It was then I knew. Something in that box had to do with my father. I took a deep breath.

"When I first met your father, I wasn't like I am now. It may be hard for you to believe, but I was . . . *fragile* . . . one crack away from breaking entirely. I had struggled for a long time with depression and panic attacks. Your father was very patient. There were some days when I screamed at him so much, I lost my voice. Other days, I couldn't even leave the house. I was another person, Lex. I don't know who that person was anymore."

I wasn't sure what to say. A few months ago, I wouldn't have believed her, but after seeing her so broken when I had returned, I knew she was telling the truth.

"For some reason, after we had you, everything shifted. I stopped yelling so much. My anxiety got better. I felt truly *happy*, something I had given up on ever feeling again. I was so excited that I threw myself head first into work and didn't look back. I didn't leave any room in my life for your father."

I nodded. My mother began opening the second box, tearing away the tape from its edges. Caught by the light, miniscule particles of dust fell to the ground like tiny stars.

"What's in the box, Mom?" I was so afraid to know the answer, but the question was unavoidable.

"I couldn't lose you, Lex. I was so selfish. I thought if you knew your father wanted to see you, you would leave me—and then I would go back to that *other* person, the one I was before you. By the time I realized what I had done, it was too late to take it back. I thought you would hate me. When you asked me if he ever thought of us, it broke my heart."

"What do you mean *wanted to see me*?" I tried to take the edge out of my voice, but it cut through anyway. I had been choking back anger at my mother for so long that it seeped through inadvertently.

From the box, my mother removed a handful of letters, followed by another and another. They were all opened, addressed to me. In the left-hand corner, a name: William Knightley. My father.

My mother put the thick stacks of letters into a bag—eight years' worth of letters. "These are yours," she said, handing it to me. I wasn't sure what infuriated me more—realizing that my mother had hidden the letters from me for so long or thinking of her opening and reading each one, knowing that it would never reach me.

A hot coal of rage seared inside my stomach, pushing its way into my throat. Before I knew it, I was shouting and crying at the same time, my voice shattering the air like a rock through a window. The words were coming too fast to think, too fast to stop. "How could you do this to me? How could you possibly think this was okay? I've spent *years*, practically my whole life thinking I did something wrong, that Dad abandoned *me*. You let me think that. *And you read my letters!* I never knew you could be *so* selfish."

I stood up and flung the bag onto the ground. The letters scattered at my feet. The impact startled me, but it felt strangely satisfying to throw something. My mother watched me helplessly.

"Why now, Mom? Why are you showing me these *now*?" My voice shook as I tried to stamp out my fury before I completely lost control.

"Because I realized that by keeping them from you, I wasn't loving you. I was hurting you. Quin helped me realize that. He cares about you, Lex, enough to risk losing you. That's the rarest kind of bravery. You're right—I've been selfish and I don't know why. But I hope that someday you can forgive me."

My anger slowed to a simmer, tears running hot down my cheeks. "I think you should leave," I said, avoiding her eyes.

"This is the last letter." My mother placed a single envelope on the table. Unlike many of the others, it wasn't yellowed with age. "It's from your eighteenth birthday, right before they suspended what remained of the postal service."

She paused, her face pained with guilt. "I'll be in the kitchen if you need me."

Still crying, I removed the letter from its envelope.

> *Dearest Lex,*
>
> *I can hardly believe it, but today you are eighteen! I know it's cliché, but it seems only yesterday that I held you in my arms. I can't imagine you at eighteen, but I know for sure that you are beautiful, smart as a whip, and kind and generous. You always were those things. Now, a confession:*

When I first started writing you, all those years ago, I thought you were angry with me for leaving. Your mother told me that you didn't want to talk to me, so after a while, I stopped calling. I thought it was probably easier for you without me there to muddle up your life. Then so much time had passed, I didn't even know how to be in your life anymore. Now I know that I was a fool. I failed you completely. I should've tried harder, done more, been better. I don't want to believe that it's too late, but it might be. I won't be able to write anymore, Lex. The mail service will stop here next week, not that it matters anyway—I don't think you've been receiving my letters. That, more than anything else, devastates me. If I'm wrong, and I hope I am, you can always, always call me.

Love,
Dad

P.S. There's something for you inside. I hope you'll wear it close to your heart, where I wish I could be.

At the bottom of the letter were my father's address in Boston and his telephone number. I fingered the locket around my neck, tears welling in my eyes. My father must have known that my mother would give it to me. It occurred to me that my mother probably missed my father just as much as I did, but was too stubborn to admit it.

Next to the box marked *Dishes*, I noticed my mother had conveniently placed our portable telephone, which we hardly ever used anymore. Through my tears, I managed a half-smile. Somehow, some way, I knew I would forgive her. The alternative was simply inconceivable.

I stoked the smoldering remnants of the fire in my stomach, allowing my outrage to give me momentum. Without thinking, I dialed the number at the bottom of the page. It rang and rang and rang—each ring like an electric finger reaching through the void, striking my heart.

Then, a voice. "Hello?"

Even though eight years had passed, virtually an eternity, I recognized it instantly.

CHAPTER FIFTY-SEVEN

SNAGS

THE NEXT MORNING, I FOUND my mother in the kitchen, looking at a map of Alcatraz. Quin had marked certain areas of the Guardian Force headquarters in red ink. My mother had been studying that same map for at least a week—usually with intensity—her eyes squinting in concentration.

Now her stare was vacant, her thoughts elsewhere. When I sat down at the table, she looked at me child-like, her eyes pleading for forgiveness. Seeing that look stirred a cauldron inside me. In it was anger, of course, but there was so much more—guilt, betrayal, and that unspeakable connection that always pulled me back to her.

Of course, there was no hiding the telephone call. As usual, I spilled my secret.

"How *is* your father?" she asked. It was her only question.

I didn't know how to answer. We had talked for over two hours. How do you sum that into a word? "He's good, I guess. He wants to see me." I added, "He asked about you."

It wasn't entirely accurate, but seeing my mother's face brighten made my stretch of the truth worth it. My father had confirmed the reports from SFTV. Boston had been under martial law for at least a year. Small, clandestine factions of the Resistance were active, but the military quickly squashed any public demonstrations. My father recounted his surprise in seeing my mother's face on a Resistance flyer. I imagined it must have been a welcome shock. When I told him she had changed a lot, he simply said—"*Oh*"—curious, but not brave enough to ask. I hinted that we were working on something important, but I resisted the urge to tell my father everything. My mother was right . . . we didn't know who was listening.

I pretended to eat my breakfast, as I watched my mother with melancholy. Her expressions, her mannerisms, as familiar to me as my own. And yet, with all that she kept hidden, she was always reminding me that she was a stranger. In her hand, she turned her cell phone over and over nervously.

Soon Quin, Elana, and Edison were awake and joined us at the table. No surprise, my eyes gravitated to Quin. His face was unshaven, shadowed with stubble, his hair mussed. Even so, I felt a brutal tug of longing. I noticed that he was carrying an unmarked file folder. I looked at it curiously. Our eyes met for a moment, and he gave me an easy smile. A surge of warmth traveled through my body.

Clearing her throat nervously, my mother set the phone down on the table with intention.

"I heard from Carrie," she announced.

My mouth hung open.

"Why didn't you say anything?" I asked. My voice came out sharper than I intended, accusatory. Everyone's eyes turned to me.

My mother tried to appear unaffected, but the hurt in her eyes was palpable. "I wanted to make sure *we* were okay," she said, turning to me. "I thought that was more important."

My shoulders slumped in embarrassment, my eyes downcast. I felt so childish.

Breaking the awkward silence, much to my relief, Elana asked, "What did Carrie say?"

"She sent me an encrypted email," my mother explained. "A few snags in the plan, unfortunately. There was a break-in yesterday at the Resistance lab. The whole place was ransacked. Luckily, the Resilire data was in a vault and was untouched, but most of the lab was destroyed, including one of the compounds needed to complete the formula."

"A break-in?" Quin asked skeptically. "That seems unlikely with all the security."

My mother nodded. "I agree. The Council suspects that Augustus was involved. Apparently, since our last communication, Dr. Bell uncovered several emails between him and Jamison Ryker. It seems all the while he was blackmailing them, Augustus also was trying to broker a deal with the Guardians for the flash drive. Ryker was furious that he hadn't received it from Augustus as promised and told him that he was as good as dead."

"No wonder he ran away," I said. "The only worse enemy than Augustus is Ryker."

"So this compound . . . do you have it here?" Quin wondered.

My mother nodded. "I told Carrie that Lex would bring it to her. I can't risk the three of you being seen. If you were caught, the whole plan would be in jeopardy."

"But she can't go alone," Elana added.

"I'll be okay, Elana," I assured her.

My mother's face was pensive, deliberating. "No, Elana is right. Someone should go with you."

Edison began, "I'll g—"

Quin's forceful bellow easily overshadowed Edison's voice. "No, I'll go."

"Don't mind me," Edison sneered. "I forgot—I'm not allowed near your *ex*-girlfriend." He emphasized the *ex*, twisting the knife and waiting for Quin's reaction.

Quin paused and took several audible breaths before speaking contritely. "Sorry, Eddie. It was rude of me to interrupt you. If it's okay with you, Lex, I would like to go."

I looked at Quin, and we both laughed nervously. "It's okay with me," I replied.

"Then, it's settled," my mother said. "Let me get the compound. Max will be on this side of the Golden Gate Bridge to meet you."

A few minutes later, Quin pulled up in the jeep we had stolen on the way home. My mother decided it was safer than using her car.

Before I got in the passenger seat, I felt my mother's hand on my shoulder.

"Lex, are we okay?" she asked with undeniable puppy-dog eyes. "It's miserable when you're mad at me."

"We're fine, Mom," I said flatly. Seeing her disappointment, I reluctantly added, "You know I always forgive you eventually."

My mother grinned sheepishly.

As we pulled back from the driveway, I sighed, exasperated. "Ugh. She can be so annoying sometimes."

Quin chuckled. "Like mother, like daughter," he teased.

I rolled my eyes, preparing a clever comeback, but Quin's pensive expression gave me pause.

His voice serious, he said, "You're really lucky, you know? Your mom . . . it's so obvious that she loves you."

I nodded. "I know. It's just that sometimes she has a funny way of showing it. She hides things—really *important* things. She's not as perfect as you think." I wanted so badly to tell Quin about my father, but I felt myself holding back. I feared being broken again.

As we approached the bridge, Quin was silent. Maybe he was holding back too.

Just before the Golden Gate, he parked the car at the lookout spot where we planned to meet Max and then turned to me.

"I don't think she's perfect," he admitted. "I heard about your letters."

"*You did?*"

"One day, when we were in her lab, your mom asked if you ever talked to me about your dad. Then she told me about the letters. She was really afraid to tell you, but I told her that you would understand."

I shook my head in disbelief. My mother had confided in Quin. I wondered if I would ever fully understand her. In some ways, it made sense though. Despite my best attempts, as with my mother, I knew I would spend forever trying to crack Quin's code.

"I talked to him yesterday," I offered. "It was . . . *strange* . . . but good."

"I'm really glad, Lex," Quin said wistfully. "I know how much that means to you. I want you to be happy. I mean, that's what your mom wants too."

I was suddenly aware of my body leaning in toward Quin. *Did I mean to do that?*

As he spoke, Quin was inching closer to me as well—so close that I could see a nick on his chin where he probably cut himself shaving. The ends of my hair were brushing against his shoulder, our lips a fingertip's length apart. His eyes were yearning, drawing me in.

I felt paralyzed by indecision. *Kiss him*, half of me implored. *Do not kiss him*, the other half insisted. *Kiss him. Do not kiss him. Kiss him.*

Sighing, Quin sat back against the seat. Just like that, the moment was gone.

He shook his head. "I'm sorry. For a second, I thought . . ."

There was a knock on the window—it was Max—and we both jumped.

"Hey, you two. Didn't mean to *interrupt*." Max raised his eyebrows. "Good thing I'm not a Guardian anymore," he said sarcastically.

"Yeah, good thing for *them*," Quin shot back at him in a transparent attempt to deflect attention.

Quin opened the door and embraced Max.

"We've missed you," I told him.

"Speak for yourself," Quin teased, mussing Max's hair.

"What's it been like at Resistance headquarters?" I wondered, as I handed Max the bottle containing the compound.

"Lonely," Max replied, only half-joking. "A lot of people have given up. I guess Dr. Bell isn't quite as charismatic as Augustus . . ."

"Or diabolical," I added, smiling.

Max and Quin chuckled.

"And the break-in?" I wondered curiously.

"Definitely an inside job," Max confirmed Quin's hunch. "Dr. Bell suspects that Cason may be working with Augustus. Even though we've been watching him closely, we can't prove it."

"Figures," I said, recalling Cason's fierce loyalty to his unscrupulous leader.

"How about with you?" Max asked, his eyes darting between us.

From behind Quin, I gave a tiny shake of my head, hoping Max would ask nothing more.

"Pretty boring," Quin said, his voice monotone.

"Yeah, I can see that," Max responded dryly. "You were *so* bored waiting for me, you didn't even see me coming." He winked at me.

Quin offered no response. Instead, he turned to me. "We better go. There's probably another helicopter patrol coming soon." On cue, in the distance, we heard the muted, methodical chopping of blades cutting through the air.

As we drove back, I couldn't take my eyes off Quin. He stared straight ahead as if I wasn't there.

A few blocks from my house, I reached to touch his arm, but stopped myself. I turned the radio on—the one remaining station owned by SFTV played a continuous loop of oldies from the 2020s—hoping to drown out my continuous replay of our almost interlude. It was useless. The only thing I heard was my own voice. *I should have kissed him.*

Without a word, Quin suddenly veered down a side street, jolting me back into the present.

"Police," Quin warned, screeching the car to a stop in the middle of the block. "We have to get out."

I jumped out quickly, my heart racing. Quin was a few steps behind. His eyes looked panicked.

The city police rarely patrolled our neighborhood. With crime rampant elsewhere, the jails were overcrowded and understaffed. Traffic stops were not a priority, and I hadn't seen a police car since our return, but there was no mistaking the screaming siren.

"In here." I pulled Quin inside a fenced yard. The house was abandoned, its windows obscured by weeds taller than us. The thick overgrowth scratched at my arms.

Pressed together in a clearing near the fence, we peered out through the slatted boards, both of us breathing hard. The police car passed without stopping, without even slowing down, completely oblivious to our stolen vehicle.

I looked at Quin, trying not to laugh.

He shrugged, smiling at himself. "What can I say? Old habits die hard, I guess."

"We should probably walk back anyway, just to be safe," I said, extricating myself from the weeds and opening the gate.

On our way back, I found myself telling Quin all about my conversation with my father. It felt good to confide in *someone*, but not just someone—*him.*

When we reached the cul-de-sac, I stopped. "Quin, about earlier, I—"

"It's okay, Lex. I get it. You don't have to explain. You don't owe me anything."

He walked inside before I could finish, before I could give a voice to my feelings. *I should have kissed you.*

CHAPTER FIFTY-EIGHT

THE PLAN

ONE WEEK LATER, MY MOTHER'S telephone dinged.

"Carrie," she said, her eyes widening. Her voice was charged with nervous excitement.

The text was intended to be cryptic. "Project at 80%."

My mother and I looked at each other for a moment, dumbfounded, before we called out to the others. The drug was close to completion.

Quin, Edison, and Elana rushed into the room, hearing the urgency in our voices.

"We need to talk more about *this*," my mother said, pointing to the map. "Carrie has almost wrapped things up."

The room seemed to collectively hold its breath. My mother looked to Quin expectantly.

Speaking with authority, he addressed the group. "If Carrie finishes by the end of this week, then we can plan for next Monday. Like we talked about, it's probably best for us to use darkness to our advantage. We can hide our boat *here*." Quin traced an X on the map with his finger. "At night, they reduce security at the lab." Quin pointed. "I used to do that watch myself, and if we time it right, we can get in and out without being noticed. Max, Edison, and I can easily disable the guards, if necessary."

Quin smirked in Edison's direction. "Well, at least it will be easy for Max and me," he added.

Edison rolled his eyes.

Quin continued, directing his words to my mother. "Then, Elana and Edison can lead you and Carrie to the distribution point."

My mother nodded. "What about the . . . *demolition?*" she asked, clearly uncomfortable in admitting that we were planning to blow up the laboratory along with all the research the Guardian Force had relied upon to perfect their program.

Quin replied, "Carrie will bring the explosives from the armory at headquarters. Once we're inside and the drugs have been swapped, we'll set the charge to explode the lab shortly after the meeting begins. That way, we'll minimize the casualties from the Guardian Force."

My mother insisted we harm as few recruits and members of the Guardian Force as possible. She contended that they were being victimized as well—their vulnerabilities exploited—but more than that, I think my mother felt guilty about the damage already done. Though in some ways I agreed, I thought that she was being naïve. After all, given what Carrie had discovered about some of the permanent brain damage caused by Agitor and Onyx, we didn't really know how, or *if,* the Guardians would react to Resilire.

Elana's face was puzzled. "What happens after that? Ryker will be furious, and we can't predict how the Guardian Force will respond even if their emotions are no longer altered." I was glad I wasn't the only one who was concerned.

"That's where the video comes in," my mother explained. "The Guardian Force will have some special entertainment during their meeting that I hope will open their eyes to the ugly side of their recruitment and expose Ryker for the tyrant he is."

Quin furrowed his brow in concern. "Dr. Knightley, I respect what you're trying to accomplish with the video, but I think what Elana is saying is that even without the drugs, not all of the Guardian Force will react the way you're hoping. I've heard you say that people . . . that emotions . . . are unpredictable, and you're right."

I waited for my mother to react. She wasn't accustomed to others questioning her judgment.

Surprisingly, she nodded. "Quin, you're absolutely correct. I can't be certain what will happen. That's why I asked Carrie to involve Dr. Bell. Early Monday morning, once the plan is underway, Dr. Bell will inform Admiral Bennington of General Ryker's multitude of crimes—executing rejected Guardian Force recruits and proceeding with this program despite documented evidence of its volatility. The Resistance headquarters has all the data to support these claims."

"Why not just contact him now, Mom? Let the military deal with Ryker." I was annoyed. Not only was my mother's plan unnecessarily dangerous, but Quin had assigned everyone else a role. My name was noticeably absent.

Both Quin and my mother shook their heads. Quin addressed me. "Lex, if we don't destroy the Guardian Force research, the government will build it again, bigger and better this time. There's always going to be another Ryker waiting in the wings."

"Fine." I knew he was right. "Then, what about *me*?" I asked, gesturing toward the map, not bothering to disguise my irritation.

Quin's jaw stiffened slightly. He took several long, deep breaths, and I watched the tension fade from his face. "Lex, you said yourself that it's risky." His voice was calm and measured, but he avoided my eyes. "You're not trained for this."

My aggravation gnawed at me. Quin clearly considered me useless.

Trying to keep the peace, my mother interrupted, "Quin, Lex is right. We'll need her."

Quin nodded, but I could see he was troubled. "Then she can go with you," he conceded.

As I left the room after the meeting, I saw that Quin lingered behind. I assumed he was planning to talk to my mother, probably to tell her how *untrained* I was. I waited outside the door, listening.

My mother spoke first. "I know you're worried about her. But she's tough, like me. She'll be fine." I smiled at her words.

When Quin didn't respond, I cautiously peeked around the corner. He was sitting at the kitchen table, his head down in his hands. My mother stood behind him, patting his shoulder. He lifted his head, and I quickly skirted out of sight.

"If anything happened to her. . . " Quin didn't finish his sentence.

I wanted so badly to hear his next words, but he kept them contained somewhere inside himself.

"I know," my mother said empathically. "I love her too, Quin."

CHAPTER FIFTY-NINE

A SETUP

THAT AFTERNOON, MY MOTHER CALLED me into the living room. She had a curious smile on her face.

"Would you mind doing me a favor?" she asked. "I promised Quin that he could read our poem, the one we like. I thought he might enjoy it. Could you bring the book down to him?" She gestured toward the lab.

"Okay," I agreed.

Quin was sitting at the table, reading, when I walked in. I hadn't been alone with him in a few days. Recalling their conversation after the meeting, I immediately suspected that my mother had planned this.

He looked up, startled. "Hey," he said, cautiously. "I didn't see you there."

I walked over and sat next to him. Casually, he scooted his stool away from me. It was probably unintentional, and I knew I was being silly, but it hurt.

"More recommended reading," I joked, handing Quin the poetry book. His lips curled slightly in a smile, and he nodded.

"You know, I didn't mean that you couldn't handle it," Quin said, referring to the meeting. "I know you're more than capable."

I didn't know how to respond without admitting my eavesdropping, so I changed the subject. "What are you reading *now*?"

"It's my dad's file," he said. "Your mom gave it to me last week. Did you know she went to see him again a few years ago?"

"No," I said, trying to disguise the perturbation in my voice. I vaguely remembered my mother taking a trip a few years ago to L.A. for a psychiatric conference. She must have made a secret stop at Dellencourt.

He gestured to the file in his hand. "I guess my dad has his own book. It's almost as sad and pathetic as mine. It's weird, but I never thought of him as a person before. I always saw him as a monster, but he had a really hard life."

I looked at Quin with interest, hoping he would continue. Just being with him, I felt lighter.

"His father was really strict, like over the top. When my dad misbehaved, he would make him stand for hours in the corner. He told my dad that he was worthless. And, of course, my dad saw a lot of violence between his parents. No surprise there."

"Does it help to know about your father's past?" I felt I already knew the answer. My mother's revelations about herself made it easier to let go of her mistakes.

Quin nodded. "I can't say I forgive him. I'm not sure that I ever will. The past is a hard thing to shake." He gestured toward his electronic file, the *Book of Quin*, sitting on the table next to him. "But I hate him a lot less now. Your mom told me that when she went to see him, she realized that she might've been wrong about him. She said he'd changed a lot, and he asked about me . . . if she knew anything about me."

"It's funny how someone's past can make you see that person differently," I said, thinking of something my mother had told me. She said people were like icebergs, showing only a tiny tip of themselves to the world. If you took the time to look beneath the surface, you would really *see* the vastness of everything else—dark, cold, and hidden—and understand.

Quin added, "I guess I'm seeing myself a little differently too."

As we talked, I could sense there had been a change in Quin. It was subtle, like a slight redirection of the wind. Whatever had been balled inside him so tightly was slowly coming unwound.

"So . . . tomorrow's my birthday," Quin announced, his voice small and boyish. "Number twenty."

"Quin! Why didn't you remind me?" With everything that had happened, I had completely forgotten it was already June.

"It's not really that important," he said. "I usually just try to ignore it and hope it will go away." He laughed.

"Well, that's completely unacceptable, Mr. McAllister," I frowned at him. "I have an idea, but it's going to require you to be alone with me. I'm not sure if you can handle that." I was definitely flirting, testing the waters.

"I think I can force myself to get through it," he joked. His eyes were playful, and I was encouraged.

"Okay." I tried to make my voice sound nonchalant as if I wasn't completely beside myself with excitement. "Then meet me tomorrow night, after lights out, and bring *this*." I gestured to the *Book of Quin*.

He nodded, grinning. "Alright . . . sounds mysterious."

"By the way, I'm proud of you," I said. "Everything that you've been doing . . . it's really brave."

His face reddened, and he shrugged. "I figured it was time. I know I messed things up with you, but maybe one day, I'll get it right."

His voice sounded resigned, but I thought I saw a question lingering in his eyes. He continued, "I still have a long way to go, but I want to *love* someone. I'm starting to think that I could actually be good at it."

Imagining Quin loving someone else froze my heart, iced it over. I could feel it give way, cracking inside me.

"What if I don't want you to love anybody else?" I asked.

Before Quin could answer, I stood, taking a step toward the stool where he was sitting. He was leaning back casually against the table. I positioned myself between his knees, carefully placing one hand on each. I hadn't touched Quin in weeks. It was intoxicating.

Kiss him. Heart and mind spoke together, finally synchronized.

I waited for him to move away, but he didn't. I imagined him counting in his mind as I would have—one thousand one, one thousand two. Before he got to three, I leaned in and kissed him along his jaw, letting my lips mark the space between his chin and his ear. He sighed softly, and I smiled to myself. I was better at this than I thought. Then I gently kissed him on the lips, *once.* I felt his body tense. Sitting up, he wrapped his arms around my hips, locking me in close to him.

"You shouldn't have done that," he said, shaking his head.

"Why?"

"Because now I just want to do it again." Quin's eyes were intense, but his lips hinted at a smile.

I grinned, slowly extricating myself from his arms before he could follow through with his threat. "That's kind of the point," I said.

CHAPTER SIXTY

BEST BIRTHDAY EVER

"WHERE ARE WE GOING?" QUIN asked, his voice light and energized. In his arm, he carried his file, as I had asked him to.

"You're not allowed to ask any questions," I teased. "Just trust me."

"Okay," he agreed.

Even though it was June, the night air was crisp, a slight breeze tickling my skin. Quin was wearing his leather jacket, and I had on one of my favorite sweatshirts, stretching its arms to cover my hands.

We walked to the marina, a little less than a mile from my house. The moon was just a sliver, and it was so dark I couldn't tell where the sky ended and the ocean began. I could hear the water lapping gently against the pier. There were several boats docked there. Most had been abandoned; one had been left unlocked. Before I had left for San Francisco, I liked to climb inside it and pretend I was on a houseboat in the middle of the Pacific Ocean.

"So we're here," I announced to Quin.

"And what exactly are we doing *here*?" Quin volleyed back at me.

"Well, I've been thinking about your file . . . the *Book of Quin.*" I made air-quotes with my fingers. "Yesterday, you were saying that the past is hard to shake, but I don't think the past is holding on to you. I think that it's you who needs to let go." I gestured to the tablet in his hand.

"What do you mean?"

"My mother once told me that holding on to the past is like walking around with a pebble in your shoe. You can still keep walking, keep moving forward, but that pebble is always there nagging at you, begging for your attention. After a while, that pebble is all you can feel. Sometimes, you just have to stop walking for a minute and get rid of it once and for all."

"So this is my pebble, huh?" Quin said, smiling.

I nodded. "I think it's time to let it go."

Quin's face was pensive, considering my words. "I can't believe that I'm saying this, but I think you're right. Every time I read this thing it brings me right back there." He shook his head, dismayed by his realization. "So what do you propose, Ms. Knightley?"

I pointed out into the vastness of the ocean. "The perfect place for a pebble," I said.

Quin took a breath. "Here goes," he announced.

With a running start, he launched the *Book of Quin* high into the air. I couldn't see it, but I heard it fall with a splash. I imagined it sinking slowly to the bottom, burying itself in the sand.

Quin was laughing, his face lit with a wide grin. "That felt good," he admitted.

His laughter was infectious, and I giggled. "Maybe twenty won't be so bad after all," I said, still looking out at the dark waves. "Happy birthday, Quin."

As I finished speaking, there he was, standing in front of me. His eyes were an invitation, but he didn't wait for me to accept. Before I knew it, Quin was kissing me. Aside from our brief moment in the lab the day prior, it had been *so* long. It was like before, but different, *better*. Saying nothing, I took Quin's hand and began leading him.

"Where are you taking me?" he asked playfully.

"You'll see," I replied, squeezing his hand tightly.

I led him to the boat, my pretend houseboat. Inside the cabin, it was darker than I had expected. I set my flashlight in the sink, face up, casting a small circle of light around us. The instant I slid the cabin door shut, Quin pushed me against it, kissing me with urgency. His hands were alive again in my hair, under my shirt, conveying everything unsaid between us.

"Wow." Quin whispered, his kisses softening, becoming tender. "I missed you." He ran his fingers through my hair, smoothing it back.

"I missed you too," I said. "*Obviously.*" I pulled him toward the cabin's small pullout bed.

"Did you know this would happen?" he asked, his voice equal parts confusion and awe.

I smirked. "I thought it was in the realm of possibility." Then I confessed, "I hoped it would."

Without hesitation, I added, "Quin, I love you."

"You do?" he asked, doubtful.

I nodded.

"You know, nobody has said that to me since I was six. I might need you to say it again." Quin gave me a boyish smile.

"I love you," I repeated.

Quin pulled me in close to him. I could feel the soft leather of his jacket on my cheek. "I love you too," he said aloud, his voice certain.

He began whispering his kisses against my neck, ever so slowly meandering his way back to my lips. It was torturous in the best way.

Taking a step back from me, Quin took off his jacket. I watched him carefully, barely breathing. He pulled his T-shirt over his head and tossed it aside, then flopped down casually on the bed. I exhaled.

He seemed so calm, as if the whole world wasn't about to break wide open. Grinning, he beckoned to me with his hand. Quin was right, when I'd invited him here, some part of me must have known this would happen. I had imagined it many times. Still, I felt like another person, an alternate me. This was *happening*.

I walked toward him, biting my lip, nervous. He took my hand and guided me onto his lap, sitting so my legs fit closely on either side of his body. His face seemed content, relaxed. I tried not to think that he had done this before—I tried not to think at all.

"What are you thinking?" Quin asked. Obviously, my efforts had proven unsuccessful.

"Nothing," I lied.

He gave me a skeptical look. "Tell me," he encouraged.

I sighed. "Just that you seem so calm."

Quin widened his eyes at me. "Are you kidding?" he asked, incredulously.

He took my hand and placed it on his bare chest. A man's, not a boy's, his body was different than I had expected, so real that it terrified and thrilled me simultaneously. I could feel his heart beating fast, its rhythm speaking to mine in a language that I understood—its wild pounding so much like my own, both comforting and exciting me.

I noticed a small scar on his shoulder and one on his side. I traced them with my finger.

"Tell me about your scars," I said.

"Okay, *Doctor* Knightley," he replied, with pretend seriousness.

He displayed the knuckles on his right hand. "This one, I think you already know about."

I nodded. "Punching the wall at Riverbend," I said.

"This one," he pointed to his shoulder, "is from a fight I had when I was thirteen. It happened at one of the foster homes I lived in. This bigger kid pushed me, and I fell against a table."

"And this one?" I asked, lightly grazing the side of his abdomen where his muscles were taut. He grabbed my hand, laughing.

"A fight," he said again, still chuckling.

"Do you have any scars that *aren't* from fighting?" I teased him.

He held up his elbow. There was a thin, white line on it, barely visible.

"Skateboarding, when I was ten."

"Then that's my favorite," I declared.

"*Is it?*" he asked, a playful lilt in his voice. "Maybe you haven't seen them all yet."

Quin gave me a sly grin. I could feel my face warming, but I smiled back. Putting his hands around my waist, Quin moved me gently from his lap to the bed, paper-weighting himself on top of me. He was addressing all of my senses. I saw his brown eyes, lit by the flashlight, twinkling with tiny flecks of amber and gold. I heard his breathing, quick and even. I felt his warmth, his heaviness, so solid like an anchor grounding me. I could smell him—summer morning, crisp and fresh, but with a promise of heat.

He whispered to me, punctuating each word by putting his lips on mine. "Best. Birthday. Ever."

CHAPTER SIXTY-ONE

CALL IT EVEN

"GOOD MORNING, EVERYONE," QUIN CHIRPED, a wide grin on his face.

"You're certainly chipper this morning, McAllister," Edison observed.

Ignoring Edison, Quin leaned over from behind me, putting his hands on my shoulders, and kissed me on the cheek. In a softer voice, he added, "Good morning, Lex."

"Oh . . . *that* explains it," Edison infused his voice with mock drama. I waited for him to follow his remark with something mean or sarcastic, but he didn't. He just smiled.

Quin had never kissed me in front of my mother before—or anyone else for that matter—but she didn't seem to mind. When I glanced at her, she winked at me. I grinned back at her conspiratorially, inwardly feeling satisfied. For once, I had a secret I would keep.

From across the table, Quin and I exchanged a story with our eyes, one that belonged only to us. It had been early morning by the time we had returned from the marina and snuck back inside the house. Quin lay in bed next to me, running his fingers through my hair. It felt so good that I tried not to fall asleep, but when the sun awakened me hours later, Quin was gone. On my pillow was my poetry book, with a small piece of paper marking the dog-eared page. As I read Quin's handwriting, I felt giddy.

"Twenty is my favorite year so far. In case you forgot, I love you."—Q

I had folded the note carefully and returned it safely to the book. Since first seeing it that morning, I had mentally reread it a hundred times. My body was sitting there, having breakfast, but every other part of me was with Quin.

Edison cleared his throat loudly. "Uh, earth to Lex . . . come in, Lex."

I felt my face instantly redden, and I glared at Edison. "Sorry. Did you say something?"

Quin chuckled to himself, eating his toast hurriedly. "Edison just asked if you wanted to accompany us on a run. We're taking Artos."

"Oh," I said, trying to be casual. "Sure."

Five miles later, Artos was exhausted. He lay panting on the porch, lapping up water from a bowl in between breaths. Quin sat next to him, his face glistening with sweat. Elana and Edison stood near the door stretching. For the third time that week, Edison had beaten all of us back to the house.

"Edison, you're getting really fast," Elana said, giving him a playful punch on the arm.

He nodded. "I ran track in high school for a while, but I got kicked off the team for drinking." I was surprised to hear Edison publicly admit to any flaws in his character. It seemed as if he immediately regretted his disclosure because he quickly added, "And I got pretty good at running away from *this* guy." He gestured toward Quin.

Quin shook his head. "I think it was the other way around, Van Sant. You were—" Quin stopped himself. Turning to look at Edison, he continued, "You know we both acted like idiots. Why don't we just call it even?"

Edison looked surprised, almost disappointed. He smirked. "Man, McAllister, what's gotten into you? I can't keep this bitter rivalry going on my own."

Quin shrugged, glancing in my direction.

"Looks like love is in the air." Edison couldn't resist. "C'mon, Red, let's go inside before Quin tries to hug me." We all laughed.

When they left, I sat next to Quin, letting my knee touch his.

"That was big of you," I said.

He grinned, shaking his head in agreement. "You were right. He's not *that* bad. But I'm not sure Eddie will know what to do with himself without a sparring partner."

Quin put his hand on my knee. I saw the thin scar across his knuckles and touched it, smiling to myself.

"I got your note."

"Did you like it?" Quin's voice was eager, seeking my approval.

I nodded and looked up into his eyes.

"Can I kiss you, even though I'm sweaty?" he asked.

I laughed. "Quin, you don't have to ask my permission. From here on out, you can just assume that I'm going to answer *yes* to any question that starts with, *can I kiss you.*"

"I like that rule," he said, lifting my chin gently and bringing his lips to mine.

"Quin! Lex!" My mother's urgent voice traveled from the kitchen interrupting us mid-kiss. She pointed to her cell phone on the kitchen table. Her apprehension evident. "There's a message from Carrie."

I picked up the phone and looked at the screen, showing it to Quin. There was one word—*Resilience*, the code word we decided on before she left. It signaled that Carrie's part of the plan was complete and ours was about to begin.

CHAPTER SIXTY-TWO

SUNDAY

IT WAS THE LONGEST DAY of my life. Time seemed to barely pull itself along as if slogging through thick mud. And yet, the passing of each hour only sharpened my apprehension. I wanted time to pass. Then I wanted time to stop. No matter what I wanted, those hands continued their inevitable measured crawl around the clock's face.

I spent most of the day walling out my fear by pretending to be a disinterested onlooker, observing everyone else. Though my mother tried to contain her nervous energy, her body would not quietly hold its tension. Like a trapped animal, she paced, tapped her fingers and talked incessantly about nothing.

Edison and Elana were a study in contrasts. Edison was a box, holding his contents in tightly, concealing his emotions beneath a flat and stoic exterior. Meanwhile, Elana's face gave it all away. Her brow was permanently furrowed, her body on high alert. Typical Quin, he was reserved, his eyes distant. When I watched him, I felt alone, knowing he was somewhere only he could go. I was surprised that, when our eyes met, he *saw* me, his gaze intense.

We planned to depart from the marina at 3 a.m. A couple of hours before midnight, we ate dinner. Well, Quin and Edison ate. The rest of us picked at our food, pretending to make conversation. Quin talked us through our plan once more. Afterward, I retreated to my room to make a journal entry.

June 9, 2041

I've had so many firsts lately, so many experiences that have forever shaped the person that I am. I know tonight promises more firsts, though I have no way of knowing how this will all end. Our plan is dangerous. Even though I don't want to admit it, I know some people will probably get hurt. But more than that, more than anything, I'm most afraid of losing someone I love. Being without my father for so long was one thing—I knew he was still there, even if he was always just out of my reach. Death, on the other hand, is another country, completely unreachable. I've never lost someone that I love before, not that way, and the thought of it actually happening is unbearable. I don't know how my life would continue, and yet, the worst part is that it would . . .

There was a knock at my door. It was my mother. I closed my journal, my entry unfinished.

"I thought I might find you in here," she said softly. "I just wanted to make sure you're okay with all of this."

I shrugged. "What choice do we have?" In my mind, the question had no answer.

"Lex, we *always* have a choice—no matter what," my mother replied, sitting down on the bed next to me. "I guess I just want to know that you think I'm doing the right thing by going forward with this. I want to do something that you can be proud of."

Instantly, my eyes brimmed with tears. "Mom, I've always been proud of you—even when you think I wasn't or shouldn't have been. You always did the best you could."

She pulled me in close to her. "It means a lot to hear you say that. You're the only person in the world I need to hear that from."

Another soft knock at the door interrupted us. My mother released me, wiping tears from her face. It was Quin.

"Sorry to interrupt, but it's almost time," he said matter-of-factly.

My mother nodded, giving me one last squeeze before she stood and left the room.

Quin lingered in the doorway, one foot in, one foot out, contemplating his next move. Finally, bringing both feet inside, he closed the door behind him and walked toward me.

"Lex," he began, his voice hinted at so many emotions—I felt them all.

"You don't have to say anything, Quin. I *know*."

"No, you don't *know*," he said, sitting next to me, taking both of my hands in his. Half-smiling at me, he added, "Even if you do know, let me tell you anyway."

"Okay."

He took an audible breath. "I want to tell you that, since I met you, my whole life has . . . well, it's started making sense again. It hasn't made sense for a long time." He paused. All that was past seemed to travel through his eyes. "I'm so scared right now that something could happen to you, but in a strange way, that makes me glad. It's good to have something to lose."

I squeezed his hands tightly. "You know, you're not the only one with something to lose. You are . . ." All words seemed flat and insufficient, but I selected one anyway. "You're *special* to me." *Special?* Not even close.

He nodded and leaned toward me, pressing his forehead to mine. "Let's talk about something else," he whispered.

"Alright." I hoped he would kiss me, his lips always a welcome distraction, but he continued speaking.

"When this is all over, there's this thing I need to do. I can't do it without you. Will you promise me something?" He addressed me quietly, his face serious. I listened with intention, keeping my eyes on his.

"I promise."

CHAPTER SIXTY-THREE

DREAD

IT TOOK OVER AN HOUR to maneuver our small dinghy into view of Alcatraz. The water was rough, spitting cold spray at us, jostling us left and right. I felt queasy, taking deep breaths of the salt air until the churning in my stomach passed. Halfway through, we cut the engine and rowed toward the shore.

Quin had positioned us on the south side of the island, completely opposite the lab, near the Agave Trail. According to Quin, the Guardian Force rarely used this part of the island. We would wait here, unnoticed, until the lighthouse flashed its beacon three times, signaling a change in watch. Carrie and her team would meet us at our second position, just behind the building marked Model Industries on the map. Quin had scratched through the name, his red pen spelling out Lab/Research Facility.

Just before we reached the shore, Quin jumped from the boat, the frigid water lapping around his knees. He towed us in and anchored us to a rusty metal stake driven between the rocks. Apparently we weren't the first boat to visit this side of the island. We pulled a tarp over us, leaving a small opening to stay in view of the beacon.

"Is everyone okay?" Quin looked only at me as he spoke.

I nodded. Though his eyes comforted me, I wished to be somewhere, *anywhere*, else.

"How long do we wait?" my mother asked.

Quin consulted his watch. "The change in guard should happen around 5 a.m., a little less than an hour from now."

From behind me, I heard Edison's voice. He made a feeble attempt to lighten the mood. "So how does it feel, McAllister? This is quite a homecoming."

Quin laughed nervously. "I could ask you the same, Van Sant."

"Well, I never thought I'd see this place again," Elana said. Her voice quivered noticeably.

I patted her arm, trying to comfort us both.

No one else spoke. We sat quietly, listening to the waves break on the rocks. It was almost peaceful. *Almost.*

Just as Quin predicted, at exactly 5 a.m., the lighthouse beacon flashed three times, illuminating the sky with an eerie yellow glow. Quin and Edison pushed us away from the rocks and rowed to the west. As the black waves roiled around us, I looked toward the city. A few lights flickered back at me in response. Their distant twinkling made me feel lonely and disconnected, conjuring a feeling that I had lost something essential without even realizing it yet. Overwhelmed with melancholy, I turned away.

As we passed the lighthouse, advancing to our second position, my stomach flip-flopped. There was no boat awaiting us, no Carrie, no Resilire.

"*Where are they?*" Edison gave a worried voice to my observation.

I looked to my mother. She shrugged helplessly. "I told them 5 a.m.," she insisted, her voice wavering.

"Don't panic," Quin soothed her. "I'm sure they'll be here."

We anchored our boat and waited.

"Look," Elana directed, pointing out into the darkness. In view, but still a mile or so away, I spotted another boat. Trailing behind it, I saw another smaller raft with several large containers inside it.

As they drew closer, Max waved to us. Carrie sat next to him, her face exasperated, nearly frantic. Cason Caruso and Hiro Chen were on the boat as well, along with several armed men I didn't recognize. Seeing Cason, I was alarmed, but I momentarily withheld my suspicions.

"Fancy meeting you here," Max whispered, punching Quin on the arm as we drew their dinghy alongside ours.

I edged my way over toward Max, nearly losing my balance in the wobbling boat. Quin grabbed my arms to steady me.

"Careful," Quin said gently, holding me to him a little longer than was necessary. I saw Max watching us closely, reading the signs.

As we embraced, with an ear-to-ear grin, Max reminded me, "I told you he would make it right."

I nodded, smiling back at him.

"What happened? Did you oversleep?" Quin teased Max, then addressed Carrie with seriousness. "Why are you late?"

Carrie took a deep, frustrated breath and considered Cason with disdain. "*He* insisted on coming."

"I am a part of the Council . . . *remember?* I have every right to be here." Cason glared at Carrie. Judging by their mutual disgust, I imagined this argument had been going on for hours.

"We don't trust you," Max countered. "You're working with Augustus."

"Even if that was true, you *obviously* need me . . . if this is the team you've assembled to take down Ryker," Cason said, clearing his throat, as he turned toward my mother. He eyed us with condescension. "I'm confused," he asked her. "Are you the psychiatrist or the crazy one?"

His arrogance infuriated me. I wanted to punch his face just to witness his surprise.

"Hey," Quin cautioned him, "this is the team. We don't have time to argue. You're either with us or you're not."

Cason offered no reply. He had been momentarily silenced.

Having extinguished one fire, Quin tried to calm Carrie. "He's here now—*like it or not*—and we do need him."

"Humph." Carrie glowered at Cason, but nodded her assent.

One of the unfamiliar armed men reached inside the raft and produced a gun, offering it to me. I took it in my hand without hesitating. But in my mind, I saw a flash of Elliot's face—not the cold, slack face of a dead man, but the animated face of living Elliot from his photograph. I remembered the ambush—my hesitation—I still wasn't sure I could pull the trigger again, even if I had to.

Practically reading my thoughts, Quin told me, "Don't even think about it—use it if you need to." I wondered if he was also giving himself permission.

It took almost all of us to pull the small raft ashore and unload its contents: a large container with thirty vials of Resilire—enough to vaccinate the entire Guardian Force, recruits included—and two plastic cases housing the explosives. Quin, Max, Cason, and Edison went ahead of us.

The rest of the team followed behind, except for Hiro. From Resistance headquarters, he had already ensured that the two cameras near the lab were on a running loop, playing the security footage from the same time on Saturday night. He would wait on the boat until we returned, using his computer to access the internal Guardian Force network. Once the meeting began, Hiro would upload the video to the screens inside the debriefing room.

The night air was cold, and the wind off the water, colder. Even though I was breathing heavily from the hike, my teeth chattered. I could see Quin up ahead, his silhouette barely visible. Suddenly he stopped, holding up his hand to signal the rest of us. His unexpected movement sent a whoosh of adrenaline coursing through me as if it had been injected straight into my heart, each pump sending panic through my veins.

Quin was looking at something near the rocks—an object glistening, caught by the moonlight. He lowered his hand and walked toward it, his weapon drawn. We all followed cautiously. As I approached, the object came into view, revealing itself. It was a watch . . . on a man's wrist . . . with a Guardian tattoo visible beneath it.

Quin reached down and touched the man's face, checking for signs of life. I imagined his skin was so cold. Just past the man, floating in the shallow water near the rocks, were several bodies, likely executed Guardian recruits.

"He's been shot," Quin told us. "He's . . . *they're* . . . dead." Quin released the man's body. It drifted toward the others, where it log-jammed against them.

I felt nothing. Well, not exactly *nothing*. A muffled cry of dread rose up in my throat. It wasn't for the recruit, but for myself, as I realized that just like for him, *for me*, this night would have no real end. It was like the first tip in a long line of dominoes. Whatever happened, there was no going back.

CHAPTER SIXTY-FOUR

THE LAB

THE MODEL INDUSTRIES BUILDING ROSE up from the northwest corner of the island. Three stories tall, it had once served as a work site for inmates. Now it was coated in thick rust from years of exposure to the salty sea winds. According to Quin, behind its ancient walls, the building had been updated and modernized. The lab was located on the upper level, accessible by an elevator that was secured with a biometric identification pad, similar to the one at Resistance headquarters.

We planned to try Edison's fingerprint first. It had been only a month since his abrupt dismissal, and we were hopeful his print hadn't been deleted from the system. Edison had even agreed to wear his Guardian recruit uniform, marked Greenhorn 558 on the sleeve, just in case a change in plan required him to blend in here.

After cutting a small hole through the thirteen-foot, razor-wire fence, Quin waited as we all crawled through cautiously. Once we were safely inside, Cason halted us, pointing to two armed men walking near the back entrance to the building. They were patrolling the perimeter of the lab.

When they were out of sight, we filed into the building, and Quin set the timer on his watch. The patrol required six minutes to complete, giving us about five and a half minutes to swap the drugs and get out unseen before the guards returned.

Quin led us down a long, narrow corridor to the elevators. Initially, he had intended to stay behind, but when everyone else appeared reluctant, Quin volunteered to place the explosives. Max, Cason, and two of the other armed men remained on the first floor to neutralize the guards if they returned earlier than expected. Though their weapons were at the ready, we were all clear on one thing: It was essential not to raise suspicion.

Edison placed his finger against the elevator's keypad, as the rest of us watched without breathing. There was a short beep as the floor numbers lit up in green. The words *Identity Confirmed* rolled across the small screen. Edison grinned with relief and pushed the number three. The elevator jolted to a start, and I met my mother's eyes. We appeared to be having the same thought—so far, the plan had gone perfectly. *So far.*

The Guardian Force lab and research facility was immense. As soon as the elevator doors opened, I noticed a massive generator occupying the right corner of the room. It quickly occurred to me that the source of the power outages was right here. The demand for electricity required by the pharmaceutical companies' manufacturing equipment would have easily overwhelmed the power grid. With that generator, the Guardian Force had ensured that at least one part of the island would never go dark.

Behind a glass partition, there were at least twenty large steel drums connected with sections of thick pipe. Each drum was marked—Agitor, Onyx, or Emovere—and notated with a batch number indicating its strength and composition. Hundreds of computers, most of their screens dark, lined the walls.

My eyes were drawn toward one of the lit screens. At the top, large block letters read *Recruiting*. An Internet site was open, a red flag marking one of the headlines, *"Fire Consumes Home: Fifteen-year-old Girl, Lone Survivor."* Trauma, no family—essentially an ideal Guardian Force recruit. I shook my head in disgust.

Quin pointed us to a tray of vials marked with Monday's date, June 10, 2041. My mother and I began swapping out the glass vials, handing the castoffs to Elana. As we worked, my mother's hands shook. She bobbled one of the vials, catching it just before it met its end on the cement floor.

"Mom, relax," I whispered, even though my own fingers were pulsing with apprehension.

"Four minutes," Quin announced. In the otherwise silent room, the echoes of his voice unnerved me.

I watched as Quin placed the explosive charges—one under a lab table, the other inside the nearby server room, out of sight behind a tangle of wires. The charges had been carefully shaped to contain the impact since my mother was determined to minimize damage to the other buildings. The timer was set for 7:05 a.m., shortly after the start of the Guardian Force debriefing. When Quin's work was done, he looked up at us eagerly.

"Three minutes, ten seconds. Let's go."

We hurried from the lab back down to the first floor where the others were waiting.

"Two minutes," Quin said calmly.

Outside, there was no sign of the guards. A faint sliver of sun was just beginning to emerge on the horizon. I couldn't believe our luck. We were already on the trail heading back to the boat when I heard the faint beep of Quin's watch.

CHAPTER SIXTY-FIVE

LUCK RAN OUT

ON THE WAY BACK TO the boat, I felt light, overcome with relief, almost giddy. Still, there was that undeniable lump of dread sticking in my throat. I tried to push it way down inside myself, but as we passed the executed recruits' resting place, I felt my eyes pulled to the water where the bloated bodies floated near the rocks. I attempted to resist the urge to stare. The longer I looked, the harder it was to contain my foreboding.

Hiro was partially concealed under the tarp, his face lit by the computer screen. His eyes told the story. Our luck had run out.

"I can't do it," he said, frustration sharpening his voice. "I've tried everything. There's no way around their firewall."

No one spoke. Everyone's eyes turned toward my mother.

"So you haven't been able to upload the video?" she asked. "The meeting starts in less than an hour."

Hiro shook his head, dejected.

Cason climbed aboard the boat. "I'm done here," he announced. "In about an hour, the lab is going to blow, and Ryker will either be dead or in handcuffs. That's what I came to do."

The armed men from the Resistance nodded their heads in agreement.

Carrie clenched her fists and looked at Cason. "*I knew it,*" she said. "You *were* here for Augustus . . . doing his dirty work . . . getting rid of Ryker."

Cason laughed haughtily. "Maybe I was. Maybe I wasn't. Either way, Ryker's minutes are numbered. Who cares about the stupid video?"

"*I care,*" my mother replied. "The Guardian Force needs to know the truth. Once the government arrests Ryker that video will never be released. I know how these things work."

"Mom . . ." I tried to silence the desperation in my voice. "As much as I hate to admit it, I agree with Cason. We did everything we came to do, and we're all okay. Please, let's just leave now."

Frustrated, my mother approached Hiro, snatching the drive with the video download from his hand.

"I'll do it myself if I have to," she said, resolute. She produced a copy of the map from inside her pocket and began walking determinedly toward the main buildings with no concern for her surroundings. I knew she was heading for the Quartermaster building, marked on the map in Quin's handwriting with the words *Monday Debriefing/Injection site.* Just a few years ago, the building was derelict, barely standing. Quin said it had been demolished, a state-of-the-art meeting complex erected in its place.

"You really *are* crazy!" Cason called after her. He had already begun to untie the boat. Hiro, still sitting inside it, eyed him with uncertainty.

I surveyed the area with alarm. We were making too much noise.

"Cason, shut up!" Edison's voice was an urgent whisper.

Immediately, I turned to Quin. His eyes were following my mother.

"She's going," I assured him.

"What should we do?" Elana asked me. Her face was distraught.

"We can't let her go alone," Max answered for me. "She'll never make it back."

Saying nothing, Quin began walking briskly, trying to catch up to my mother. I followed him, Max and Elana close behind me.

I heard Edison groan. "You've got to be kidding me." But I knew he would follow.

When I turned to look back, I saw Carrie standing by the boat. Her mouth was open. She seemed undecided. Then one of the armed men grabbed her by the arm, pulling her aboard. She shrugged off his grasp, but she didn't protest, and I didn't blame her. In another life, I was on that boat too, watching Alcatraz disappear behind me. But in *this* life, everyone I loved, with the exception of my father, was walking in the opposite direction. Though there was only one choice, I knew one thing for certain—this wasn't going to end well.

Quin was running now. He quickly caught up to my mother and pulled her into a small shed behind one of the nearby buildings. As we approached, I could faintly hear his voice addressing her.

". . . just run off like that. You're putting us all in danger." His tone was gentle, but firm.

When we opened the door behind them, I finally saw my mother's face. She had the look of a reprimanded schoolgirl.

"I'm sorry," she said to all of us. "I just . . . I want to . . . I *need* to do this."

While she was speaking, I heard the crunch of gravel as boots approached the shed. Quin held his finger to his lips, and I quieted my breathing. Elana grabbed my arm, her fingertips making deep indentations in my flesh.

A deep, unfamiliar voice came from outside. "Is someone there?"

Nearest the door, Edison waited patiently for the turn of the handle. When it came, he pulled the Guardian inside and covered his mouth. The man's eyes were wide with surprise, Edison's hand containing his scream. Edison wrapped his arm around the man's neck, holding tight until the man's legs stopped moving. The Guardian collapsed to the ground in a heap, his face as purple as a bruise. On his uniform, I saw his identification, Legacy 188.

Exhausted, Edison supported himself against the shed's wall, breathing audibly. Quin and Max bound and gagged the man using pieces of his uniform and dragged him to the corner of the shed where he remained, his head slumped awkwardly to the side.

My mother was near tears, her eyes wild. I grabbed her shoulders with intent.

"Mom, you have to pull it together. If we do this, we have to be smart about it. Look at what just happened." I gestured toward the crumpled Guardian.

She nodded, slowly regaining her composure. "I'm okay," she said unconvincingly.

Quin peered from a small hole inside the shed's wall. He looked at his watch before speaking in a hushed voice.

"It's 6:45. The meeting starts in fifteen minutes. The injections usually start early. In fact, they've probably already begun." My mother's face brightened.

Quin continued. "Ryker detests lateness so most of the Guardian Force will be there in five minutes. We're going to have to split up. Lex, you and Max will cover us from here on the hill." Quin pointed to a spot on the map marked *Water Tower*. "The rest of us will go inside. Once we deal with the guard in the control room, we can access the video monitors from there."

I took a deep breath before speaking. "I'm going inside, Quin." I was surprised at my voice. I sounded certain.

Quin bit his lip. I imagined that he considered talking me out of it, but he didn't try. There was no time.

"Elana, you stay with Max." He glanced sternly at me, the look in his eyes a reminder of just how impossible it was for him to say those words.

Turning to Edison, Quin said, "We'll need you to get us in." He pointed to the badge on Edison's uniform, and Edison nodded.

Quin left the shed first, gesturing for us to follow him. Down below us, a remaining few members of the Guardian Force were running toward the Quartermaster building. Late for their meeting, they scurried like ants. We waited for most of them to disappear into the building before we began our approach. Max and Elana maneuvered cautiously toward the base of the water tower, positioned just above the Quartermaster building.

As the rest of us watched, concealed behind the wall of the building, Edison fell into line, jogging behind two Guardian Force recruits, his uniform camouflaging him perfectly. Abruptly, one of the recruits turned to him.

"Hey man, do you know if Ryker's here yet?" The recruit asked nervously.

Edison shrugged. "No clue," he responded, allowing the recruit to skirt into the doorway in front of him. Edison held the door, pausing for a moment before calling us over.

Inside, Quin pointed down a long hallway. "Debriefing," he whispered.

I listened for voices, footsteps, anything, but I heard only the hum of the air conditioner and the sound of my own breathing, rapid and labored—just on the edge of panic. *Not now*, I warned myself.

We went opposite of the meeting room, down another long hallway. My mother and I walked in front, our guns at our sides, while Quin and Edison kept a permanent watch behind us. I noticed that almost all the doors were secured with a biometric keypad like the elevator.

"The third door on the right," Quin whispered.

Suddenly and without knowing why, I felt my body tense. The tiny hairs on the back of my neck rose in alert. From behind, I heard a familiar voice, General Ryker. He was late to his own meeting. There was another voice as well, a woman's voice.

Instinctively, I pressed my body to the wall, still making my way toward the third door. My mother was up ahead, almost there. Quin and Edison were frozen against the wall behind me, their guns ready.

"We need to call the lab," the woman's voice said. "There's something off in the dosing. A lot of them seem . . . I don't know . . . *restless* or something."

"Do it," Ryker commanded. "I'll be in shortly." The sound of his boots faded into silence.

I relaxed for a second—less than a second—but far too long. When I looked up, a towering steeple of a man had my mother's arms pinned behind her; her weapon was secured in his waistband. Another member of the Guardian Force, stocky and red-haired, had his gun pointed at me. Quin and Edison were gone.

The red-haired man spoke, fixing his eyes upon me abnormally. "Lower your weapon. Set it on the floor, and slide it to me." His voice was ice. If he had been injected with Resilire, it certainly wasn't working.

I complied with his order, watching my gun scuttle across the floor like a large insect. As the man reached down to pick up the gun, taking his eyes from me for a moment, I heard Quin's voice.

"Lex, get down," he directed.

I dropped to the floor, the impact jarring me just in time to feel a bullet whiz past. As the shot struck him, the towering man fell, a red mist exploding from his chest. He released his grip on my mother and collapsed to the floor, pulling her down with him. His gun dropped within feet of me. I crawled on my belly, inching toward it.

Hidden behind a corner, Quin and Edison continued to exchange fire with the red-haired man. The bullets careened around me, cracking the air like a whip. Though Quin had explained that most of the rooms in the complex were bullet and soundproof, I was shocked, but grateful, that somehow all this bedlam attracted no attention.

"Stay down, Mom!" I yelled to her forcefully so that she could hear my voice through the volley of gunfire.

Taking the towering man's gun, I aimed for the red-haired Guardian. He was dragging my mother through an open doorway, firing shots at me over his shoulder. Without hesitating, without even a thought of Elliot, I squeezed the trigger. The red-haired man collapsed to the ground.

My mother tossed the flash drive to me as two more Guardians rounded the corner, already firing their weapons.

"Go," she implored me.

Her voice left no room for debate, but turning from her felt unnatural. I felt riveted to the floor, rooted to my mother. It took the zip of a bullet to compel my legs to move toward the third door on the right. Quin and Edison approached from behind me, their footsteps urgent.

"Eddie, go with Lex," Quin directed. I started to protest, but Quin had already vanished into the other room, along with my mother.

Edison quickly accessed the control room with his fingerprint, the door's keypad lighting up in a familiar green. Opening the door with one hand, he cautioned me with the other. Inside the room was a girl crouched under the table. Fear had drained her face of color. She had a Guardian tattoo.

"She's been injected with Resilire," I told Edison. "She's afraid. Look at her."

Edison ignored me, jamming the door closed with a chair. Instantly, the door shut out the alarming sounds from the hallway behind me. General Ryker's barking voice and hurried footsteps were cut off by stony silence.

Edison considered the girl.

"Give me your gun," he demanded. She handed it to him gingerly as if it might explode. He secured it in his waistband.

When Edison spoke again, his words were pointed and razor sharp. "If you move from that spot, I'll blow your head off."

The girl nodded, curling herself into a tight ball.

Inside the room, along the wall in front of us, were at least thirty monitors, each displaying a different room within the building. I easily spotted the screen displaying the debriefing room. At least three hundred Guardian Force members and recruits shifted anxiously in their seats. They *did* seem restless.

"Lex, the drive," Edison called to me. He was standing in front of a sprawling desk, an oversized computer in front of him.

I handed it to him, and he inserted it into a port on the side of the computer. With a few clicks, he opened the file.

"It should be playing *now*," Edison announced with one final keystroke.

I directed my attention to the debriefing room, observing as one by one, the Guardians became still and focused. Their eyes were turned upward, watchful.

Edison rushed over to me, pointing to another screen with urgency. "Turn on the audio," he instructed.

I flipped the switch, General Ryker's voice suddenly booming from the screen.

"It's quite ironic, don't you think? Seeing both of you *here*?" As he considered my mother and Quin, I watched Ryker's usual expression of harsh disdain morph into a twisted sneer.

My mother was standing a few feet from Quin. There was a scrape on the right side of her face, her eye swollen shut. Quin held his right arm tightly, his fingers bright red with blood. Behind them, one Guardian pointed a gun barrel at their heads, while another lay lifeless in the corner.

I felt a searing heat rising in my throat, burning its way into my mouth. I gagged, my stomach riding waves of nausea.

General Ryker addressed my mother first. "It's been a while, *Doctor* Knightley." He pronounced her title, mockingly. His contempt sounded personal as if they had met before, though my mother had never mentioned it.

"*You* are the very reason that we are standing here today. Am I not correct?" His question wasn't meant to be answered. "We have you to thank for Emovere." He paused for dramatic effect as if he was performing a scene. "And yet, here you are, trying to destroy the very thing that you gave birth to."

"This is not what I intended. You know that, Jamison." My mother addressed him by name in a surprisingly familiar way. Now I was convinced. *They knew each other.*

The room began a slow, lopsided spin with pinpricks of black exploding across my field of vision. I squeezed my eyes shut and opened them again, hoping to reset myself.

"Lex, we have to do something." I heard Edison speaking from behind me. "He's going to kill them both."

I murmured in agreement and tried to stand, but Edison stopped me as I stumbled.

"Lex." He evaluated me with concern. "You're bleeding."

I'm bleeding. The thought set off a siren of pain that had been silent until then. Instantly, my fingers went to the wound just along the side of my abdomen. My shirt was warm and sticky with blood.

Edison ripped a section of his shirt and held it tightly against my side. "Keep putting pressure here," he instructed. "I'll be right back."

Feeling helpless, I watched Edison leave the room. Then I felt the earth shift beneath me. One thousand one, one thousand two—and it was over.

"Did you feel that?" I directed my question to the fearful Guardian hidden under the desk.

She nodded, and I knew. The bombs had detonated—their impact conveniently resembling an earthquake. I wondered if anyone would suspect otherwise. On the screen, I saw my mother glance furtively toward Quin.

General Ryker's soliloquy was suspended, his face quizzical. He addressed the armed Guardian positioned behind Quin. "What was that?" he asked, breaking from his theatrics.

The Guardian shrugged. "Earthquake, I guess. It felt like an earthquake."

"Initiate the security protocol," Ryker commanded, pointing to a red switch on the wall, "just in case." He refocused his eyes toward Quin and my mother. "I want to be sure we aren't interrupted."

The man depressed the switch, and I heard a click from the door inside the room. After taking a few breaths to steady myself, I approached the door and tried the handle, jiggling it at first, then depressing it frantically with all my strength. It was locked. My side was screaming at me—the blood had soaked through Edison's shirt. Through the muddle, my thoughts sluggishly assembled themselves.

I was trapped. In here.

Quin and my mother were trapped. In there.

With Ryker.

General Ryker resumed speaking, still addressing my mother. "Yes . . . well, you never could quite make up your mind about what side you were on. After all, you ran from Crim-X straight to Zenigenic. Did you honestly think you were taking a step *up* the moral hierarchy?"

"It was always clear what side you were on," my mother responded, her words dripping with disdain.

"You're right, Doctor. I am nothing, if not loyal," Ryker turned his eyes to Quin. "Speaking of *loyalty* . . ."

Quin tensed. His fists clenched into tight balls, his jaw set and hardened. I desperately wanted to protect him. My breath quickened. I couldn't let this happen. *Think.* I willed myself to quiet my mind.

On the screen, I could see Edison frantically trying to get inside the other room. Just like my door, it was locked— the keypad apparently deactivated.

The keypad.

Edison fired his gun at the door, the bullet blistering the doorframe. It didn't go through. Even so, General Ryker turned, firing several return shots before continuing.

I ran to the door, banging on it to get Edison's attention. *The keypad.* I repeated the words in my mind. Then I said them aloud. Then I screamed them. It was useless . . . he couldn't hear me.

Ryker's voice taunted me from the screen. "Legacy 243, Quin McAllister. I consider you a personal failure—a traitor, of course, just like the good doctor, but worse. Does the doctor here know about the things you did? The people you hurt? All to set up the fall of the Resistance, the very group you now claim as your own. Without Legacy 243, the city of San Francisco would never have been evacuated, the Resistance never forced underground."

Quin said nothing in response. His face was stilled, unchanging.

I was breathless, defeated. I collapsed by the door, my wound burning. From inside the room, the Guardian spoke in a meek voice. "If you press the intercom for the hallway, he can hear you." She gestured to one of the buttons near the screens.

As I struggled to my feet with my eyes fixed on that button, Ryker continued, "That's not even the worst of it. You were one of the finest recruits the Guardian Force has ever seen. You were made for *this*, Quin. Don't try to tell yourself otherwise. When you left, you spit in the face of everything we both worked so hard for." Ryker was shaking his head at Quin, his condescension evident, even under his mask of pretend hurt.

Quin answered Ryker, his voice clear and strong. "I'm not *made* for *this*. You're right—I was good at it—but you convinced me that I didn't have a choice—that I had to be like my father . . . that I had to be like *you*. Now that I know I can, I choose something else."

I didn't wait for Ryker to reply. "*That one*," the Guardian directed me. Depressing the button, I yelled, "Edison, take off the keypad!"

I watched the screen with desperation. At my direction, Edison crouched by the door, pulling at the keypad with ferocity.

Ryker was silent, but the expression on his face made my brain buzz with alarm. Up until then, he seemed angry, yet disinterested, almost bored. Now his eyes were lit from within—dark windows offering a terrifying glimpse of the fire raging inside him.

Quin saw it too. Ryker was on the verge, teetering right on the edge of explosion. Turning swiftly, Quin lunged toward the Guardian and rammed him into the wall. Stunned, he loosened his grip on his weapon, relinquishing it to Quin's hand.

Quin fixed the weapon on Ryker as he removed my mother's gun from the Guardian's waistband, striking him forcefully in the face with it. The man staggered and fell to the ground. My mother looked on, dazed—her face pale and vacant.

"Are you really going to shoot *me*, Legacy 243?" Ryker asked, considering Quin with condescension. "I don't think you have it in you anymore."

"Put your gun down, Ryker," Quin ordered.

Ryker's high-pitched laugh sounded maniacal. "Looks like we've got ourselves a stalemate, Doctor," Ryker announced, glancing toward my mother. "Maybe I should just shoot you first."

Ryker pointed his gun toward my mother, then back to Quin, then at my mother again. His lips curled in a fiendish grin, toying with them, a devilish game of cat and mouse.

Edison had pried one corner of the keypad loose, but the rest wouldn't budge. Feeling panic pressing down on my chest, I pushed the intercom button again. "Hit it with your gun! Hurry!" Edison began striking the fixture repeatedly with the butt of his gun.

Suddenly, I was overcome by exhaustion. I looked down at my side and felt queasy. Half of my shirt was drenched red.

From behind Quin, the limp Guardian began to stir. I watched in horror as he rose on wobbly legs and plodded toward him.

Look behind you. Look behind you. Look behind you. The words pressed insistently into my throat, but I didn't have the strength to say them aloud. For a brief moment, I came up for air, the scene crystallizing in front of me. As if my entire world was only *this*, I saw everything happening clearly, but not until several moments *after* it happened. It was as if my mind was on a tape-delay, taking its time to catch up with my senses. It was a feeling of reverse clairvoyance.

I saw Quin fire his gun just as the Guardian struck his arm, sending the bullet careening wildly toward Ryker, striking him in the shin.

I saw Ryker recoil in pain. His eyes were narrowed and unforgiving. He held tight to his weapon, the muscles in his arms taut like wire.

I saw Quin's eyes widen ever so slightly. A pall of fear passed across them like a shadow. His mouth opened—suspended in an "*O*."

I saw Ryker's finger depress the trigger—how quick he must have moved, and yet how *slow*, how deliberate. Each millisecond, each millimeter, a decision point.

I saw my mother take a step, walling herself between Quin and Ryker. Her arms were outstretched toward the screen, pleading.

I saw the bullet make impact, my mother's chest a firework of red. She clutched her hands toward her as if holding a small child. Her face contorted in the agony of realization.

I saw my face reflected in the screen in front of me. I knew it was me, but *those eyes*, they *were* my mother's.

My own face was the last thing I saw before I saw nothing.

CHAPTER SIXTY-SIX

HOW?

I DREAMED THAT MY MOTHER died. I simply *knew* in the same way that old bones can sense a change in the weather. And yet, there she was, next to me.

"My mother died," I said, speaking to her as if she was a disinterested observer.

She only nodded.

In my dream, I began to cry. My tears felt hot. They burned like acid.

My mother spoke, her voice removed. "You have to go on *without* her."

"I can't."

"Of course, you can." She turned to me. On her chest, a small rosette of blood was blooming. I considered it in horror.

"*How?*"

There was no answer.

I awoke in a strange bed, my head pounding and a machine marking the continuous beeping of my heart. I instantly knew Quin was there. His arms contained me and I breathed him in. Lifting my head slightly from the pillow, I groaned. It hurt.

"Quin?" my voice sounded far away from me as if it had come from someone else.

I knew I needed to speak, to ask a question, but the words I wanted to find were out of reach. He pulled me tighter to him, smoothing my hair from my face, and some of the words came.

"My mom? Is she . . . okay?"

Quin shook his head "no." Though he didn't speak it, the word echoed in my mind.

"Lex, she died yesterday." He paused, waiting for my reaction. "She was shot . . . so were you. Do you remember?"

I heard Quin's words, but it took a moment for the impact to reach me, like the gradual fallout from a bomb. *My mother was dead. I had been shot. Did I remember?*

I nodded to Quin. No matter how much I didn't want to, I remembered.

"Ryker?" I asked. "Is he . . . *dead?*"

Quin's voice was gentle. "No, but he was wounded. Edison shot him in the stomach through the spot behind the keypad—just like you told him to. Admiral Bennington's team disarmed the Guardian Force and arrested him."

Still feeling groggy, I propped myself up against the pillow, surveying the room. Edison, Elana, and Max were standing in the corner, watching me with worried eyes.

Quin whispered to me, "You saved me Lex . . . you and your mom."

"And Edison," I added, trying to muster a smile, even as my eyes welled.

"*And Edison,*" Quin agreed. His tone was begrudging, but he and Edison shared a conspiratorial grin.

"I thought it was a dream," I told Quin. He didn't say anything. I was glad.

I turned my face toward his chest, burying it in the crook of his arm. The tears came.

CHAPTER SIXTY-SEVEN

EASIER, NOT BETTER

THE NEXT MORNING, MY FATHER arrived from Boston. Admiral Bennington had personally arranged his travel. I was sitting on the hospital bed, flanked by Quin and Elana, when he arrived. Somewhere inside me, I felt excited, but my exhaustion was so overwhelming that the feeling was muted, colorless. My father was different than I remembered, and yet, so much the same. His sandy colored hair, now peppered with gray . . . soft lines around his eyes.

"Lex." He said my name deliberately—like a pronouncement he had been practicing for years.

Elana quickly excused herself from the room, giving me a tiny wave before scurrying out.

"I should go," Quin said, glancing nervously from my father to me, but he didn't move.

"Stay," I commanded, latching onto his forearm.

"You must be Quin," my father said, extending his hand.

Quin nodded. "How did you know?"

"Well," my father began, sitting on the side of the bed and taking my hand, "Lex's mother told me about you."

Both Quin and I raised our eyebrows in surprise.

"You talked to Mom? When?" Saying *Mom* aloud induced fierce pangs of longing for her.

My father sighed. I noticed his eyes were red and swollen at the edges. He had been crying. "She telephoned me a few days after you. She said there were some things she needed me to know. I got the sense that she was about to do something dangerous. Your mother was nothing if not practical." He smiled to himself.

"What did she tell you?" I asked.

My father looked at Quin. "For starters, she said that you were awfully fond of my daughter."

Quin beamed. "Yes, sir," he replied, looking at me affectionately.

My father continued, "And she told me that she read my letters, every single one of them—not that I was surprised. She said it made her feel close to me, even though she was still angry with me for trying to take you away." My father looked at me, his eyes moist. "That was never my intention, Lex. For a long time, all I wanted was for us to be a family again."

I nodded. "Mom loved you," I said. "*Still.*"

My father pulled me in close to him, holding me. Though I couldn't see his face, I could feel him unraveling. "I, uh, want to . . . talk to the doctor . . . and find out when we can get you home. I'll see you in a minute." He stood and quickly left the room, his hands shielding his eyes.

"Are you okay?" Quin asked, after a moment.

"I guess. I just . . . I can't believe my mom. She kept so many secrets. Why didn't she just tell me?"

Admiral Bennington had confirmed that General Ryker and my mother had worked together on the Crim-X project. Now *this*. My mother's withholding still hurt. It made me wonder if I had ever really known her at all.

Quin put his arm around me, and I nestled in close to him. "Not everybody is as good at talking as you, Ms. Knightley. Just keep that in mind."

I laughed, but tears came to my eyes. "Is this ever going to get any easier?" I asked. More than anyone, I knew that Quin understood.

Quin nodded. "*Easier,* but not better."

CHAPTER SIXTY-EIGHT

HEROINE OF THE RESISTANCE

"YOU'RE LUCKY," THE DOCTOR SURMISED as he re-bandaged my side. "You lost a lot of blood, but the bullet went right through muscle. You should be as good as new in about six weeks."

I watched my father's face soften with relief.

After he said goodnight, I lay in bed, staring blankly at the television. Another rerun. Closing my eyes, I pressed against my wound until it ached. Despite my grimace, there was something oddly comforting about the pain. Its source was tangible. It was expansive. It could fill almost any emptiness. I wanted to sleep, but I was afraid to dream, afraid of hearing my final question—*how?*— still unanswered.

When I opened my eyes, my mother's face looked at me from a small box at the upper left of the television screen. The words *Heroine of the Resistance* scrolled beneath her. I sat up in my bed, instantly wide-awake.

"Good evening from SFTV. I am your host, Barbara Blake, reporting live from Alcatraz Island, former headquarters of the United States Guardian Force, where we have a breaking news update."

Just behind the perfectly groomed Barbara Blake were the burnt-out remains of the Model Industries building that had been leveled in the blast. Somewhere in those mountainous piles of rubble were the shreds and shards of all the Guardian Force research.

"Just three days ago, Dr. Victoria Knightley and a small team of crusaders took on the insurmountable task of defeating General Jamison

Ryker and his rogue Guardian Force. Though our government sources have repeatedly confirmed that the program was originally intended to *protect* our city, under the supervision of Jamison Ryker, the Guardians were subject to a cruel and exploitative experimental protocol using Emovere and other banned substances."

I shook my head in dismay. Not surprisingly, the government hadn't stopped spinning their own version of events, disavowing any direct connection to Ryker's methods or the use of emotion-altering substances. Whatever their agenda, it certainly didn't involve transparency or the truth.

"Dr. Knightley, true heroine of the Resistance, exposed us all to the harsh reality of the Guardian Force. Tragically, she lost her life for her cause." Barbara Blake cast her eyes downward in disingenuous despair.

I imagined my mother sitting next to me. I knew she would have rolled her eyes at the term *heroine*—bristling, not at the word, but at the irony of it all.

General Ryker's picture appeared. He was wearing his full military garb, and his face was expressionless. Instantly, I recoiled, seeing another image—Ryker pulling that trigger. In the last few days it came to me often, flashing from the recesses of my mind, each time as horrifying as the last. I took a deep breath, and it was gone.

"In the days since Dr. Knightley's passing, an official government investigation has revealed numerous indiscretions and blatant criminal activity on the part of General Ryker and his lieutenants. Our sources tell us that Ryker manipulated the government's policies on terrorism to justify his use of private information to identify and recruit candidates who had experienced trauma. Additionally, those inside the Guardian Force have reported that General Ryker ordered the executions of at least two dozen rejected recruits, often dumping their bodies in the San Francisco Bay."

I clutched the side of my bed and gasped. On the screen was a picture of Augustus. He was wearing a suit and a familiar, slick smile.

"Within the past twenty-four hours, our sources have also uncovered a second hero of the Resistance, a mysterious figure, Mr. Augustus Porter. Mr. Porter has presented compelling evidence that, as the elected leader of the Resistance, he learned of General Ryker's evil schemes and planned to release video evidence of those wrongdoings before he was unfairly ousted from power. Though he graciously insisted that tonight's broadcast be devoted to honoring Dr. Knightley, we are fortunate that the humble Mr. Porter has agreed to be interviewed for tomorrow evening's report."

My eyes widened in disbelieving disgust. Just as my mother had predicted, Augustus had slithered out from under his rock. He was somewhere, coiled and watchful, readying himself for a well-timed strike.

"Tonight, let's take a moment to remember two true champions of our once-glorious city, Dr. Knightley and Augustus Porter. And please tune in tomorrow night for my exclusive interview with Mr. Porter. This is Barbara Blake, signing off for SFTV."

My mother's picture—the one from her Zenigenic badge—lingered on the screen until it faded to static. I closed my eyes, but I didn't sleep. Instead, there was a memory turning in my mind.

I was eight and my mother was running late. It was already dark outside. I stood on our porch and watched the headlights pass without stopping. My father appeared unconcerned. To him, her return was inevitable. But I pictured her car mangled on the highway, her body lifeless. Worse, I tried to imagine my life without her, but I couldn't. There was only blankness, a string of empty days that I simply knew I wouldn't live through.

I never told Elana, but from that moment, I knew exactly what she meant about the *worst thing*. The *worst thing* was a bullet to the soul, a black hole in the middle of life, swallowing everything in its path.

I clicked open the locket around my neck, holding it close to my face—and closer still—until all I could see was my mother smiling back at me.

No matter what was coming—Augustus, Ryker, or some other nameless terror—I wasn't afraid. *I knew.* I had lived through the *worst thing.* If you can live through that, nothing else can touch you.

CHAPTER SIXTY-NINE

THE DOG-EARED PAGE

IN THE WEEKS THAT FOLLOWED, I returned home. My father moved back into our house in Tiburon. Though his face was becoming a familiar sight to me now, I still found myself occasionally jarred by his presence. Sometimes I just sat and watched him, observing his mannerisms, trying to locate pieces of myself in this kindred stranger.

Elana visited me often. She was living with her mother in Marin, and she rode her bicycle to my house at least once a week. When I had seen her last, she had seemed buoyant, even more radiant than usual.

"Have you seen Edison?" I asked her. I hadn't talked to him in a few weeks since he had returned home. He was attempting to reconcile with his father.

Elana nodded, her face turning red.

"Why are you blushing?"

She laughed. "Edison sort of asked me on a date."

"On a *date*?

Her smiled broadened.

"Elana! I thought you didn't like him. You said he was obnoxious."

"He totally is," she said, still grinning. "But, it kinda works for him."

We both chuckled.

"Are you sure you're ready for that? Dating, I mean?" I asked, recalling our earlier conversation.

"Not really," Elana admitted. "But it helps that we were friends first. I even told him what happened to me . . . *all of it*."

"How did he react?"

Elana smiled. "Well, first he offered to . . . *seriously injure* those guys. He didn't say it that nicely, of course."

"Sounds like Edison."

"Then he just listened to me. It was actually sweet. A little *strange*, but sweet."

"Who would've thought Edison was so enlightened?" I joked.

"What are you two giggling about?" Max interrupted our laughter, Quin following close behind him. My father had allowed Max and Quin to stay with us—*temporarily*, as my father repeatedly emphasized to Quin—until we could all figure out what would come next.

"Edison," Elana answered.

"Say no more," Max deadpanned.

Quin chuckled and sat down next to me on the bed.

Eyeing us watchfully, Max grinned. "Let's leave these two lovebirds," he teased, linking arms with Elana.

After they left, Quin sighed with contentment as he lay back on my pillow. I lay next to him, not speaking. Our hands were linked between us. Feeling jealous, Artos jumped onto the bed and nudged his way to the middle, settling comfortably against Quin's leg. Slowly I turned my head to look at Quin. Though we were touching, his eyes seemed to be somewhere else.

"Hey, Lex," Quin said, noticing my gaze. His voice was tender, his eyes present again.

"Hey, yourself," I teased, the words calling to mind a distant, precious memory.

Quin guided my face to his and kissed me softly.

"I want to show you something," he said.

From my bedside table, he produced my mother's poetry book. Since she died, I hadn't opened it. It was too hard. He handed it to me.

"Open it."

I looked at him quizzically. "Just open it?"

"You know which page," he directed.

My fingers easily found the dog-eared page. Pressed inside was Quin's note. I held it, looking up at him warmly.

"Not that," he said, shaking his head. "Although . . ." He kissed me again.

Pushing him away from me gently, I turned my attention back to the page. Written in the margin, in my mother's nearly illegible cursive handwriting, it read:

"Quin isn't the only one who loves you, in case you forgot." —Mom

EPILOGUE

QUIN WAS SITTING NEXT TO me, his fingers interlaced with mine. He was squeezing my hand tightly. On his wrist was a not-so-familiar tattoo. I thought Max had been joking that first day when I met him, but he had convinced Quin to turn his Guardian Force badge into a dragon. Max was right—it did look pretty tough. Quin said it reminded him that we can't change the past, only the way we perceive it. For me, it was like the scar on my abdomen, a reminder that no one can pass through this life unmarked.

I scooted closer to Quin. The room was cold and colorless, the building so sterile, I wondered how it could sustain life. And there was something else—a heaviness—as if the air was thick with hope long-discarded, an endless parade of days wasted in a self-inflicted purgatory. I glanced toward the door. It was marked in large black letters: *Dellencourt Visitation Room.* Despite knowing that I could walk through that door, leave at any time, the sense of feeling trapped was tangible. Still, I had promised Quin I would do this with him. And being here, a place where *she* had been, somehow, I felt closer to my mother.

"Visitor for George McAllister?" The throaty voice bellowed from a heavyset woman in police garb. Expressionless, she gestured toward a door marked with a large number five.

Through the door's small window, I saw a man. He bore a faded resemblance to the mug shot in Quin's file. His eyes were surprisingly human, not the dark, cold marbles that I remembered. Quin and I both stood.

"I'll be right here if you need me," I said, touching Quin's hand. I added, "My mom would be so proud of you."

He nodded and turned from me, taking an audible breath.

"Quin?" He paused, listening. "I love you."

"I know," he replied without looking back. There was an undeniable certainty in his voice.

"*Oh, do you?*" I teased.

He glanced back toward me, a wide grin on his face. "How else do you think I made it here?"

I beamed at him, my heart surging. His words were unexpected, but true. Love was the *how*.

Without hesitation, Quin opened the door and walked through it.

COMING SOON

The adventures of Lex Knightley continue in Prophecy, the second book in the Legacy series.

Now that you have finished my book, won't you please consider writing a review? http://amzn.com/1452520402 Reviews are the best way readers discover great new books. I would truly appreciate it.

If you would like to receive a notification when the second and third books in the series are released, please sign up for Ellery Kane's newsletter: http://eepurl.com/bigOYr

ACKNOWLEDGEMENTS

A HEARTFELT THANK YOU TO:

My editor, Ann Castro, and the team at AnnCastro Studios for giving the book its polish.

Laney Dobbs, Dawn Blacker, and Melissa Diedrich for giving this first time author a bit of confidence.

Last, but *most* and *always*—to Gar, *my* Quin McAllister—in plot and in life, for giving me the *how*.

ABOUT THE AUTHOR

Ellery Kane is a forensic psychologist residing in the San Francisco Bay Area. She spends her days evaluating violent criminals and trauma victims. *Legacy* is her first novel.

Printed in the United States
By Bookmasters